DECEPTIVE TRUTH

THE COWBOY JUSTICE ASSOCIATION: SERIALS
AND STALKERS, BOOK FOUR

OLIVIA JAYMES

DECEPTIVE TRUTH

Copyright © 2021 by Olivia Jaymes

1

Knox Owens flinched as the barred doors behind him slid shut and locked with a loud metallic clang. He'd already signed in and turned over his firearm for safekeeping, and he was traveling farther into the prison where uniformed guards stood watching his every movement with suspicion.

Gray. Everything around him was a particularly depressing shade of greenish-gray. The floors, the walls, even the ceiling. It only added to the overwhelming air of despair, sadness, and gloom mixed with more than a whiff of desperation. It was almost physically painful to be standing in these surroundings. It was as if there wasn't enough oxygen in the room, and he had to struggle for breath, his chest excruciatingly tight.

If these gray walls could talk, the stories wouldn't be happy. The gloom was that palpable; deeply dark and oppressive.

He didn't want to be here, and he resented the hell out of it. It was all he could do to keep going forward rather than turn back and forget all of this bullshit. He didn't need to actually show up at the parole hearing. He'd already written his letter to the parole board. They knew his feelings. They weren't a deep, dark secret.

But he'd promised his younger brother that he would be there. If it had been anyone else, he would have said fuck it and not even showed up, but he couldn't do that. Not to Randy. His brother said that it was important that all the family be there. Family was important to Randy. He still believed that the Owens clan could be happy, loving, and close. Knox had given up on that dream a hell of a long time ago. In a funny way, he admired his brother's optimism. Randy never gave up hope.

His entire family put the *fun* in *dysfunctional*.

To keep his own sanity, Knox spent as little time with them as possible. It had been over a year since he had seen Randy and more like two since he'd seen any of the others. He doubted anything had changed. Nothing ever seemed to. Luckily, he'd moved out of Montana for his job and that gave him a good excuse to stay away. He was always busy. It wasn't a lie. Even when he'd lived in Montana, he'd been the first guy to raise his hand to volunteer to work holidays. Getting shot at by criminals was far superior to spending Christmas Eve with his relatives.

Damn, I'm getting pessimistic in my old age. In a few years, I'll be yelling at kids to get off my lawn.

"You made it. I told Mom you'd be here."

Randy threw his arms around Knox and they hugged, slapping each other on the back.

"I did. How's business, little brother? Life treating you good?"

"Busy as all hell. Julia sends her love."

Julia was Randy's wife, a lovely woman who handled the paperwork side of the family business. Randy ran a heating and air conditioning company. Knox had even invested in it at the beginning to help his brother get a start. He was certainly the most successful of the Owens kids and he deserved it. He'd worked hard for it.

"Tell her I said hello."

"Tell her yourself," Randy shot back. "Come and visit. See the kids. They miss their Uncle Knox."

Randy and Julia also had three rowdy boys that liked to climb Knox like a tree and play wrestle in the middle of the living room floor. Every time he visited, he had to rest the next day. He didn't know how his brother survived. Those kids kicked his ass and then some.

"I miss them too. I'll make some time."

Eventually.

Randy jerked his thumb toward an open set of double doors. "We're all assembled in the waiting area."

"Who all is here?" Knox asked, delaying the inevitable as long as possible. He didn't want to go in there. Already a tension knot was building in his gut. When the Owens were all together the only certainty was uncertainty. Literally, anything could happen. Usually it was bad.

Randy shrugged. "Pretty much everyone. Patty, Diana, Sara, Cal, and Roman. And Mom, of course."

There was no *of course* about Knox's mother being there. Their dad had left Alexa Loudon Owens years ago when Knox was only a teenager. Since then, Benjamin Owens had been married four more times, and always to the nicest women that Knox had ever met. Every one of them had been far younger than Ben and had somehow missed - or ignored - all of the red flags that came along with him. They were genuinely nice and sweet and they seemed to think they could change or save Ben by loving him a lot. If they'd asked Knox, he would have told them that it was a waste of time but no one ever had and he, for the most part, kept his mouth shut.

Benjamin Owens could be a smooth, charming son of a

bitch when he wanted to be. He could turn on the suave, debonair side of him as if flipping a switch. He could also be meaner than a snake, and twice as cruel. He only thought about himself and he'd been a lousy father and husband, not giving two shits about the long line of destruction in his wake.

That's how Ben had ended up here. Drinking and driving. They'd told him for years to stop but he didn't care. He'd been arrested several times but somehow, he'd always get his license back. Then when he didn't, he'd drive anyway, railing against "the system" and saying that no one was going to tell him that he couldn't drive. Eventually, he'd hit someone while driving drunk and they'd died. He'd been sent here.

Now he wanted out.

Knox was against it. His father wasn't capable of remorse for his actions. He'd never had any before. He didn't learn from his mistakes. He didn't empathize with others. He was a goddamn sociopathic narcissist, and this was the best place for him.

Randy slapped Knox on the back again. "Come on, let's go join the others. Mom's been talking about you all day."

"I highly doubt that."

Alexa had never seemed all that fond of Knox when he was growing up. He'd lost count of the times she'd told him to leave the house and not to come back until bedtime. Apparently, he gave her a headache.

Now as an adult, he didn't think that was the case. He was pretty sure it wasn't him that did that. It was the gin. That was her drink of choice because she thought others couldn't smell it on her. She was wrong.

"Is she here with Rock?"

Rock was Alexa's man friend of sorts. They'd been together for many years, and he seemed to drift in and out of her life whenever it suited him. Knox had known him since he was twenty but he still didn't know the guy's real first name. Everyone called him Rock.

Randy didn't have to answer the question because Knox could clearly see his mother and her shady boyfriend standing in the corner of the large room. At seventy Alexa looked a decade older, lines deeply embedded around her eyes and mouth, and Rock didn't look much better, although he still had a few pounds of muscle packed onto his large frame.

The better question was why Alexa was here at all. She and his father had been divorced for years. Ben was on his fifth wife, a lovely woman named Patty who was also in the room waiting for the hearing. If asked, Alexa would say she was here to support her children, but Knox had a gut feeling that she'd never quite got over her first love.

His older brothers Cal and Roman were talking to Rock and Alexa, but Roman excused himself and hurried over to Knox.

"You made it. We were beginning to worry about you."

I drove slow because I didn't want to be here.

"To be honest I'm still not sure why we're all here anyway."

"To show support," Roman replied quietly. "That we believe in Dad's rehabilitation."

"But I don't believe in it and if you're honest, you don't believe in it either."

"People can change," Randy argued, also keeping his voice low. "Everyone deserves a second chance."

"I wholeheartedly agree," Knox said. "But how many chances has Dad had? About a million? He's blown through them all and doesn't give a shit."

Cal joined the group, a scowl on his face. "Then why are you even here then?"

Sadly, his brother took after their father. Women, booze, gambling, and who knows what else. Cal was the center of his own universe and everyone existed to simply orbit around him.

Knox kept his distance as much as possible. His brother destroyed pretty much everything around him without a thought or care in the world.

"Because Randy asked me to be here," Knox replied evenly. "I'm here for him, not for Dad."

That scowl didn't budge, only deepening. Cal jerked his head toward Alexa. "What about Mom? Aren't you here for her too? This has been really hard on her."

Knox was used to being the black sheep of the family. The scapegoat. Everyone blamed him for whatever was going wrong in their life even if he was a thousand miles away. Cal, on the other hand, had always been the golden child. He'd never done anything wrong in their parents' eyes.

Knox's gaze traveled to his mother who had lit a cigarette and was sitting in one of the metal folding chairs. "I can see that it's been hard on her. I can also see how she's handled it. Her face is bright red from the gin."

"It was just one to help calm her down," Cal said, but Knox had already brushed past his siblings and walked up to his mother.

"You can't smoke in here, Mom. This is a no smoking building."

Her eyes narrowed and she swayed slightly in her chair, not answering right away as if she had to figure out who the hell he was before she did.

"It's just one cigarette," she finally said. "It's not hurting anyone."

Rules were always for other people. That's what Knox had learned from her and Ben when he was growing up.

"For Christ's sake, put it out before they march you outside," he growled. "For once, can't you just do what you're supposed to?"

Rock stepped forward. "Your mother–"

Knox didn't give a shit what Rock thought.

"Just put it out. You can smoke later."

Stomping away, Knox didn't spare a glance over his shoulder. This was why he didn't spend time with his family.

"I see you're your usual charming self," Patty said as she joined him, giving him a hug. He allowed it because he truly liked her. He still thought she was out of her mind for standing by his dad, but he did like her. She was a good person and she deserved a hell of a lot better. "How have you been, Knox?"

"I've been good. Busy with work, but good. How about you?"

Patty was only a few years older than Knox. Attractive with short dark hair and hazel eyes, she always had a smile and a kind word for everyone. No matter how much of a jerk they were.

"I'm doing well. Nervous about today, of course." She gave him some side eye. "I'm surprised to see you here. Randy must have been very persuasive."

"He was and this was a mistake. I shouldn't have come here."

She placed her hand on his arm and leaned closer. "I know about the letter you wrote to the parole board."

Instinctively, he stiffened, suddenly wary of her friendly mood. "It's not a secret. I told Randy what I was going to do."

She nodded. "You did and he told me. Ben's lawyer reached out to me and I told him that you were going to send a letter, and to let me know when it arrived."

"I'm not sorry, Patty. Someone had to say it. Come on, you have to know the truth by now. My dad isn't ever going to change. He says he's found religion. I think it's just another in a long line of con jobs. He's played and abused every one of us. How can you let him continue?"

From the conflicted expression on her face he could tell that she did know the truth about her husband. She just didn't want to admit it. Then she'd have to admit that she'd been wrong hanging in there all these years.

"He's done good things too."

Knox could feel the heat on the back of his neck as his anger simmered. It wasn't her fault though. This was all Ben.

"I can't think of any recent things. He's left you with two young kids and no income. Let's not even mention all the other kids my dad has fathered and not bothered to support or care about. How many is it now? Ten? Or is twelve? I've lost count of the women he's left behind while he skips merrily through life without a thought to the consequences."

"He's paid his debt to society."

"That's a matter of opinion. And even if he has, he has a mountain of outstanding debts he needs to deal with."

Unfortunately, it wasn't Knox's opinion that mattered today. It was all up to the parole board.

"I wish you and your father could reconcile," she sighed. "He is your father, after all."

An accident of biology.

"There's more to being a father than being a sperm donor," Knox replied, the words blunt. "Being a father means being there for your kid, and he sure as hell was never there for me."

"He was young," Patty argued. "He's learned as he's aged."

"Good for him. The best thing he can do is be a better parent to his younger children. Clearly, I'm a lost cause at this point."

She opened her mouth to defend Ben again but Knox shook his head and put up his hand to stop her from wasting her breath.

"Please don't. I'm not going to change my mind and neither are you. Can we just enjoy seeing each other again? I don't have any issues with you."

He tried to give her his best smile and Patty simply chuckled. "You've got as much charm as your daddy. I think you could get away with anything."

She thought she was saying something nice but...

"I'm nothing like my father. I don't use my charm against people."

Ben did it to get his way and if he didn't get what he wanted, he acted like a toddler having a tantrum.

She finally let it drop and they chatted for a few minutes about innocuous subjects like the weather and who might make the playoffs this year. Patty was a die-hard sports fanatic.

"I wrote a letter too," Patty said abruptly when the conversation had begun to lag. "After I heard about yours. I wrote a letter saying that Ben sounded like he'd changed. I said that his children needed him."

Knox didn't know what to say at that point. He didn't think Ben was anyone to look up to, but clearly Patty with her sunny optimism saw something that he'd never seen.

"I shouldn't have come here," he said instead. "This was a mistake. I wanted to be here for Randy but I can't pretend that I think Dad should get out."

This time he walked away to the other side of the room, shoving several quarters into a coffee vending machine and drinking down the vile liquid in just a few gulps. He barely noticed the burn on his tongue and the back of his throat, his attention on his family and staying a few feet away from them. This is how they always ended up. Him on the other side of the room counting the minutes until he could leave.

I'm an adult. I can leave now if I want to. But what about Randy? That's why I'm here.

I can do this. I can stay until this is done. For him. Then I'll leave.

Sometimes he wondered if it was really him that was the issue and not his family. They didn't seem to have the problems with their father and mother that he had. They didn't seem to think that Cal's behavior was all that bad. It was always Knox calling them out and everyone else telling him to apologize and stop being so mean. They told him that he didn't understand the importance of family.

Maybe I don't.

Tossing the empty paper cup in a trash can, he turned as a man walked through the set of double doors. He walked directly over to Patty and leaned down to speak, their heads together. Without a backward glance, he walked out again.

Smiling widely, Patty stepped into the middle of the room.

"He's been granted parole. Ben's going to be free."

2

*ne year later...*

CHRIS MARKS SLAPPED Knox on the back and grinned. "She's a keeper, my friend. You need to hold on to this one."

Knox and his friends, Chris, Luke, and Ryan were having a fun night out with their significant others. They'd gone to a movie and then ended up at a sports bar that had tons of gaming equipment. So far Knox had lost three straight air hockey games to his new girlfriend Jenna. Far from being put out about it, he was actually quite proud of her. She was damn good at the game. He liked that she didn't feel the need to pretend to lose to him or some such bullshit to try and protect his ego. That was such crap.

My masculinity isn't that fragile, thankfully.

"You just want everyone to be married like you are," Knox replied, signaling the waitress for a refill. He'd already had one beer and that was his limit tonight. He was drinking soda as of about ten o'clock. "It's like a cult. First marriage, then a baby, and then a minivan. I'm not driving a damn minivan so you can just forget it."

"They're very practical," Chris laughed. "Lots of space."

"It's not for me. You and Ryan can compare models to your heart's content though."

Ryan's fiancée Mariah was currently six months pregnant and they were deep into decorating the nursery and buying car seats. Knox was pretty sure he'd heard his friend talk about buying Mariah a minivan. Did Mariah even want one?

"Seriously," Chris said. "Jenna's fantastic. Smart, funny, beautiful. She's the whole package. And you've got a great meet-cute story for the grandkids."

They did have a great story. Knox had been hanging out at a local sports bar watching a game and he'd headed to the men's' room during halftime. On the way back, they'd literally bumped into one another, sending Jenna's drink down both their shirts. After her effusive apology and a stack of napkins to clean up the mess, Knox had bought her a new drink and asked her to join them. He'd also asked for her phone number, which she'd given with a smile. That was three weeks ago. So far, so good.

Jenna had said she wanted to take it slow and Knox was fine with that. It was far better than a few other females he'd dated that had practically had the wedding planned after a few dates. He could be patient. As far as he was concerned, Jenna was worth it.

Because he liked her. Really liked her. More than he could remember liking any other woman in his memory. She was everything Chris had said and more. He found himself thinking about her at the most inconvenient times of the day. There was something about her that he couldn't quite put into words, but he felt comfortable with her in a way that he hadn't with anyone else he'd ever dated. She challenged him too, making him think about things in a new way. She was wickedly intelligent and incredibly gorgeous. She was also funny as hell and she could probably have just about any guy that she wanted.

It appeared that she wanted Knox.

Which is just fine with me.

She only had one flaw that Knox could see. She wanted to talk. Specifically about their relationship. Several times now she'd said that they needed to have a serious discussion.

Knox didn't "do" serious relationship discussions if he could avoid it. He especially didn't want to have them in the early days of dating. If she wanted to know where their relationship was going she was going to have to wait and see, just like him. Luckily, so far, he'd been able to get her away from the topic using diversionary tactics. Kisses, joking, whatever would work in the moment. If they continued dating, they'd eventually have to have some sort of conversation but he wasn't looking forward to it.

It really didn't make much sense to him either. Jenna swore she wanted to take things slow, but then she also wanted to have a serious talk.

Which was it?

"I think we'll wait on the grandkids. We've only been dating three weeks."

"It looks like it's going pretty good. She fits into our strange little group very well."

"I'm not sure that's a good thing," Knox laughed. "I wouldn't call us mainstream or even normal."

"Who wants to be normal? I don't," Chris declared.

"You're well on your way, bro."

Jenna, Mariah, Ella, and Shaw were finished playing a game where they shot water into a clown's mouth and inflated a balloon. The first one that burst won a prize and Shaw was holding a large pink stuffed elephant proudly and showing it to her fiancé Luke.

Jenna shrugged and laughed at her loss, settling into the chair next to Knox. She looked beautiful this evening, dressed casually in blue jeans and a white button-down blouse. She wasn't petite or delicate, instead tall, leggy, and athletic. She had that California-girl look with her pale blonde hair, almond shaped blue eyes, and golden skin, although she swore to him that she'd never stepped foot in that state.

"I didn't win," Jenna said, mock pouting as she linked their arms together and rested her chin on his shoulder. "Shaw's a champ at that game. She traded in three small prizes for that giant one."

"I can buy you a stuffed animal," Knox offered, snuggling closer and taking in her heady scent, a mixture of florals and fresh rain. "Hell, I'll buy you two."

Jenna nudged his shoulder. "Thank you, but I'm okay. Just a little disappointed. I'm simply too competitive for my own good. I want to win everything."

"There's nothing wrong with that as long as you're not body checking people to knock them out of the way."

Giggling, she pressed a quick kiss on his jaw. "I thought about it but I controlled myself."

He waggled his eyebrows, his pulse quickening. "Control is overrated."

"Think so?" she whispered, her breath warm on his cheek and her fingertips skating along his arm. The skin tingled in her wake. "What would losing control look like?"

"We'd definitely be closer," he said, his lips brushing her ear. "A lot closer."

They'd been taking it slow but he wasn't against taking a big leap in their relationship. Right into his king-sized mattress. He could already see her long blonde hair tousled on his pillows.

Damn, he wanted her so badly it hurt.

She glanced over at their friends. "I don't think we can do that here. They might not let us back into this place."

"Are you suggesting that we would be indecent in public?" he chuckled, tangling their fingers together. He wasn't a big fan of public displays but there was something about this woman... He could barely keep his hands off of her.

"I think you were suggesting it."

"Actually, I was suggesting that we go somewhere else. Somewhere far more private."

"Private sounds good. But we can't just blow off your friends. That wouldn't be nice."

His friends were currently cock blocking him, and they probably didn't even realize it. Luckily, Mariah was yawning and clearly getting tired. She and Ryan were sure to call an end to the evening quite soon. It was already midnight and none of them were party animals anymore.

"I can wait."

But not for much longer.

Knox had a feeling that tonight was going to be fucking fantastic.

THE CLOSER JENNA and Knox got to her home the more nervous she became. Right now her stomach was tied into a painful knot and her heart was racing so fast it threatened to jump out of her chest and take off out of the car. She kept telling herself to breathe slowly and calm down but it wasn't working in the least. She was terrified her dinner was going to make an uninvited second appearance.

Things were moving far too fast, as in lighting speed, but Jenna didn't seem to know how to slow them down. Her relationship with Knox had taken on a life of its own and it only seemed to gain momentum with each passing day.

She liked him.

Really, really liked him. A lot.

He was intelligent, funny, kind, and sexy as hell. He was the kind of guy that she'd always hoped to find but hadn't had any luck until that night in the sports bar when she'd spilled her beer on both of them. Instantly, she'd been charmed by his flashing smile and easy laugh. He was far too handsome for his own good, but he wasn't arrogant about it. He definitely knew he was attractive but he'd never treated her as if she was lucky to be with him. He was a great person and she loved spending time together.

She was also lying to him.

It wasn't a teeny tiny lie, either. It was a big whopper and she was deeply ashamed of herself. So many times she'd tried to talk to him and come clean, but somehow he'd steer the conversation in another direction and the next thing she knew the truth hadn't come out.

Tonight, she couldn't put it off any longer. Because it was one thing to date a guy that didn't know the unadulterated truth, but she couldn't make love with him under these circumstances. She couldn't be intimate with him and lie to him all at the same time. It simply wasn't who she was. This time she wouldn't let him quiet her. She was going to say what she had to say and he was damn well going to listen.

Then he'd probably tell her that he never wanted to see her again. She'd be heartbroken because she'd really come to care for Knox Owens. She hadn't planned it, and it sure wasn't convenient or even wanted but here she was. She liked a man and she was probably going to get dumped tonight.

It's your own fault. You should have been honest from that first moment.

I just didn't expect to...like him so much. I thought he'd be different.

She had intended to be truthful. She'd never intended to

keep her secret, but that first evening had just been so fun that she hadn't wanted it to end. Then on their second date, she'd honestly tried but when she'd said that she had something she wanted to talk about, he'd managed to keep her from talking. Mostly by kissing her, but it had been extremely effective. That had pretty much been his habit thus far.

She'd say they needed to have a serious talk and he'd start the romance.

And Knox Owens was a great kisser. He knew what he was doing and he absolutely knew that spot on the back of her neck that made her shudder and lose the ability to put sentences together. He could turn her into a pile of jelly with one smoldering look. The sex was sure to be off the charts too.

Not that she was going to find out.

Jenna had allowed this to go too far, and too long. Knox wasn't going to be a happy man. He'd probably be furious and she honestly couldn't blame him.

I'm to blame. Me.

Those words echoed in her head as she led Knox into her condo and switched on a few lights and the television. She couldn't seem to relax so instead she went into the kitchen to get them both a drink. She needed to move around. It was the only thing keeping her sane at the moment.

"Beer, wine, water, soda? I think I'm going to have soda," she said, keeping her hands busy by dumping ice into a glass. She was so distracted she didn't realize Knox had come up behind her until she felt his arms around her waist and his solid frame pressed up against her back.

His body heat immediately penetrated the thin cotton of her shirt and sinking into her skin.

"I'll take a soda too but why don't you let me fix them?" he said, his lips close to her ear. She could feel his breath against her cheek and her stomach did a full flip in her abdomen at his close proximity. "You go and relax."

This - right here - was her problem. When Knox was close like this she could barely think straight. How was she supposed to have a serious talk with him when she was a drooling, aroused mess? It wasn't fair. She was only human after all.

She opened her mouth to object and tell him that she couldn't relax, but that sounded dumb so instead she did as he asked, leaving him in her tiny kitchen while she tried to get settled on the couch. She grabbed the remote on the coffee table and began to surf through the channels, skipping over a steamy romance movie and landing on a comedy she'd never actually watched all the way through. The canned laugh track always grated on her nerves but she'd put up with it tonight.

"What are we watching?" Knox asked when he settled next to her on the couch. He placed two glasses on the coffee table in front of them and then leaned back against the cushions, his arm tucked around her shoulders. He felt warm and solid and reassuring at this moment. She wanted to lean on him and tell him all of her troubles. She wanted him to know the truth.

And then she wanted him to want to still see her even after he knew.

She was dreaming.

"Uh, I'm not sure of the name. It's supposed to be funny."

Except that she wasn't laughing. She was far too jumpy to enjoy the lighthearted banter of the actors. Any other day she would have probably loved it.

Knox leaned closer, his hand skimming down her arm and raising goosebumps on the flesh with the simple contact. "Jenna, are you okay? You seem a little off."

I am a little off. Or way off.

"I don't know what you mean."

She was lying through her teeth.

"Okay, I was just concerned, that's all."

He was being nice and she wasn't. Dammit. This wasn't what she wanted.

"That's sweet, but I swear I'm fine." She leaned forward and grabbed her soda, taking a drink. She'd managed to make it all awkward and weird between them. "Is there anything that you want to watch? I think there's a game on another channel."

"I'm not fussy."

He wasn't and she liked that about him. He was definitely a man that picked his battles.

"I know you'd rather watch sports."

He shrugged. "I'm good either way. Did you have fun tonight?"

That was an easy question.

"I did. Your friends are a lot of fun." She paused and then took a deep breath, plunging forward. "It must be great working with them day to day."

"It is. They're great guys and I'm lucky to be a part of the team."

"I would...love to hear more about your work. It sounds so interesting."

So far Knox hadn't been all that forthcoming about his job. She hadn't tried to strong-arm him into talking but this time she'd just went for it and asked.

"It can be interesting and it can be boring as hell too. A lot of computer research and digging through old, dusty file folders. There are some weeks I barely leave the office."

"And when you do?"

His brows rose. "Are you thinking about becoming a cop? I swear I'm not holding anything back. It's just not that exciting like it is on television and in the movies."

"You mean you aren't Dirty Harry?"

"Not even close," he laughed. "Personally, I'm not fond of having a gun pointed at me. None of my friends enjoy it either."

"That sounds wise."

"I think we'll live longer."

"Are you working on anything interesting now?"

Rubbing the stubble on his chin, he grimaced. "I'm between major cases at the moment so I've been helping the other guys. When the next big one comes up, it's mine."

"Like a murder?"

"Like a murder," he confirmed with a nod. "And if that happens, I might have to be out of town for a bit. I do tend to travel a lot for my job."

Knox had mentioned that early on but so far, he'd only had to fly out once for a few days.

"So...how do you do it? I mean...what are the steps to solving a crime? Like murder, for example."

"You want to know how I would solve a murder?"

He seemed genuinely puzzled by her question.

"Yes, I'm intrigued. I've watched that crime channel a few times but I've never known any cops before. So what would you do first?"

His eyes narrowed suspiciously and her heart leaped into her throat. "Are you one of those crime junkies that find serial killers fascinating?"

"No, not at all. I'm just very interested in your job. You don't have to answer if you don't want to."

His expression relaxed and he gave her a slow, sweet smile. "It's okay. I just wanted to make sure you weren't one of those murder groupies."

"I don't even know what that is."

"I get the fascination but for the most part my job is pretty routine."

"Except that you catch the bad guys."

"I try."

"No matter who they are." He frowned at her reply so she rushed forward. "For example, if the killer were a billionaire you would still arrest them, right?"

"Absolutely."

"Or a famous actor."

"Yes."

She was beginning to sweat on the back of her neck. "Or...a family member."

He looked puzzled again but he nodded in agreement. "Yes, if someone is guilty of murder it wouldn't matter who they were."

"I'm glad you feel that way."

Sweat trickled down her back and the room spun for a moment and then righted itself. She wasn't going to let him put her off again. She had to come clean. She had to tell the truth. She couldn't go on this way; it was tearing her apart bit by bit. She was falling for this man and he didn't have a clue...

"I would hope most people feel that way, Jenna."

Curling her fingers into a fist, the nails cut into the palms creating a small hurt to distract from the gigantic hurt in her heart. Her chest had closed up, squeezing her ribs against each painful thump.

"There's something we need to talk about."

"Jenna—"

He started to move away but she grabbed his hand. "No. Stop. I mean it this time. We need to talk."

There was panic in his expression as if he wanted to run.

"Listen, I really like you, Jenna. A lot. Can't we just take our time and see where the relationship goes? Do we need to define it right now? I'm not seeing anyone else if that's what you're asking."

At first, she was confused by his words. They didn't make any sense. Then when she'd had a moment to wrap her addled brain around them, she realized that they were having two quite different conversations.

Christ on a unicycle, he thought she wanted to discuss their relationship?

Really, Knox? I mean, you're hot and everything. But it isn't all about you.

"That isn't what I want to talk about. I don't want to discuss where our relationship is going."

Because it was about to crash and burn. In full pyrotechnic gory glory.

Frowning, he shook his head, seemingly perplexed. "Then what do you want to talk about?"

"My sister."

"Your sister?" he echoed. "What about her? I didn't even know you had a sister. You've never mentioned her before."

"She's not my real sister," Jenna explained. "Her family sort of took me in and adopted me. She's my best friend in the whole world and I don't know where she is. I haven't heard from her in almost six months."

"Six months? How come? Did you argue?"

Jenna shook her head, her throat growing tight with emotion. Tears burned the back of her eyes.

"No, we didn't argue. She was going out for a date with her ex-boyfriend. To have coffee. She said she would call me the next day. She never called and I never saw her again. She's disappeared and no one knows where she is."

Knox didn't reply, his brows still pinched together as if he was trying to make sense of what she was saying.

"She'd been dating her boyfriend for several months," Jenna went on. "No one really liked him, but she'd make excuses for him. We all thought he was bad for her."

Still silence, although Knox had pulled away from her, his expression turned wary.

"His name was Callum. Lori was dating your brother, Knox."

Levering to his feet, Knox walked over to the front window that overlooked the small patch of yard outside her condo. He looked outside and then back at her.

"She was dating my brother?"

"When she disappeared," Jenna confirmed. "So you probably know where I'm going with this."

Her voice was shaky and she had to hold her hands together to keep them from shaking.

"Let's pretend that I don't. Where are we going here?"

He hadn't budged from his spot by the window. If it was awkward before on the couch, now it was downright frosty between them.

He hated her. She'd expected this but she hadn't figured on how much it would hurt. Like a knife slitting open the flesh to the elements.

I really liked you, Knox. For real.

"I need your help," she finally replied. "I need you to help me find Lori."

"You want me to help you find your sister?"

His tone gave nothing away, although that ice wall was still firmly between them.

"Yes, and I think your brother was responsible."

In for a penny...

This time he took a step forward, his eyes narrowed. "Say that again, please."

She could feel the tears beginning to spill over, her fear, sadness, and despair all coming to the fore at once. It was all too much.

Didn't he realize just how desperate she had to be to come here? To him?

"I think your brother is responsible for my sister's disappearance and I want you to help me prove it."

3

The universe had to be playing a dirty trick on Knox. Some sort of not-very-funny prank and some game show host-type of guy was going to jump out of a closet or from behind the couch and yell, "Gotcha!" any second.

Except that didn't happen.

Jenna simply sat on the couch crying, her shoulders shaking with the strength of the sobs. His first instinct was to go to her side and comfort her, but then he remembered that the reason she was crying was that she thought his brother Callum had killed her sister.

What in the ever-loving fuck was going on?

"I think I'm going to need more information than you've given me."

A big part of him wanted to march out her front door and never come back but there was a little voice in his head that was saying that he needed to shut up and listen. He needed to know this story because it was too crazy to be true.

Although my brother is a total loser. But I don't think he's a killer.

But it was that tiny shred of doubt that kept Knox's boots planted on Jenna's living room carpet.

Jenna scrubbed at her red, wet cheeks with a tissue. "I can tell you what I know."

Knox glanced at his watch. "Then get to it because I'm rapidly losing my patience here."

The romantic mood of earlier was completely gone. Knox was pissed. He didn't like surprises. At all. The vast majority of surprises in his life hadn't been positive.

"Lori told me and Michelle - Lori's twin - that she had a new boyfriend. She really liked him and she couldn't wait to introduce us to him. She was working in Douglas at the time for a marketing firm. She said she met him at a coffee shop. When I went to visit her, I met him. Your brother, Callum Owens."

"You don't know for sure that he's my brother. He could have been lying about his name."

She nodded in agreement. "That's true but you and he do have a strong resemblance. His hair is darker and he has more lines around his eyes and mouth."

"He's older."

"Anyway, I met him and at first, he seemed just like Lori had described, charming and funny. But then it got a little weird. He seemed rather controlling and not so nice. The more I heard about him, the less I liked how he treated her. Eventually, I spoke up and she admitted that she'd had some doubts about him as well. She told me of a few incidents that made me worried."

"Violence?"

"No," Jenna said with a shake of her head. "Not actual violence, but sort of threats. Like he could understand why a guy might smack his girlfriend or cheat on her. Stuff like that. He was constantly turning every argument around on her and making himself the victim. It was always about how she needed to change and somehow he never did. I'm not sure if you get what I'm talking about."

Unfortunately, Knox did. He'd seen his father pull that shit on his mother countless times. He'd tried it with Knox and his kids too. Hell, he'd pretty much tried it with everyone and sadly, it worked more times than not. Now that Knox was savvy to his dad's manipulation it didn't work anymore. But in the past? Far too often.

Ben Owens liked to get his way, and he wasn't above some sketchy shit to get it.

"I get what you're saying. But being a lousy boyfriend doesn't make a person a killer."

His tone was aggressive, but shit...what did she expect? That he was going to roll over and just accept a crazy accusation like that? She was dreaming.

"There's more," Jenna continued, still sniffling from her earlier crying. She turned her head away from him, her expression stormy. "Both Michelle and I tried to convince Lori to leave Cal. He was getting more out of control, yelling and having tantrums when she wouldn't do what he wanted her to. Eventually, she did. At that point, she was staying mostly at his place although she had an apartment there, so she packed all of her stuff when he wasn't home and left him a note that their relationship was over."

Knox hadn't been around his brother's romantic relationships much, but he still had an inkling how Cal had reacted.

"And that was the end?"

Jenna shook her head. "Not at all. I guess Cal had a meltdown of sorts. He called all of her work friends when she wouldn't answer her phone. She'd blocked him. He called from other numbers and when she wouldn't answer those messages, he started showing up at her worksite. He said he just wanted to talk, explain himself. She told him it was over, but he wouldn't give up. Eventually, she said she'd meet him for coffee just to hear him out and give him closure. She said he kept saying that he needed *closure* and only she could give it to him. He just wanted ten minutes of her time."

Jesus H. Christ, Knox could almost hear his brother's voice whine the word *closure*. Cal was completely convinced his wants and needs were the most important in the world.

I wonder where he got that idea? Oh right, my dad.

"What happened when she met him?"

Jenna stood, her arms wrapped around herself as she walked over to the window where Knox was standing.

"That's the thing. He says that she never showed up. But there were witnesses that said that she did. All we know is that she disappeared after that. Just...gone."

He didn't want to hear this, but his cop brain was already whirling, trying to make sense of the mystery. He couldn't fucking help himself.

"What did you do? Did you call the police?"

"Michelle did. They said that it wasn't against the law for a woman to disappear."

That sounded...strange.

"They didn't look for her? Talk to anyone?"

"They did. That's how they found witnesses that said that she showed up at the coffee shop. Michelle received a text from Lori a few days later saying that she was going to take some time to clear her head but then we didn't hear anything else. The police said that it wasn't against the law for a person to voluntarily leave their own home, but we know that she wouldn't do that. She wouldn't just disappear, Knox. We pushed the police detective and he questioned a few people, but nothing came from the investigation. They say it's still open but I don't know what they're doing about it. When Michelle or I call, they never have anything new to tell us. They said we should be patient and Lori will get in touch with us when she's ready."

Was Jenna in denial about her sister? Sometimes people do strange things when under pressure.

"She just disappeared? Just...poof...gone? Did they go to her apartment? Talk to her friends?"

At the very least, they had to have spoken to his brother Cal. Was he under suspicion? Knox had to admit that it didn't sound good. He could - kind of - see why she thought that Cal was responsible for her sister's disappearance. And possible murder. Except that Lori could be alive and well and hanging out at the beach for all they knew. Jenna had jumped to the worst-case scenario.

"You've jumped to a lot of conclusions here, Jenna," he finally said when she didn't continue with the story. "The first is that your sister is dead. She might not be. She might be out there trying to get a little bit of peace and quiet. Let's hope that's the case. The second is that Cal is responsible. While I agree that my brother can be an asshole, he's never been violent in all the time that I've known him. A pain in the ass? Absolutely? A woman killer? No."

Her lips turned down and a few stray tears streaked down her cheek. "I thought you'd be open-minded. I thought you'd be different."

"You thought I'd be down to put my own brother behind bars? Why did you think that?"

She threw up her hands and groaned loudly. "Because Lori talked about how Cal complained about his brother Knox. He said that you weren't loyal to the family because you didn't think your father should get parole."

That sounded like Cal.

"So you thought I'd be more helpful when you came to me with your accusations?" A thought occurred to him. "Wait, did you know who I was that night in the bar?"

It was all becoming a hell of a lot clearer. He didn't need her answer. He already knew he'd been set up.

Licking her lips, she nodded. "I did. I found out where you

worked and I followed you to that bar. I watched you for a few days and then that night I made sure to run into you."

She'd stalked him. Fuck. He was a member of an elite serials and stalkers task force and he'd been completely taken in. He'd had no fucking idea. The heat of his anger had his stomach churning and the back of his neck hot. He was pissed the hell off. At her and at himself.

He'd been taken in by a pretty face.

I'm such an idiot. Too horny for my own good. This is what I get when I think with my dick.

"I was so desperate," Jenna said, her voice rising with emotion. "I couldn't eat or sleep. I was going crazy. We weren't getting any answers from the police and it seemed like they'd given up. Nothing was happening. We hired a private investigator but he didn't seem to be getting anywhere, just taking our money. Lori had talked about you and how you were this amazing cop. I just...I know it's bad...I just...I just hoped..."

Her voice trailed away, and she'd turned so her back was to him. From the shaking of her shoulders, he could tell she was crying again. This time so quietly he could barely hear.

Fucking hell.

"I didn't intend to like you. I didn't intend to fall for you."

Her head was in her hands and her voice was muffled but Knox understood her words. This was a nightmare. He hadn't intended to like her either. Not as much as he had.

Had? Was it already past tense?

Fuck, yes. She'd lied to him.

"But you did lie. Every time we were together you made that decision."

She whirled around, her cheeks red. "I *tried* to tell you so many times, but you always shut me down. Changed the subject. Kissed me. Said we could talk about it later. I tried, Knox. Fuck, the only reason we're having this fight now is because I wouldn't let you divert me again. You tried to do it again but I wouldn't let you. Because I've wanted to tell you the truth from the beginning. I never expected it to go on this long. I was planning to tell you that first night."

Well...shit. So that's what she'd been wanting to talk about? He'd assumed...

You know what they say about assuming. He'd made an ass of himself.

But she'd stalked him, dammit. He wasn't taking the blame here. This was all on her.

"Don't turn this around on me. You planned all of this," he spat out. "You watched me and stalked me. Lady, that's some mental case behavior right there. You should seek help right away. You've got problems."

Her chin lifted and her blue eyes had turned gray. She was mad. Tough shit.

"The only problem I have is that my sister has disappeared and might be gone forever. She was dating your brother and he's lying about her being at that coffee shop. I've done my research and I know that the most dangerous person in a woman's life is the man she's seeing. That makes him my number one suspect."

"You have suspects?" Knox's tone dripped with sarcasm. "Why didn't you say so? Tell me, Sherlock, how you came to this conclusion. Was it elementary?"

The hurt look on her face was almost his undoing. Twenty minutes ago he'd adored this woman but at the moment he didn't like her very much. But that didn't mean he was happy about being a jerk. But he wasn't feeling all that regretful at the moment either. She'd brought this on herself. Did she think it was going to be all rainbows and kittens?

"You don't think that your brother lying about seeing Lori is suspicious behavior?"

Scraping his fingers through his hair, he tried to get his

temper under control. Being pissed off wasn't helping the situation.

"I haven't talked to my brother about this but perhaps he had already left the coffee shop by the time your sister arrived," Knox explained as patiently as he could muster. "Maybe she got there earlier and left. Maybe he didn't see her. Or perhaps, and this is the big one, the eyewitnesses mistook another woman for your sister. Eyewitness accounts are notoriously faulty and shouldn't be relied on. What I'm trying to say here is that neither you nor I truly know what happened that day. We can't draw any conclusions."

"That's why I need your help."

Her voice was so low he almost didn't hear her reply. A heaviness took up residence in his chest. This whole situation was a cluster fuck.

"This wasn't the way, Jenna."

This time she turned back around so he could see her face, now streaked with tears, her mascara running down her pale cheeks. She looked lost, sad, and alone and for a moment he wanted to reach out to her, pull her into his arms and tell her that everything was going to be okay. He'd make sure that it was.

Then he remembered that she'd lied to him.

"I think I'm going to go home," he said taking a step back from her. There was still a part of him that had feelings for her but he was determined to stomp that feeling into the dust. "I wish things could have been different."

She visibly shook but she didn't argue or beg, simply brushing past him to the door. She opened it and stepped back.

"I think you're right. It is time for you to go. I'm sorry that I ever thought that you might help me. I'm sorry that I intruded on your life. It won't happen again, I can promise you that."

Shit.

He didn't want it to end this way, hating each other.

"I'm sorry–"

"You said that." She nodded toward the door. "I'm sorry too. This was all a big mistake. You'll never hear from me again."

There was really nothing left to say so he kept his mouth shut, grabbing his jacket and slipping it on as he headed out the door. He was halfway to his car when he heard it.

"Take care, Knox."

He turned on his heel but the door was already closed. Clearly, he was imagining things. She was inside and there was no way he could have heard anything she said with a door between them.

It was over. Jenna was the past. It was just all so much a mess.

He'd never see her again. That was good. He didn't need crazy in his life.

There were plenty of fish in the sea.

4

"I told you that it was a waste of time. There was no way he was going to help you."

After a good cry, Jenna had poured herself a glass of wine, settled on the sofa, and called her sister Michelle. She was emotionally battered, her usual enthusiasm gone. She'd convinced herself that Knox would help, that he would see how desperate she was.

She'd been wrong.

She wasn't angry with him. And he certainly had the right to be mad at her. She had lied to him. She couldn't sugarcoat her own actions here. She'd been in the wrong, although she'd hoped he see that it was for a good cause. He hadn't, of course, and he hated her now. She sort of hated herself too. She'd let Lori down. She'd failed.

"I thought he might see how much we needed his help," Jenna replied softly, taking a small sip of the wine. She wasn't a big drinker but she'd felt the need of it tonight. It was probably a lousy idea. Drinking alone wasn't a healthy habit. "I thought... Shit, I don't know what I thought."

Somehow in her mind she'd built Knox up to be their

knight in shining armor who was going to rush in and help them solve this mystery.

I'm an idiot.

"Sometimes you are so optimistic and naive," Michelle said, her tone gentle. "It's a beautiful quality but it can get your heart stomped on. Did you really like him?"

The million-dollar question.

"Yes," Jenna admitted, although it pained her to do so. "I did really like him. He's a great guy. Even if he won't help us."

"Did he yell? Was he furious?"

Jenna would have preferred it if Knox had yelled. She'd seen the muscle that ticked in his jaw and known that he was angry. Very angry, but he'd kept his tone calm, if not more than a little sarcastic.

"No, he didn't yell. I don't think that's how he gets mad. I think he's the type that goes cold."

"Oh honey, I'm so sorry that it ended up this way. I wish he would have said yes. But..."

"Right, he was never going to do that."

"It's his own brother, Jenna," Michelle reminded her. "He's not going to help us put his brother in prison. He was never going to help us."

Not sure what she was going to do, Jenna could only wallow in her own misery. She'd been more than desperate that night she'd "run into" Knox at that bar. The words hadn't been invented yet for what she and Michelle had been feeling. They only knew that their sister disappeared, the cops didn't think it was a big deal, and that Lori would never do that to them. She just wouldn't. Their entire lives they'd barely gone a few days without contact of some sort. The idea that Lori would go off somewhere by herself and not contact anyone was absurd.

"What are we going to do next?" she asked Michelle. "We're going to have to figure out how to do this on our own."

"That's what we've been doing," Michelle pointed out. "And we haven't done such a great job."

"We could hire another private investigator. I was going to offer to pay Knox, after all. Maybe we'll have better luck this time."

"I guess we could do that. I don't know anything about hiring a good one though. We picked the wrong one last time."

They'd picked the first person who had returned their calls.

"I'll do the research," Jenna offered. "It will give me something to do and help me feel like I'm not just sitting around helpless."

"That's the control freak in you."

"I'm not arguing that. But I have to do...something."

As the oldest twin, Michelle had always been the most calm and patient. Lori had been the one with the softest heart. Jenna was far more a person of action, never wanting to sit still for too long. She and Knox had been alike that way.

Don't think about him. He's gone. And hates me.

"We're going to find her," Michelle said. "I just know we will. She's out there somewhere."

Then why hadn't she contacted anyone?

At first Jenna had been convinced that Lori *was* out there, but as the weeks and then months had gone by her hope had leaked away, leaving a terrible feeling of foreboding. Nothing would keep Lori from calling them or coming home except...something very bad. Something deadly. Each day had chipped away at Jenna's hope until she had none left. Now she wanted answers and for someone to pay for whatever heinous thing they'd done.

"I want you to be right. I want that more than anything."

"We'll find Lori and we'll bring her home. You have to believe."

Michelle always said that Jenna was the optimistic and

naive type but she was displaying quite a bit of both of those traits at the moment.

Jenna wanted to believe. It was just about the only thing keeping her going.

It was time for Plan Z. Getting Knox to help them hadn't even been Plan A through D. That's how desperate they were. But Jenna wouldn't give up.

Time for a new direction.

KNOX WAS in a foul mood on Monday morning. He'd spent most of the day Sunday pissed off as well. With everything that had happened with Jenna, he couldn't clear his head. He couldn't even enjoy his damn day and that made him even more frustrated and mad.

He wasn't supposed to give a damn about Jenna and her situation. He was supposed to break the relationship off and walk away, no looking back. That simply hadn't been the case, however. He'd been brooding about it since he'd walked out of her home. He couldn't seem to think about anything else.

He was so tired that he'd contemplated calling into work. Not for very long, though. After all, he hadn't missed a day of work in years. So instead he'd dragged his tired ass into the office and slugged down a couple of cups of black coffee on an empty stomach. That turned out to be a huge mistake because by ten in the morning his nerves were jangled and his guts were hurting. His mood was on a swift sled downhill.

So when Chris asked him about a case file, Knox didn't respond all that well. He growled at Chris and then proceeded to chew his co-worker a new asshole for merely having the audacity to ask if the folder was on Knox's desk. That earned him a trip into Logan's office to *talk about it*.

"I thought you and Chris had put your feud behind you,"

Logan said, pointing to the guest chair in his office. "I thought you two were friends now."

With a tired sigh, Knox lowered himself into the chair. "We have and we are. That was just me being an asshole."

Poor Chris was currently in Jared's office probably getting the same grilling. Knox would have to buy his friend lunch to make up for this.

Perched on the edge of his desk, Logan glowered down at Knox. His boss didn't like unrest on the team.

"Why are we acting like an asshole this morning?"

Scraping his fingers through his hair, Knox had no choice but to answer. If he didn't, Logan wouldn't give up. The man was like a dog with a bone when it came to shit like this and Knox already felt like a perp under a bright light being interrogated. It would be easier to get this over and done with.

"I had a rough weekend. Didn't get much sleep."

Logan's brow quirked up. "Party a little too hard?"

If only that was the issue. Knox could take a few aspirin and eat some greasy tacos. He'd be better by mid-afternoon.

"Let's just say that my new relationship has come to its inevitable but messy end."

"She dumped you."

Logan didn't phrase it like a question which only served to irritate Knox a bit more.

"Actually, it was me that called an end to it."

Standing, Logan rounded his desk and sat down in his over-sized leather chair. "That's too bad. I guess I'm confused then as to why you're in a shit mood. If you ended it, then why are you upset?"

"I don't know," Knox blurted before he could stop himself. "Dammit, I don't mean that. I mean...maybe. Shit, I don't know."

Frowning, Logan leaned forward, his elbows propped on the desk. "If you don't mind my saying, you seem like you don't know whether to scratch your watch or wind your butt.

Whoever this woman is, she's got you confused as hell. Are you sure you wanted to break up with her? Was this some sort of weird impulse? Were you drinking? Did you argue?"

Knox had been thinking about it all night and still wasn't quite sure how to describe it.

"I wouldn't say we argued. But we had a disagreement."

"Okay, so you ended the relationship over this disagreement but now you're having second thoughts."

Was he? No, he'd done the right thing. Jenna was a liar. Plain and simple.

"I'm not having second thoughts."

Logan's brows shot up. "Then you're going to have to help me out here because I can't see why you're being such a shit to everyone today and acting like a bear with a sore paw."

Knox's hesitation must have clued Logan in.

"Is it personal? You don't have to tell me about it. I respect your privacy. What I will say is whatever it is, try to leave it at the door. You can't take out your frustrations on everyone else in the office."

Do I want to talk about it?

Knox would trust Logan with his life. That was a fact.

"It is personal," Knox admitted. "But I'm not keeping it a secret. It turns out that Jenna didn't bump into me by accident that first night at the sports bar. She knew who I was."

"She knew who you were?" Logan echoed. "I'm not sure I follow you."

As succinctly as he could, Knox explained what had transpired the night before all the way to the point where he drove away and then spent the entire night tossing and turning.

"She wanted you to help prove that your brother had something to do with her sister's disappearance? That's one wild story."

"I certainly didn't see it coming. I was shocked."

"Did you even know Callum was dating this woman?"

Knox shook his head. "I haven't seen him since...you know..."

Logan was well aware of Ben Owens and his issues.

"And you're certain he wouldn't do anything like this?"

That was a question that Knox had been chewing on all night. He hadn't much liked the answers he was coming up with either.

"Callum is a grade-A narcissist and all-around asshole. I definitely believe he could be verbally and mentally abusive to his partner, but I've never seen him get violent with a female. I don't think he would kidnap and then maybe kill his girlfriend. I do see him making her wish she'd never started dating him to begin with."

"You and I both know that behavior can escalate."

"True," Knox conceded. "I just don't see it with Callum. I'm not trying to protect him or anything. Believe me, I have no delusions about what a dick he is, but I don't think he's a kidnapper or a murderer."

"So that's that."

Logan had...something in his tone. Like he wanted to say more but he wasn't going to.

Dammit.

"That's that," Knox agreed. "I told Jenna that I wasn't going to help her. She lied to me, after all. And stalked me too."

For some reason he felt like he needed to justify his decision to Logan. It was a good decision. Sound. He didn't need to defend it or himself.

"So you're walking away? Just letting it go?"

"Of course, what else would I do?" Knox paused for a moment. "What would you do?"

Rubbing his chin, Logan shook his head. "I don't think I should weigh in here. This is a personal issue for you. You said so yourself."

But now Knox really wanted to know. He respected Logan's opinion as a boss and as a friend.

"I wouldn't mind your thinking on this."

Logan didn't answer right away, still rubbing at his chin, his lips twisted.

"I think," he finally said, his words measured. "I think that my curiosity would get the better of me and I'd have to look into her claims. Aren't you the least little bit curious as to what happened to her sister? It's not even my brother being accused and I'm curious as hell."

Knox had mostly been concentrating on Jenna's betrayal, but he had found his mind wandering to the myriad of possibilities a few times.

"A little," he admitted. "But I don't think that I should get involved. From what Jenna says, the cops aren't even investigating this. They seem to think that her sister's gone off on her own for awhile."

Logan smiled. "And cops are never wrong."

Knox had most certainly been wrong in the past. So had every lawman that Knox had ever known. They weren't superhuman, they were fallible just like everyone else. They did their best though and they tried to do the right thing.

"I'm not sure that I want to see Jenna again."

Knox hadn't been able to shake her expression, the pain and desperation. To do what she'd done...

Stop. Don't make excuses for her.

Shrugging, Logan sat back in his chair. "Then don't. I'm not suggesting that you do. Just look into the case, do a little research. See how you feel after that. You don't need to make any decisions right now. In fact, you don't need to make any sort of decisions today or tomorrow or the next day. If this woman has been missing for months, she's probably not going to suddenly reappear in the next week or so. And if she does, then this is all a moot point, isn't it?"

Right. Knox didn't need to give himself a headache thinking about all of this crap. He could just sit with it for awhile and maybe, down the road, he might think about looking into the case.

For his own curiosity. Not because he wanted to help Jenna.

"Sure, that's what I'll do. There's no hurry at all."

Logan stood, which meant that the meeting was over.

Knox ducked out of the office and went back to his desk, determined to get his head in the game. Last night was over, Jenna was out of his life, and he had more important work to occupy his time.

He'd think about it all later. Much later.

5

Luckily, Chris Marks was an easygoing guy and despite the fact that he and Knox had been at each other's throats in the morning, by midday they were friends again. They decided to head out for a late lunch around one-thirty, both of them starved.

"We could just go to the sports bar," Chris suggested as Knox started the car. "It's fast and cheap, and I could go for a cheeseburger."

Except that was where Knox had met Jenna. He didn't need the reminder today.

"How about we hit the pizza place," Knox suggested. "My treat."

"Then I'm in," Chris laughed. "I love a lunch I don't have to pay for."

The pizza joint wasn't far and soon they were shown to a booth in the back. They ordered a large with pepperoni and extra cheese.

"So did Logan rip you a new one?" Chris asked when the waitress had bustled away to get their drinks.

"Not really. He just told me to keep my bad moods out of the office."

"Very restrained of him. But you were in there for awhile. Did you get a new assignment?"

"No, we just chatted."

Chris' brow quirked up. "Chatted? Now you have my attention. What in the hell were you *chatting* about?"

Knox might as well tell his friend the truth. He was going to find out sooner or later anyway.

"Jenna and I broke up over the weekend."

Frowning, Chris shook his head. "You asked Logan for romantic advice? I guess he must know something. Ava has stayed with him all of these years."

"Shit, no. I didn't ask him about that. We talked about why we broke up. It's what put me in my bad mood."

"That was my next question," Chris said as the waitress slid their sodas in front of them. "What the hell happened with Jenna? She's amazing. Great. Oh hell, did she dump you?"

That was the second person today who had assumed that Knox was the *dumpee* instead of the *dumper*. It was starting to piss him off.

"No, she did not dump me. I'm the one who ended it."

Chris held up his hands in surrender. "Excuse the hell out of me. I didn't mean to offend you. I just...well...shit...you seemed really into her Saturday night. What in the hell happened after you went home? It must have been one big blowout. Did you find out she's married or a secret government agent?"

Both of these would have been preferable to the reality.

"Jenna and I didn't meet by chance that first night. She knew who I was."

"You're not exactly a celebrity. How did she know who you were?"

"Because she'd been following me," Knox replied with a

sigh. "I'll tell you the story but you're probably not going to believe it."

He recounted the details from Saturday night all the way to when he walked out. Chris didn't say anything while Knox spoke, just nodding as if he heard shit like this every single day.

"You don't even seem shocked," Knox observed when he was done. "Not even a little bit."

"I am surprised but I wouldn't say that I'm shocked. Very little can do that after the crap we've seen in this job. Also, you've told me from your own lips that your brother is a piece of work and an asshole. It's hard to be shocked that he might be wrapped up in something nefarious, isn't it?"

"Cal is a grade A asshole but kidnap and murder someone? He's never done anything even remotely like that."

"Has he ever hit anyone?"

Knox shrugged away the question. "Sure, we all have. We beat up on each other growing up all the time."

Chris laughed and shook his head. "No, I mean someone else. I get that siblings are shits to one another, although I never could have gotten away with hitting my sister. My dad would have grounded me for life for something like that. I was asking if he's ever hit a stranger. Bar fights? Domestic violence? That sort of thing."

"There have been a few tussles," Knox admitted. "Mostly drunken bullshit, especially when we were younger. I don't know if there's been anything recent because I try not to spend any time with my family if I can help it. As for anything domestic, I don't know that either. I do know that he's a terrible boyfriend. He cheats and lies and those are his good qualities."

"He sounds like a real charmer," Chris said sarcastically. "How does he attract women?"

"The same way my dad does. In the beginning they're all suave and debonair. They're the greatest boyfriend in the history of romance. They bring flowers, shower them with gifts and compliments. They only show who they really are when they think they have the female totally in love with them. Then the women keep thinking that my dad is going to change back into that great guy but he never does. He just keeps getting worse until they finally can't take it anymore or they get too old for him and he moves on to another victim. Cal learned from the best."

"Your dad sounds..." Chris' voice trailed off. "I have no idea how you turned out so normal."

"Neither do I, but then I wonder if I am all that normal. Maybe I'm as fucked up as they are, but I don't know it."

"You aren't fucked up. You're a pain in the ass, but you're not a liar and a cheat."

"My younger brother Randy turned out pretty normal too. I try and stay in touch with him, and my sisters aren't too bad. At least one of them is fairly normal. The other has a temper and frankly, I don't like to be around her when she yells."

Knox didn't like it when anyone raised their voice, to be truthful. After watching his mother and father fight for years, he didn't like angry confrontation, yelling, or fighting of any type. He liked to keep the peace if at all possible.

Chris leaned forward in his chair. "Was it bad? Did you and Jenna have it out? Did she cry? Damn, it rips my heart out when Ella cries."

"It wasn't bad. I stated that I was angry and disappointed, and I told her that our relationship was over. She did cry though."

Knox could still see Jenna's tearstained face in his mind. It was going to be a while before he could forget it.

"I hope you weren't too hard on her. She must have been so fucking desperate to do something like that. I can't even imagine what she and her sister have been going through, not knowing what happened to their own sibling, and the police not really doing anything about it. It had to have made her crazy."

"Are you making excuses for her? Because what she did was some serial killer shit."

Chris threw back his head and laughed, causing a few heads nearby to whip around to see what was so funny. Apparently, it was Knox.

"Are you seriously equating what Jenna did with someone like Wade Bryson? Because I don't think I can listen to anything you have to say if that's what you're trying to do. Listen, I know you're upset about her searching for you and then not telling you who she was, but you've already admitted to me that you now realize she was trying to talk to you, but you kept derailing the conversation. You have a part in this, too."

Knox didn't want to hear that any of this shit was his fault.

"This is all on her," he argued. "She should have found a way to tell me who she was."

"How should she have done that?" Chris asked, his expression somber. "This is a serious question. You've told me that you recognize that several times she's started to tell you and being the playboy, man about town, baby, don't get hooked on me kind of guy that you are you made sure that she couldn't keep talking. All because you thought she was going to ask you some bullshit question like *where is this relationship going* or *are you seeing anyone else*? And you were such a pussy about that you wouldn't let her talk. So tell me how she's a serial killer again because I'm not seeing it. What I'm seeing is a woman so fucking desperate she was willing to ruin her blouse with beer and talk to you in a bar. That's it. All of us really liked Jenna. She seems like a good person."

Knox didn't want to talk about what Jenna might or might not be.

"Lots of women would happily talk to me in a bar."

Chris's grin spread across his face. "That's what this is about, isn't it? You're all butthurt because you realize that she wasn't dating you because she was all starry eyed and admiring your male physique. She bumped into you because she needed your help. Shit, this is about your bruised ego. Full stop."

"That's not it," Knox denied with a shake of his head. "That's not it at all. I just don't want to date someone like Jenna. That's all."

"Fine, you don't have to date her." Chris paused but Knox could tell that his friend wasn't done talking. "But can you honestly tell me that you're not the least bit curious? Come on, we live for cases like this, and now one's been thrown right in your lap. You don't even want to look into it? Just a few hours of research? You're a stronger man than I am. Maybe I'll look into it then. I definitely have questions that I'd like answered even if you don't."

"Knock yourself out. I don't want to get Jenna's hopes up by doing any sort of research for this. Don't you think that would hurt her even more?" Knox pressed. "It would be cruel to make her think I was going to help when that's not my intention at all."

"That's true," Chris conceded. "Although I would argue that you don't know whether you would proceed with the investigation. You just think that now. After some research, you might change your mind."

"I'm not going to change my mind."

"Fine."

"Good. Because I'm not going to."

"I didn't say shit. It's fine."

"I know it is so stop busting my balls about it."

"I'm not doing anything," Chris laughed. "You're doing it to yourself."

The waitress arriving with their lunch gave Knox a reprieve from replying. They both dug into their food and the conversation drifted toward more innocuous subjects like work and the weather.

He felt badly for Jenna but he wasn't going to investigate this case. End of story.

After they finished their meal, Chris and Knox went back to the office. Since Knox was between cases, Luke asked him for help looking through old missing person cases from the 1990s which only served to keep reminding him about Jenna's sister. All day long.

By the end of the day, his mood wasn't much better than it had been that morning. He needed a couple of ibuprofen and a good night's sleep. A hot meal wouldn't be amiss either.

What I need is a distraction.

For a moment he thought about heading down to the local watering hole near his apartment but then decided against it. He was crabby and tired, not the ideal state to drink. Plus he was at the point in his life where he was getting tired of the whole...bar thing. He was beginning to notice that he was a lot older than many of the other patrons. It was a sure sign that it was time to move on and grow the hell up. With the exception of Jenna, the women he'd met lately weren't the type he'd want to date for more than an evening or two.

And he'd stopped having one night stands over a decade ago.

He packed up his briefcase and was heading to the exit when Chris appeared, holding up a file folder.

"Looks like I have some reading this evening," he said with a mischievous grin. "Don't worry. I won't say anything about it to you tomorrow."

Knox knew what was in that damn folder. Chris was between assignments as well and helping other people out, so obviously he'd taken a few hours and done some research on Jenna's sister.

Son of a bitch.

Knox wasn't going to have a drink at a bar. He wasn't going to have a peaceful evening in front of the television with some greasy takeout.

He was going to be reading that goddamn file.

Because he couldn't take it anymore. Chris was right. The curiosity was strong. This wasn't about helping Jenna. This was about clearing his obviously fucked up head.

"Give it to me."

Chris blinked at him innocently.

"Give you what?"

Knox didn't need this shit.

"Just fucking give it to me."

Chris's gaze moved to the folder in his hand, a shocked expression on his face as if finding it there was a complete surprise.

"You mean this?"

Knox held out his hand. "Just give it to me before I kick your ass."

Laughing, Chris glanced over his shoulder. "Don't let Logan hear you say that. We're supposed to be a team, and you're supposed to be keeping your pissy moods out of the office. That didn't last long, did it?"

Sighing, Knox hung his head. "Just give me the folder before they find your body in a shallow grave."

"You wouldn't be that careless," Chris scoffed. "None of us would. If you killed me, they'd never find the body."

"That's true. I'm already thinking about dump spots."

"How about that place by–"

"For fuck's sake, give it to me and go home to your wife."

This time Chris handed it over.

"It actually looks pretty interesting. Let's talk about it tomorrow after you look through it."

Knox shoved it into his briefcase. He wasn't a happy man.

"I'm just going to look at it. I'm not going to help Jenna."

"Sure, just keep telling yourself that. Who are you trying to convince? Me or you?"

Me. Most definitely me. Damn.

6

It had been a shitty day and all Jenna wanted was to order in some dinner and then take a long, hot bath. She planned on scrubbing her skin raw. After spending less than an hour interviewing a potential private investigator, she felt dirty. Icky. He had to be the sleaziest guy in the entire state. Possibly the whole country. Within five minutes of being in his company, she'd wanted to vomit.

I won't be hiring him.

He hadn't taken the news well either. When she'd finally managed to make her way around him and to his office exit, he'd realized she wasn't going to hire him, he'd become angry and nasty. He'd actually had the audacity to grab her by the arm and that's when the shit got real for Jenna. She didn't like anyone she didn't know to touch her. It was a thing from her childhood. She'd jerked her arm away and almost yelled the place down, her anger bubbling over. He'd finally backed away but not before calling her a whacko. She hadn't bothered to return the favor, instead taking the opportunity to flee.

Even now, more than an hour later her heart was still

pounding and the adrenaline still pumping through her veins. She'd been in fight or flight mode, and she would have fought to get out of there if she'd had to. Just being enclosed in that small office with his body blocking the door had her sweating and panicking.

And if anyone was the whacko, it was him.

He'd actually thought he could convince her to sleep with him in return for his taking her case. This guy made her skin crawl.

Jenna poured herself a glass of wine and pulled out a takeout menu from the Italian place on the next block. They were reasonably priced and the portions were huge. She'd have lunch for the next day as well. She was deciding between lasagna and chicken parmesan when her doorbell rang.

She wasn't expecting anyone. Heck, she didn't even know anyone around here. She'd only moved into this short-term rental about six weeks ago. She'd relocated here to "bump" into Knox.

See how that worked out for me? I'm a terrible person.

But I still miss him. He was...more than I'd ever expected. I didn't expect to like him so much.

Cautious, she peered out of the peephole. She wouldn't open the door to strangers.

Knox. Here. At her home. She hadn't expected that. At all. In fact, as pissed off as he'd been Saturday night, she hadn't expected to see him ever again.

Jenna didn't know what had brought him to her front door but she was irrationally happy to see him. Sadly, she didn't hold out any hope that he'd changed his mind. He'd been more than adamant. No, he was probably here to tell her more ways she'd disappointed him, but that didn't stop her from opening the door.

Without a word, Knox brushed past her, striding into the

middle of her bland home. Surrounded by nothing but beige and tan, he appeared to be the most vital thing in the living room. She couldn't stop herself from drinking in his presence, far too handsome and way cockier than any human being should have a right to be. But there he was, standing there in a casual pair of blue jeans and a black button-down shirt but somehow looking like a goddamn male movie star.

It ought to be illegal to be that good looking and sexy.

With all that looks and charisma, she wondered why he was here. Surely, he'd already replaced her with a newer model.

"Knox–"

"Let me say my piece," he said, cutting her off rudely. She would have told him off but he didn't let her get a word in edgewise. His expression was intent, focused and she had a feeling he might have rehearsed what he was going to say in the car so she just gave up and let him go. She'd tell him off afterward. "I've done a lot of thinking about this whole situation. A hell of a lot of thinking and I've come to a few conclusions."

He paused slightly and she thought this might be her chance to tell him where he could stick his thoughts but then he continued.

"First, I've decided that I'm going to help you with this investigation. But...you have to have an open mind. If the investigation points away from Cal, I don't want to hear any whining from you. We'll go where the case leads us."

Dumbfounded. That was the word she was looking for. She was dumbfounded. This was the last thing she'd expected tonight.

Knox was going to help her. He'd changed his mind.

But why? She didn't ask because he hadn't shut up yet.

"Second, if your sister is found safe and sound, I'm going to be an insufferable asshole about it."

I have no doubt about that.

"And third, there will be no romance or relationship between us. I'm only helping you with the investigation. We're not a couple. We're not even friends. We're just working together. That's it. If you can't accept those conditions then I'm out."

That hurt. She couldn't deny it but caring about her own feelings seemed petty at the moment. He was going to help them find out what happened to Lori. Finally, they were going to get some answers. This was what they'd been hoping and praying for.

"I accept your terms," she said when he stopped, waiting for her reply. "And if we find Lori safe and sound you can gloat all you like. I'll just be thrilled to find my sister alive and well."

"No relationship," he reminded her. "We're not friends."

He really wanted to twist the knife.

"As I said, I accept that. Although I think it's a mistake to act like enemies. We're going to be working together. We should at least try to get along with one another. Otherwise, this is going to be unpleasant."

"I see your point. Okay, we're friends, but we're not a couple. You need to keep your distance."

Jenna rolled her eyes. "Now you're just being ridiculous. I'm not going to assault you or try to seduce you. I don't want a man who is unwilling. I get it. You're not interested. Your virtue - what there is of it - is safe from me."

She didn't bring up the fact that it hadn't been that long ago that he'd been trying to get her into bed. Things had certainly changed since then.

He held up a file folder. "Then let's get to work. I want to hear your complete story. Every detail, even the ones you think aren't important. Then we'll go through the research my friend found today."

"I was just about to order in some dinner. Should I make it for two?"

"A working dinner, not a date."

She had to stop herself from rolling her eyes. Again.

"Got it. Now what do you want?"

It was happening. Knox was going to help.

They were going to find out what happened to Lori. Good or bad. There were answers out there, and they needed to find them.

KNOX HAD ARGUED with himself for over an hour before ending up at Jenna's place. After looking through the file that Chris had put together, he could no longer deny that the case intrigued him. Everything Jenna had told him was true. Her sister was supposed to show up for a date with Cal, she didn't show, and had never been heard from again except from a lone text from Lori's phone a few days later.

No other texts followed. No contact of any kind. Her phone and purse were gone, but her car wasn't. That was a red flag to Knox. There hadn't been any plane, bus, or railroad tickets found either. She'd been seen earlier in the day by her neighbors and then she was gone. She hadn't packed anything and her luggage was tucked neatly in her closet.

According to the missing person report, Cal hadn't seen Lori that day, but the coffee shop barista stated otherwise. Lori was a regular there and they all knew her. It didn't make any sense.

This was Knox's favorite kind of case. One big mystery wrapped up in knots. He loved to pull at the strings and see what came loose. Usually it was a big pile of secrets and lies.

Speaking of lies...He could totally believe that his brother Cal hadn't told the truth. That didn't mean he was responsible for Lori's disappearance but Knox had to also admit that it made his brother look suspicious.

Not suspicious enough for the local police though. They'd taken that text as complete proof that Lori wasn't a "missing" person and they hadn't done much investigating after that. Chris hadn't been able to find much either. Knox was going to need Jenna to fill in the details because they didn't have much to go on.

She'd ordered dinner, poured him a glass of wine, and they'd settled onto her couch to talk. He made sure to keep to his end of the sofa, wanting to make sure that things stayed completely platonic. He wanted her to see that he was serious about his conditions for taking this case. To be honest, he'd assumed that she'd agree. He'd already sent Logan and Reed a text asking about taking some time off. He rarely took any vacation so he had quite a bit saved up. Just the other day, Reed had been bugging him about booking some time off so Knox didn't think this would be an issue. If a big investigation came in, he could come back quickly or fly out to the job location.

"So tell me the whole story," he said while they waited for dinner to be delivered. "Every detail. Start at the beginning. How did you meet Lori?"

Jenna visibly took a deep breath before diving in. Now that he was sitting and relaxed, he could see that she was anything but. Her whole demeanor was one of tension, her hands wringing together tightly until the knuckles were white. He had a sudden urge to reach out and press his own hands on top of hers but he instantly quelled it. Those feelings weren't welcome anymore.

It was probably just a habit. He'd get over it soon. He was like this, though. Always wanting to protect someone in distress. How many times had he stood between his mother and his sisters? Too many to count. There hadn't necessarily been violence but there had been yelling and ugly name calling. There were always tears and hurt. When he'd left that house and joined the military he'd been filled with guilt, leaving his younger siblings to deal with his neglectful and histrionic mother all alone. Jenna brought all of those unwelcome instincts out in him.

She's not mine to protect.

"I met Lori in school. We were just kids in fifth grade but we hit it off immediately. She was fun and outgoing and we had so much in common. We became best friends and spent all of our free time together. I was an only child so she became like a sister to me." Jenna paused and then grimaced. "I didn't have the best home life, to be honest. We were poor and there was never enough food in the house and my clothes were always old and didn't fit right. I was an only child and I spent most of my time alone. My mom tried to work when she could but her health wasn't great. My dad was a huge loser who never could hold down a job and was always drunk. So needless to say, I was thrilled to be invited over to Lori's house because it meant that I didn't have to be in my own home. My parents never noticed when I wasn't there so it wasn't a big deal."

Knox could understand a great deal of Jenna's story. His mother wouldn't have won any prizes either and his father was no better.

"I spent every moment that I could at Lori's house. Her family had money - lots of it - but her parents thought it was important for her and her twin sister Michelle to go to public school. They didn't want their kids to get stuck up or not realize how other families lived. They were the nicest people and they sort of adopted me. I ate dinner at their house and often spent the night. Lori and Michelle shared their clothes with me. When their parents would take them anywhere like out to dinner or to the zoo, they'd take me too. We were like the Three Musketeers. We were so close. We didn't have any secrets from one another and we wanted to be together all the time. Lori's family was amazing, and I can't imagine what my life would have been like without them. They really taught me what family meant. I didn't have any idea before that."

"They sound like wonderful people," Knox said when Jenna paused for a moment. "You were lucky."

"I *was* lucky," she said, her gaze far away, the memories painful from the expression on her face. She looked...sad...and disappointed. But mostly, she looked hurt as if she was in physical pain. Once again, Knox had to fight the impulse to reach out and comfort her. It would only confuse matters. "My parents never should have had a child. They weren't equipped to deal with me or anything to do with raising a kid. My mom was far too frail and my dad was simply a jerk."

They had much in common.

"Eventually, my mother's ill health caught up with her and she passed away when I was fifteen," Jenna continues, her blue eyes sparkling with tears. "She wasn't the greatest parent but I know that she loved me. She tried, at least. It's more than I can say for my so-called father."

The last sentence was laced with bitterness.

"Where is your father now?"

Her lips curled with derision. "At the bottom of a liquor bottle, I would imagine. I haven't seen him in awhile. The last time was two years ago. It was not pleasant so I'm not planning to do it again anytime soon."

"What happened after your mother died?"

Knox asked the question but he wasn't sure that he wanted the answer. He had a feeling that Jenna's life had probably gone downhill from there.

Instead of frowning, she smiled, wiping a stray tear from her cheek.

"I went to live with Lori's family. Tom and Anita became my *de facto* parents. They knew what my home life was like. I never tried to hide how bad it was, and after my mom died, I think they knew it was only going to keep getting worse. They actually asked my father if I could stay with them for awhile. He was thrilled, of course. I could be someone else's problem and he could spend the little money he had on booze. Later I found out they paid him a monthly allowance as well. They basically bought me but I didn't care. I was just glad that they were willing to get me out of there. Tom and Anita treated me like their own daughter. Not once did I ever feel second best."

"I never moved back in with my father but I did see him from time to time. Tom would take me over on holidays like Christmas so I could give my dad a gift. Usually my dad would be drunk and he'd yell at me. Eventually when I turned eighteen, I told Tom that I didn't want to go anymore."

There were a few more tears from Jenna and she reached across him to a box of tissues, her shoulder brushing against his arm. A bolt of electricity ran through his limb and through his veins, making him grit his teeth against the sensations that this woman could arouse.

No complications. Business only.

"How did your father take that?" he asked, hoping to distract himself from her nearness. He should have sat across the room in a chair. They needed more space between them.

"I doubt he noticed much other than Tom and Anita didn't pay him anymore. That's what he was most upset about. That's how I found out, actually. He called me to complain."

"What did you say?"

Knox had a morbid curiosity regarding her relationship with her family. It was so much like his own.

"I told him he was a lousy parent and to never call me again."

Ballsy, for someone so young, but then one of the things he'd liked about Jenna was that she was no shrinking violet.

"And did he stop calling?"

She shook her head. "No, but he did it less often. He called when he wanted money. Tom never gave it to him. I really don't know why he kept trying. It didn't make any sense to me."

"Desperate people don't always use logic."

"That's true. I wouldn't say that my father ever did."

"So what happened after that?" Knox asked. "Between eighteen years old and Lori's disappearance."

"We all three went to college. Michelle got a finance degree. She wanted to work in the family real estate business. Lori majored in marketing, and I had a double major in psychology and political science. Both Michelle and I went on to get our master's, and afterward I started working on local political campaigns. I'd always been fascinated by politics and current events. Tom had contacts and I worked hard to make my mark. From there, I was able to move on to statewide campaigns. In the meantime, Lori started at an advertising company that was owned by a friend of Tom's. That's how she met your brother."

Knox was absolutely sure that Cal had never worked in advertising. Ever.

"I'm going to need more details on that. Exactly how did they meet?"

"One of her co-workers introduced them. A friend of a friend sort of thing. They hit it off and the relationship got serious very quickly. Somehow, she convinced her firm to let her work remotely, and she moved to Douglas so she could be closer to Cal."

The expression on Jenna's face told him everything he needed to know about how she felt about Callum and Lori moving closer to him.

"I can probably guess that my brother was a shitty boyfriend," Knox groused. "He takes after my dad far too much."

He was ready for Jenna to launch into a laundry list of complaints but the doorbell rang, cutting off any reply she might have made. The break was more than welcome. He needed to get his shit together and fast. He was feeling far more than he was comfortable with. Working together was going to be a disaster unless he could keep his distance. He didn't want to be attracted to Jenna anymore.

The problem was he liked her way too much. This wasn't going to be easy. If he was smart, he'd walk out the door right now.

But I've never been that bright.

7

Jenna needed to pull herself together. She hated crying in general, and then doing it in front of Knox was even worse. He wasn't interested in her emotions clearly, and he'd practically shrank back into a sofa cushion when the tears started to flow.

I get it. He hates me. Fine.

She didn't blame him, but it didn't make it any easier. The entire situation always seemed to make her weepy, and then to add on to it, she was still attracted to Knox. She didn't want to be, but so far, her heart wasn't listening to her. Before she'd met him, she hadn't expected to like him - as a boyfriend. After all, Cal was his brother. She'd only been hoping that he was open-minded enough to listen. If he could say that his father shouldn't get parole, he just might think that his brother could be responsible for Lori's disappearance. Knox had exceeded all of her expectations and then some.

She carried the two bags of food into her kitchen, placing them on the round table in the corner before gathering up plates, glasses, silverware, and napkins. There was a heavenly scent wafting from the food and her stomach growled hungrily, demanding to be fed. It had been several hours since she'd last eaten.

"Can I help?" Knox asked, his big body looming right behind her. She could smell the clean scent of his body wash - citrus and spice. "It looks like you're having trouble reaching the glasses."

She was having trouble. This wasn't really her kitchen; it was a short-term rental. The person who had set up this kitchen had to have been about seven feet tall. She was no shorty but it seemed like everything useful was on the top shelves. She'd gotten into the habit of leaving out one plate and glass on the kitchen counter.

"Thanks, I could use a hand."

Except that this kitchen was so damn tiny they were practically playing a game of Twister as he reached over her head for the glasses and she stretched in front of his abdomen to open the flatware drawer. For a split second they were pressed together almost nose to nose, and she could barely breathe at the contact. The warmth of his body seared through the cotton blouse and blue jeans she was wearing.

He's too close. Or not close enough. I can't decide.

"I don't mean to be rude, but why do you keep your glasses on the top shelf? It's not very convenient."

She set the plates and silverware on the table. "It's not a rude question. It's a good one, actually. So here's the answer. This isn't my place. It's just a short-term rental off the internet. When I took it, I wasn't sure how long I was going to be here."

His expression shifted from neutral to something more akin to anger, but it changed back so quickly she would have missed it if she wasn't looking at him. He was obviously thinking about how she'd lied to meet him.

"So is any of what you told me in the beginning true?" he asked, his lips pressed into a thin line. "You told me that you recently moved here from Brighton Bend."

Settling into a chair to eat, she thought carefully about her answer before replying. It sounded like he wanted to catch her in more lies so he could continue to be pissed at her. If he wanted to be mad, he could do that. He didn't need to make up excuses for himself. She was a big girl; she could take it.

"I did not lie to you about that, Knox. I had just recently moved here from Brighton Bend. The only thing I didn't say was how long I intended on staying. The fact is I'm rarely in my own home. In my job, I travel quite a bit."

"You told me you're a political campaign advisor."

She sighed at his tone. "I am a political campaign advisor which is why I travel so much. My last job was in Florida. The reason I came here instead of Michelle is that she has a regular nine to five job and I was between campaigns. That's how it goes for me. I work non-stop evenings and weekends too for months and then I take some time off in between."

He finally sat down as well while she pulled the delicious smelling food from the bags. His stomach growled loudly and she had to cough to cover her giggle.

"I guess I'm pretty hungry," he admitted, helping himself from the abundant food. Knowing his appetite, she'd ordered enough for an army. Whenever they'd been together, Knox had put away a massive amount of food. "This is good."

"I've had them several times. The food has always been excellent."

They didn't speak much while they ate, simply commenting on the food a little. The tension in the room had shifted into a higher gear at some point, and Jenna was acutely aware that Knox was sitting across from her at this ridiculously tiny table. Their knees and elbow brushed even when she was trying to keep to her side. Each touch sent a frisson of awareness through her body and she wanted to scream with frustration by the time they finished their meal.

She stood to clear the table, but so did Knox.

"Let me help you with the dishes."

Oh hell, no. The kitchen was too small for them to both be in there and still keep any sort of semblance of distance.

"I got this. It will only take a few minutes. Why don't you sit down and I'll be right there."

He looked like he wanted to argue but then his phone buzzed in his pocket. Pulling it out, he thumbed the screen and then frowned before shoving it back.

"Something important?"

Knox shook his head. "Not at all. I can deal with it later."

This time he did leave the kitchen to sit on the couch while she cleared up their dinner. When she joined him, he was standing at the front window staring out at the street. The sky was pink and purple as the sun was beginning to set.

"What are you thinking about?"

It was a stupid question and she regretted asking it the minute the words left her tongue. It sounded so fucking cliché.

What are you thinking about? Is it me? Is it me?

It sounded almost desperate.

He didn't turn around right away, still staring outside. "The case. Your sister. Tell me more about your relationship with her, and hers with Cal. Did you talk to her often? See her? What did she say?"

"We talked almost every day. She talked about her job, which she enjoyed. She also talked about Cal. Things sounded really good at the beginning but then later she'd tell us that he lost his temper or that he didn't like her friends or co-workers. Honestly, he sounded controlling and toxic. She'd call us crying quite a bit about something he said. We'd tell her to talk to him about it and set some boundaries but later he'd say that he never said it or that it was just a joke and that she had a bad sense of humor."

That was Knox's dad. Right there. Cal had learned at the knee of a master. Whenever his dad had been especially shitty and someone would try and call him out, he'd simply deny that he ever said it or tell them they couldn't take a joke. Benjamin Owens thought he was a laugh a minute. Funny, but Knox didn't think his dad's humor was amusing at all.

"You encouraged her to leave him, I assume?"

"All the time. She'd try and end things but she said that he'd cry and say that he was going to do better. That he was nothing without her. She'd give in."

"And the cycle would start all over again. I've seen it may times. Not just at home but when I was a cop doing domestic calls. I don't know how many times I heard the words *but it will be different this time.* In my experience, it rarely - if ever - was. Maybe that makes me a pessimist. Or a realist. Or just damn tired, old, and full of cynicism."

"Lori has such a tender heart," Jenna said, her eyes filling with tears again. "She always tried to see the best in people all the time. She was always like that, rooting for the underdog. I mean...she took me in."

"I doubt you ever gave her a reason to regret that."

"I hope that's true," Jenna replied softly, sniffling into a tissue. "I've always wanted to make her and her family proud of me."

"I'm sure you did. It sounds like you've done well for yourself."

Both Tom and Anita had said that they were proud of her. That was more than enough reward for her hard work. They'd made everything possible.

"What do we do now? What are the next steps?" she asked, giving him a watery smile. "Now that you've agreed to help us, I can't wait to get started. I tried to hire a private investigator today but that didn't turn out well at all."

His eyes narrowed suspiciously. He must have heard something in her tone.

"What happened?"

Rolling her eyes, she groaned. "Let's just say that he got a little handsy and suggested that I could pay him in other ways besides monetarily."

His lips tightened and his blue eyes turned icy. "What was his name? I can–"

"I handled it," Jenna replied, waving away his concern. "I told him off too. He was a jerk. I have another appointment tomorrow with another investigator but I'll cancel it in the morning."

Knox frowned. "Did you ever think to hire the firm that I work for?"

She shook her head. "I wouldn't do that to you. You said you never wanted to see me again and I had to respect it even if I didn't like it."

"My firm has dozens of investigators. And they wouldn't have tried any of the crap that other guy did."

"I didn't know that." She shrugged. "It hardly matters now, although we'd be happy to pay your firm for your time to help us. It's only fair."

"I was planning on asking for time off."

"You won't have to if we hire you officially. I really don't want to take advantage of you, Knox. I know that we're lucky to have your help on this. Very lucky."

"I'd like to see that text from Lori. The last one she sent. Do you still have it? We also need a list of all her friends, co-workers, neighbors, and family. Anyone she mentioned, even if it was only casually. She could have had someone watching her, stalking her. Did she ever mention anyone that might have been a nuisance? A man that couldn't take no for an answer?"

"I don't think so but I can ask Michelle. Maybe she said something to her." Jenna paused, knowing she was about to open a can of worms. "Will you be talking to your brother?"

"Of course."

Knox's expression was giving nothing away at the moment.

But she knew better. He had issues with his family. Not the same ones that she had, but serious ones. The type that didn't get solved overnight. If ever.

"I'm guessing you're not looking forward to it."

"You could say that I'm the outcast of the family," Knox replied, checking his buzzing phone again before putting it back in his pocket. "I don't really fit in and I never did. I'm fine with it but it makes for awkward meetings and lousy holidays."

"You being the outcast is why I thought there might be even a slight chance that you'd help us."

They talked a little more about what Knox planned to do. They both decided that they needed to travel to Douglas to talk to Lori's neighbors and friends. He also talked about pulling her phone and credit card records as well.

It was almost ten o'clock when he stood and said he needed to get home. They had a great deal of work ahead of them. Jenna was too excited to sleep but she wouldn't keep Knox from getting his rest. She walked him to the door and although they'd shared a few passionate embraces in her entryway, this time they wouldn't be kissing before he left.

Nope, he was currently standing about three feet away.

"I'll call you in the morning. We'll make plans from there."

"I'm an early riser," she said, leaning against the door frame. "So you can call early if you need to."

"I need to talk to Logan in the morning about all of this before I call you."

"I meant what I said. We'll pay to hire you if it makes it easier."

They didn't say anything else, that tension between them building again. She could hear the chirp of crickets and some music being played far away. She could feel her heartbeat too. It was pounding way too fast because of this man.

"So goodnight," he said, bounding toward his car. "Call you."

He sounded just like a guy at the end of a bad date. He says

I'll call you, but he wasn't going to call. Except...he would call because he'd said he'd help. He just wasn't going to call for a date.

Jenna would rather have Knox's help finding Lori than his kisses.

But it sucked that she had to choose.

8

It was dark outside. Because it was five in the morning.

Jenna had always considered herself okay with mornings but this was a bit earlier than she was used to. In the last campaign she'd worked, there had been many late nights which often meant sleeping in the next day. She'd grown used to it.

Even the birds weren't awake yet. Smart birds.

Stretching and yawning, Jenna poured herself a large travel mug of coffee, the heady aroma perking her up slightly. She took a sip of the hot brew and sighed as it hit her stomach. Soon the caffeine would be winding its way through her veins, waking her up and hopefully helping her form words into sentences so she made sense.

She'd already showered and dressed, shoved last-minute items like her toothbrush into her suitcase, and placed her bags by the door. Knox was going to be pulling up in front of her apartment any second now and she didn't want to keep him waiting. They were going to Douglas, Montana to start the investigation, although they were planning on staying with Jenna's family in Green Falls less than an hour away.

They were driving there. As in a road trip. Jenna still wasn't sure why they weren't flying into Billings and renting a car from there. Michelle had even offered to pick them up at the airport and then lend them one of the family vehicles so they could get around but Knox hadn't been all that fond of the idea. He'd kept shaking his head whenever Jenna had talked about taking a flight, so eventually she'd dropped the subject. He was doing them a favor, after all.

Although, technically, it wasn't really a favor anymore. Two days ago, she and Michelle had officially hired Knox's firm to investigate Lori's disappearance. It was such a relief to put it in the hands of a professional team. She'd even met with Logan, Knox's boss, and he'd assured her that their team would do their best to find out the truth. He'd had a certain air about him that made her instantly want to trust him with this case.

Taking another sip of coffee, she saw headlights flash in her window. Knox was here. Grabbing her suitcase and laptop bag, she juggled her keys and coffee in her other hand as she quickly locked her front door.

"Let me help you with that."

Knox's voice was close to her ear and she had to steel herself not to react. This wasn't easy. Just being friends and all. She still had feelings for him even though he wanted nothing to do with her.

"I've got it. My bags aren't that heavy."

He didn't listen worth a damn. He grabbed her suitcase and laptop bag and was already striding back to his SUV, leaving her standing on her front step staring at the space that he'd occupied moments before. With another sigh she followed him, climbing into the passenger side. He shut the back of the vehicle with a thump and then joined her in the front seat. He had the radio going and the wide-awake disc jockey was happily telling his audience about the weather and traffic.

What traffic could there be at five in the morning?

Knox had even said that one of the reasons for getting on the road early was to avoid traffic issues. The drive was going to be around twelve to thirteen hours and he didn't want to be driving late at night.

If we'd flown, we would have been there by dinnertime.

"Can you tell me again why we're driving thirteen hours instead of taking a plane?"

Knox didn't even take his eyes off of the road to answer.

"It wouldn't have made the travel time much less," he replied, navigating toward the highway. "With flying these days you have to show up hours before your flight, then you sit and wait and hope that the airline is running on time. Then you finally get to board and sit in a seat so small that a child isn't all that comfortable. When you finally get to your destination, you get to wait again for your luggage. If they haven't lost it that is. Door to door, flying isn't that much faster for anything less than a twelve-hour drive."

"This drive is a little more than that."

"Not by much. Besides, this way we get to relax in the comfort of our own vehicle, stop when we need to stretch our legs or eat. We're not waiting on anyone else. We're in the driver's seat. When you fly, you're at their mercy the entire time."

An imaginary lightbulb went off above Jenna's head.

"You're a control freak, aren't you?"

Chuckling, he didn't deny it. "If I could fly the damn plane myself, I would."

"Do you have a pilot's license?"

"No, but that wouldn't stop me."

"You'd honestly try and fly a commercial jet? For real? Like if the pilot and co-pilot both passed out or something and the flight attendant came over the loudspeaker looking for volunteers who could fly a plane, you'd jump up?"

"Absolutely."

"That's the craziest thing I've ever heard. You'd kill everyone because of your need for control. You should seek professional help. Or a flight instructor."

"Someday I'm going to learn to fly. It's on my bucket list."

Bucket list?

"I'm intrigued. What else is on this bucket list? Skydiving? Climbing a mountain?"

"I'll only tell you about mine if you tell me about yours."

This was the playful Knox she'd come to know in the last few weeks. She adored this side of him. He was so much fun to be with.

"I'm not really sure that I have a bucket list," she confessed. "I've never written one up, but I guess there are things that I want to do. There's a lot of the world that I haven't seen yet so I want to do that. Except on a plane. I don't want to drive everywhere like you do."

Laughing, he shook his head. "What's with the obsession with flying? Can't you just sit back, relax, and enjoy the journey? I'm an excellent driver and I'll stop every time you want to without complaint. This is going to be great."

He sounded so enthused, really happy. He hadn't sounded like that since she'd told him the truth.

"You do have a point about having to hurry up and wait at the airport," she conceded. "Although I just usually take a book to read. I haven't really been on any road trips so I don't have anything to compare it to."

This time he did take his gaze from the road, although only for a split second.

"Wait...you've never been on a road trip? Ever? I don't believe that. How could that be? Didn't you go on vacations as a child? What about college? No spring breaks in Florida?"

"When we went on vacation we always flew. And no, I didn't get any wild spring breaks in sunny locations with my friends. I think my longest road trip was two hours. I went to visit a friend for her birthday."

"Then you're in for a treat," Knox declared, giving the steering wheel a playful slap. "There's nothing like the freedom of the open road. Seeing things that you can't see from an airplane window. By the end of this trip, I predict that you will be a convert."

"Are you going to take me to that giant ball of twine?"

"A giant ball of twine? I hadn't planned on it, but maybe you should put that on your bucket list."

They'd completely veered from the bucket list topic.

"You still haven't told me what's on your bucket list."

"You haven't either. I told you it was a mutual deal."

"I did so. I said I wanted to travel."

"Everyone says that. What else do you want to do?"

"I don't know, but maybe if you tell me your list, I'll get some ideas." She pointed out the windshield where it was still dark. It was going to be awhile before the sun even came up. "You and I are going to be sitting in this car for thirteen hours, Knox. Was there another topic you wanted to talk about instead?"

"I don't want to climb a mountain," he replied with a huff. "I do want to get my pilot's license. I'd also like to hike the Appalachian Trail someday."

Now they were getting somewhere. Only twelve and a half hours - give or take - to go.

MIDMORNING, Jenna had broken out her stash of granola bars but they hadn't stuck to Knox's ribs very well. By noon, his stomach was growling and so was hers. They decided to take an exit to a mid-sized town that had one of those restaurants that was supposed to be country homemade cooking and served breakfast all day. Breakfast was Knox's favorite meal of the day and he couldn't wait to eat.

The restaurant was about half full and they were seated immediately by a smiling lady who handed them each two menus - one lunch and one breakfast. Jenna opened the former while Knox went for the latter. He didn't need long to choose. He'd pretty much already decided when they'd selected this venue. Jenna, on the other hand, was frowning as she perused the offerings.

"Don't like what you see?"

If she said she wanted to go somewhere else, he wasn't going to be happy about it. He'd do it, of course, but he wasn't going to pretend that he agreed. He really wanted that bacon that he could smell in the air.

"No, it's fine," she said with a shake of her head. "I just can't decide. I haven't been here in a long time and I don't remember what I ordered then."

"So order what looks good."

He didn't see the problem.

Her frown grew deeper. "Everything looks good."

A young man sidled up to their table, order pad in hand. "Hi, I'm Steve and I'm going to be your server today. Can I get you started with some beverages?"

Knox ordered a soda - with caffeine - and waited for Jenna to take her turn but she was still scowling at the menu.

"She can't decide what to order," Knox said, placing his two menus on the edge of the table. "She said everything looks good."

Jenna shot him a glare before turning her attention to the young man. "He's right. I am having trouble deciding. But I do know what I want to drink. I'll have an iced tea, please. Thank you so much."

The young man's face split into a grin. "I can help you with that if you like. I love the food here but some meals are better than others."

The two of them were off to the races while Knox sat there saying nothing. Jenna and *Steve* were acting like they were old friends, laughing and joking as he went through the menu with her. Item by item almost. It was a bit of overkill, but it was clear that *Steve* found Jenna attractive. Knox was a student of body language and he didn't need to be a genius to see that this guy was flirting. And Jenna was lapping it up.

I'm sitting here. Does anyone remember me?

Jenna eventually settled on the pot roast with mashed potatoes. Good ole *Steve* still didn't leave the table. He was now telling her a story about a friend of his who loved pot roast.

Are you kidding me?

"Shouldn't you put our order in?" Knox asked, a little more loudly than usual. "We're sort of in a hurry."

Steve paused, finally dragging his attention from Jenna. "Oh yeah...sure...of course. I'll get it right in."

"That was rude," Jenna said as Steve bustled back into the kitchen. "What is your problem?"

"I'm hungry, and Steve wasn't going to budge. I would imagine he has other customers that need him too, by the way."

She scanned the restaurant. "It's half empty."

"He still probably had work to do. He's a server, after all." Knox should have shut up then but his mouth seemed to have a mind of its own. "You seemed pretty happy to have his attention."

Her head snapped forward and her eyes narrowed. "Excuse me? What are you trying to say?"

Shrugging, Knox wasn't going to back down. He was in the right.

"It was obvious he found you attractive. He was flirting with you...while I was sitting right here. That's really disrespectful."

"How is it disrespectful? We're not a couple."

"He didn't know that," Knox pointed out. "For all he knew, we could be married for decades with six kids and two dogs and a cat."

"He was just being nice and helpful."

Knox snorted. "Just being nice? He was way over the top, and you didn't help the situation, flirting back with him."

"I was not flirting with him. I was being nice." Jenna leaned forward in her chair. "For a cop, you have lousy people skills. It helps to be nice to your waiter or waitress. It helps to be nice to people in service positions. They already have a tough job. They don't need their actions questioned too."

"Right in front of me," Knox repeated. "As if I was invisible."

Jenna laughed, clapping her hand over her mouth. "That's what this is all about? Your delicate fee-fees got hurt? Get over it and stop being a grouch."

Steve returned with their drinks so Knox didn't have a chance to reply. The waiter smiled widely at Jenna, letting her know that their food would be out soon. He didn't say anything to Knox.

"My feelings did not get hurt," Knox said between gritted teeth when they were alone again. "I was simply making an observation that he finds you attractive and you obviously return the sentiment."

"He's just being nice and I'm being the same," Jenna said with a shake of her head. "Is this how you act when you're wired on caffeine? Because you should know that it's not a good look for you. Seriously, just drop it. I'm not going to run off with Steve at the end of our meal."

The rest of lunch was uneventful. Steve brought their food and they both were starving so they tucked in immediately, not chatting much until they were full. When Steve brought the check, Jenna grabbed it before Knox had a chance.

"I've got this one. You can get the next one."

"This place was my idea," he reminded her. "Let me at least pay half."

She placed her credit card on the table. "Nope, I've got it."

She paid and they headed back out to the car, stopping at the restrooms on the way out. When they met at the vehicle, she was holding a small styrofoam package.

"What's that?"

"Steve wrapped up some biscuits for us for the road."

Rolling his eyes, Knox climbed into the driver's seat. "And Steve just made my argument for me. He finds you attractive. Case closed."

Jenna settled into the passenger seat, placing the biscuits on the console between them. "For a guy that says he just wants to be barely friends, you sure sound jealous."

"I am not jealous."

"You sound that way."

"You're mistaken."

She reached between them, popped open the container, and pulled out a biscuit. "Then why do you care about Steve?"

Knox didn't have any answer. Because he didn't care about Steve. He'd almost forgotten the guy already.

Instead of replying, he fired up the engine and headed back to the highway. If Jenna wanted to flirt with every guy between Seattle and Douglas, she could go right ahead. It didn't bother him in the least. They were both free agents. No romantic entanglements.

But that didn't explain why he was so pissed off. He must have had too much caffeine today. That was it. Too much coffee and soda.

He wasn't jealous. Not at all.

9

If Knox had had any doubts about Jenna's adopted family having money, he didn't now. Clearly, the Waters clan had plenty of wealth to hire him and his firm with lots and lots to spare. The large, stately home sat on a huge lot surrounded by mountains and trees, set back from the road by a long, winding driveway, with a large garage on the opposite side. According to Michelle, Jenna's sister, there was a small stream toward the back of the property where they often had picnics.

So there was Michelle Waters. Where Jenna was blonde and blue-eyed, Michelle was dark-haired with soft brown eyes, the mirror image of her twin sister Lori. Michelle seemed open and friendly, smiling when they were introduced. She'd even spontaneously hugged him, whispering her thanks for helping them in his ear. He definitely heard a sob of emotion in her tone and tears sparkled in her eyes.

The unexpected person was Tom Waters, Jr. Knox was positive that Jenna hadn't mentioned having a brother at all but he was real. He had the same coloring as Michelle but appeared to be older by quite a bit. But the man was friendly, shaking

Knox's hand and welcoming him to their home. He wasn't as open as Michelle though, seemingly sizing Knox up. That was fine. In a way, it made Knox respect Tom all the more.

Despite the formality of the outside of the home, the inside was light, bright, and cheery. High ceilings, large windows, and overstuffed couches and chairs gave the house a warmth and charm that Knox hadn't expected.

Knox lifted a gold-framed photo off the fireplace mantle, studying the three smiling women in the picture, standing in front of the Eiffel Tower.

"Yes, that's us and Lori," Michelle said, standing at his elbow. "We took that on our twenty-fifth birthday. We were all on a special vacation to celebrate our birthdays. They're all within a month and a half of each other."

"You look like you're having fun."

Lori and Michelle looked almost completely alike. They wore their hair differently and it was clear they had a different fashion sense, but their features were identical. Lori liked to wear bright colors while Michelle preferred a more neutral palette. Jenna fell somewhere in the middle.

"We did. We always had fun together," Michelle said with an audible sigh. "I can't even begin to tell you how close we all were. Jenna's always been like a real sister to us. From the very first. She just...fit in if you know what I mean. Like she was a long-lost family member. Mom and Dad adored her."

"That didn't bother you?"

Knox couldn't help the cynical questions that popped into his mind. He was a cop and that made him wary when he met new people. The vibe he got from Michelle was good and happy but...

Michelle smiled wider. "No, we were thrilled. I don't expect other people to understand it. It seems like something that only happens in the movies and not real life, but we just felt this instant kinship with her. She's the most amazing person."

"I'm sure she is."

Where were Tom and Jenna? They'd disappeared. Knox was alone with Michelle, and she had a certain expression on her face. She wanted to talk about stuff. Stuff he didn't want to talk about.

Shit.

"I understand that you're upset with my sister," Michelle went on. "You feel like she lied to you and now you think you can't trust her."

He didn't want to discuss this. This wasn't her business.

"I don't think we should–"

"But you can trust her. She's the most trustworthy person I've ever known except for Lori. She's a truly wonderful person, and there's so few of those in the world."

"I'm sure she is," Knox repeated, keeping his tone even. "This is really between Jenna and myself."

Frowning, Michelle shook her head. "I know that I shouldn't butt in. Jenna would be furious if she knew that I was saying any of this but I know that she has feelings for you, Knox. She cares about you."

Knox's fingers tightened on the picture frame, the metal cutting into the flesh.

"I don't want to be rude but I can't talk to you about this." He had to change the subject. Right now. "Why don't you tell me about Lori and Cal? And about the last time you saw her?"

She nodded and stepped away, sinking down onto a sofa cushion. "I'll be honest with you, Knox. I was never the biggest fan of your brother Cal. From the very beginning, it seemed like he was trying to separate her from her friends and family. He would get upset about the smallest issues and guilt Lori into doing everything his way and on his timetable."

Yep, that sounded like Knox's brother. His dad too.

"I tried reasoning with Lori but she was in love. She kept talking about how wonderful he was in the beginning and I guess she kept thinking that he would go back to that. From what I could see from the outside, he never did though. He just became more petty and demanding as time went on. I was thrilled when she told me that she'd ended things with him. Finally, she was becoming her old self again and seeing him for who he truly was. She knew he wasn't going to magically change back."

"Smart woman."

"Lori was intelligent but oftentimes she let her heart make her decisions for her. Luckily, your brother hurt her one too many times and she'd had enough. Also, he hadn't succeeded in cutting her off from her friends and family. We were still there telling her that he wasn't any good for her. Eventually she believed us and not him."

"What happened the last time you spoke with her? Or saw her?"

Michelle took a deep breath, her hands visibly trembling. "I saw her about a week before she disappeared. All three of us had lunch in Douglas. It was a Saturday. She'd broken up with Cal and we were celebrating. Lori seemed really happy and we all had a great time. We were talking about taking a vacation somewhere warm and sunny. She didn't have a care in the world. Except for...I don't even know if I should mention this."

"Mention what?"

"There was a guy at her work. I don't even remember his name, but she complained about him that day. She said he was sort of creepy. That he seemed to have a crush on her. Jenna and I told her to ignore him."

Knox would definitely be checking him out.

"You didn't get his name?"

"Bob, maybe? Bill? Brian? It started with a B."

"I'll talk to her co-workers," Knox assured Michelle. "I'll find out about him. Now the last time you spoke to Lori?"

"The last time I spoke to her was right before she was to meet Cal at the coffee shop. She and I spoke about the vacation again and then she said that she had to go. She was meeting Cal to have a cup of coffee and tell him that there was no chance of them getting back together. It was over. I told her to call me right after and she said she would. She said that it wouldn't take much time and I told her that he was probably going to cry or beg to get her back so don't weaken. She said she was determined and that she wasn't going to get into a debate with him. She'd tell him that the decision was made and get out of there. I waited for her call but it never came. That was the last time I ever spoke to her."

"You received a text from her a few days later, I believe? May I see it?"

"Sure." Michelle stood and walked over to the end table, picking up her phone and thumbing through it. "I've saved it, of course. Here it is."

It was short and to the point. Lori wrote that she was going off on her own for a little while and she'd be in touch. She said not to worry, and that she just needed some time.

"Lori's phone was never found?"

"Her purse and phone were gone, but her car and all her belongings weren't touched."

"You're sure?" Knox pressed. "Maybe she only packed a few changes of clothing."

Although that didn't make any sense if Lori didn't know how long she would be gone. In Knox's experience, most of the women he knew would usually overpack, not underpack.

"I'm sure. Lori had the cutest overnight bag that had all these little pockets and such. If she was going to pack light, she absolutely would have used it. But it was still in her townhouse. Both Jenna and I looked through her clothes and all of her favorite outfits were still there."

It didn't make any sense for a woman to walk away with

nothing. Jared was digging into Lori's credit card history right at this very moment so hopefully they could see any patterns.

Tom and Jenna joined them in the living room again. Tom carried a tray of finger foods such as crackers, cheese, and smoked meat. Jenna had a tray of cold drinks.

"We thought you might want a snack," Tom said. "We ordered dinner but it will be about an hour before it gets here."

"Maybe we can also get some work done as well," Jenna suggested. "I've been trying to make up a list of everyone that Lori mentioned in her life like friends, neighbors, co-workers. That sort of thing. But there may have been people that you know of that I don't remember."

"We need to talk to all of them if we can," Knox said. "It's usually one little piece of information that pushes a case along. It may not even seem all that important in the beginning."

Tom nodded, his expression solemn. "We can do that."

Time to get down to work. There was a case to be solved.

Where was Lori Waters? What had happened to her?

And did Callum have anything to do with it?

"I CAN CERTAINLY SEE what you saw in him," Michelle declared, sitting cross-legged on Jenna's bed. Dinner was over and everyone had retired to their rooms to get some rest. The real work of the investigation started tomorrow. "He's gorgeous."

The last thing Jenna needed to do was sit and think about how handsome her ex-boyfriend was, especially as he was just two doors down the hall.

"He is nice looking, but there's more to him than that."

"I wasn't saying that there wasn't but...yowza. I'm just saying that I can understand why you didn't tell him the truth that first night."

Jenna wasn't sure she liked what Michelle was saying.

"I never tried to deceive him. I tried telling him the truth several times but he kept changing the subject and trying to divert me. I know he's angry with me but I'm not all at fault here. When the chips were down, and I absolutely had to tell him the truth, I practically had to tape his mouth shut so he would let me talk. I would have told him a lot earlier if he hadn't been so stubborn."

"I wasn't saying that you were trying to lie to him, but that was sort of the result of all of this, right? He's mad and you two broke up."

Sighing, Jenna rubbed at her throbbing temples. She was exhausted and needed a good night's sleep. She didn't want to talk about Knox and their abbreviated relationship.

It hurts too much.

"Knox and I are going to Douglas tomorrow. Are you going with us?"

"Unfortunately, I have to work. I wish I could though. You'll give a full report when you get back?"

"I will. I'm not really sure where we're going to start, to be honest. With Lori's neighbors, I think? Then maybe her co-workers."

"What about Cal? When are you going to talk to him? He's the one you should start with. He's the one that probably is responsible for Lori's disappearance."

And death. But we don't say those words out loud.

"I don't know," Jenna confessed. "Knox hasn't talked about that yet, but I imagine that he'll want to learn as much as he can about Lori's life and situation before he talks to his brother. So he'll know the right questions to ask."

"I guess there's no polite way to ask your own family if they're responsible for the disappearance of another human being."

"I can't imagine having to do that. I'm sure that Knox wants to prepare for that."

"And if his brother says that he's innocent? What then?"

Jenna had always assumed that Callum would never admit anything and would tell Knox that he hadn't seen Lori that last day. He'd stick to his story. It had been working so far.

"Then we find other evidence."

"You make it sound so simple."

It wouldn't be. It was going to be damn near impossible. The only thing they had going for them was Knox.

Just for the case, not for her.

He was a good man, but he wasn't her man. Not anymore.

He never really was. She'd only been fooling herself.

I'm done being a fool. Time to be realistic.

10

Knox woke up extra early the next morning. Showered and dressed before anyone else was up, he quietly left the house, leaving a note for Jenna behind. She wasn't going to be happy that he'd gone to see his family without her but some things he needed to do on his own. This was one of them.

He wasn't going to see Cal. Not yet. He needed to know much more about this case before he confronted his brother. Knox didn't believe his brother had anything to do with Lori's disappearance but he did have the feeling that Cal knew more about that last day than he was letting on. Confronting Cal without hard facts, however, was a waste of time.

This morning he was going to see his brother Randy. Not just because he wanted to spend some time with his little brother but because Randy was closer to the rest of the family. There was a good chance that he'd met Lori at one point. Knox needed to talk to someone who didn't have a vested interest in covering his own ass like Cal did.

They met at a twenty-four-hour coffee and donut shop a few blocks from his brother's home. Randy was already sitting there by the time Knox walked into the small shop. The smell of sugar and coffee hung heavy in the air and he realized that he hadn't yet had even one sip of caffeine this morning. The smiling woman at the counter took his order and said she'd bring it to him.

"I still don't see why we couldn't just meet at the house," Randy said as soon as Knox sat down across from him in the booth. "The kids want to see their Uncle Knox."

"I want to see them too, but this conversation isn't for little ears," Knox replied. His coffee and chocolate glazed donut were slid in front of him and he thanked the server before dumping sugar and creamer into the dark brew. He took a lot of shit from the guys about how sweet he drank it. "But I'll definitely be by to see them. Just not today."

"You said you wanted to talk about Cal. What's so sensitive that we can't talk about it in front of the kids? Are you pissed off at him again? Just move on from it. You know how he is."

You know how he is.

Knox was sick and tired of hearing those words. He'd heard them all of his life and shockingly, they didn't make anything better. Apparently, he was supposed to excuse every shitty thing his father and brother did...

Because that was just how they were.

They were crappy people, and the Owens family gave them a get out of jail free card. Everyone else always had to *be the bigger person.* Cal and Ben? They didn't have to change at all.

"Yes, I know how he is. We all do. But this is something a little more serious than Cal being an asshole for the millionth time."

Randy's brows rose. "Really? So tell me about it."

"First, let me ask you a few questions. Did you ever remember meeting one of Cal's girlfriends? Her name was Lori. Dark hair and eyes. She worked in marketing."

Rubbing this chin, Randy nodded. "I do remember her.

Pretty, smiled a lot. She seemed like a nice girl. Why do you ask?"

Knox still had other questions before he was ready to answer anyone else's.

"How were they together? Did they seem happy? Did they argue? Did Cal say anything to you about her?"

"I'm not sure what you want me to say. I guess they seemed happy. They never argued as such in front of the family, at least not that I saw. Cal was bossy with her. You know his usual my-way-is-the best-way stuff that we grew up with. She didn't like it much more than we did, but she never yelled at him or anything. She seemed to just ignore him and do whatever her way and let him complain about it."

That didn't sound like a healthy relationship to Knox. At least it wasn't what he wanted.

"And Cal didn't say anything to you about her? Ever? What about when you saw him with someone new?"

Randy grinned. "I do remember that. I asked him about her and he said that he'd traded up."

"I swear I cannot be related to him," Knox muttered under his breath, completely disgusted. "Our family is a fucking mess."

"Come on, we're not that bad. Every family has issues. We're not the only ones."

"We have more issues than most."

"Lighten up. We turned out okay. Our family couldn't be that bad."

The great thing about Randy was that he was determined to see only the best in people. It was also his worst trait.

"They are that bad."

"Don't use them as an excuse not to come to Dylan's birthday party on Sunday. He'd love to have his favorite uncle there. Don't say no. Julia specifically told me to tell you that she wants you to come. There will be food and the kids want to see you."

"I'll try," Knox said. "But I'm here to work on a case."

"Take a few hours and relax. Don't they give you time off?"

"They do, but–"

"No buts. Be there or Julia will call you and you'll have to say no to her."

She wouldn't make it easy either.

"So why are we talking about Cal and this woman? What's going on here?" Randy asked again. "Why couldn't we meet at the house?"

Knox gave his younger brother the condensed version of the story without going into detail about how he'd met Jenna. That wasn't anyone else's business but his.

"Wait, she thinks that Cal had something to do with her sister's disappearance? Cal? No way. That's crazy talk." Randy's eyes widened in surprise when Knox didn't immediately jump in and agree. "You don't actually think that she's right, do you? Because Cal has a quirky personality but Jesus Christ, he's not a killer. Or a kidnapper. Or whatever it is that you think he might have done."

"Quirky? You're being easy on him."

"And you're out of control," Randy sputtered, his cheeks red. "This is Cal. He's our brother. *Our brother*. He's not a goddamn killer. He wouldn't hurt a fly."

Knox had anticipated this argument. "We both know that's not true. Cal has been in lots of fights. Hell, he's spent a few nights in the drunk tank for busting up a bar. He's not a pacifist."

"Those were men, not women," Randy argued right back. "That's a completely different thing. He wouldn't hurt a female."

"We've seen him verbally abuse his girlfriends," Knox pointed out. "He has little to no respect for others. He has no empathy. He doesn't care how other people feel."

"That doesn't make him a kidnapper or a killer." Randy shook his head. "That's why you're doing this, isn't it? So you can prove, once and for all, that your brother is a piece of shit. I can't believe this, Knox. He's your brother. Where's your family loyalty?"

Knox didn't have a chance to respond. His phone began to buzz, and he reached for it in his breast pocket, checking the screen to see who it was. He declined to take the call but Randy must have seen the screen as well.

"Is that Dad? Aren't you going to answer it?"

Shoving the phone back into his pocket, Knox shook his head. "No."

"I know Dad has been calling you."

Knox knew where this was going.

"And?"

"He's upset that you haven't been returning his calls or texts."

"He's upset? Are you upset too? Because you're scowling at me."

"He's changed. You should talk to him."

It was all Knox could do not to throw back his head and laugh out loud.

"He's changed? I doubt it."

"People change, brother."

"Sure they do. If they want to change. Dad's never wanted to change. He doesn't see that there's anything wrong with the way he lives his life. Christ, he's been out...how long? Nine months? He's already driven Patty away and moved in with an even younger woman. How old is she, Randy? Is she even thirty? She's too young to see all the red flags that Dad is waving around, but eventually she will. But by then he will have spent all her money and broken her damn heart by boozing and running around. And Cal isn't any better."

"They're family. You can't turn your back on them."

"Yes, I can. Happily, might I add. They're like a drowning man, Randy. If you try to save them, you'll get pulled under too. They don't care who they hurt."

"Dad isn't like that anymore."

Knox noticed that his brother couldn't say the same for Cal.

"That's great then. Good for him. I'm glad that he saw the light."

"But you're not going to call him back?"

"Nope. I've given him lots of chances and he threw them all away. I'm done. Now, if he really has changed, that's awesome. I'm happy for him, but I don't need him in my life. I'm far more content without Ben Owens."

Randy stuck out his chin. "What about me? What about the rest of your family? Have you walked away from us too? Is that why you took this case? Is that why you've taken that woman's side?"

"I didn't take her side," Knox shot back, his frustration building. "I'm looking into this case because they hired my firm. I'm keeping an open mind. If it points in his direction, that's where I'll go. If it doesn't, then it doesn't. Listen, this isn't a game. Someone might be dead here and I'm trying to get to the truth."

"You're not being loyal."

"I'd rather have the truth than be loyal to a lie."

Pushing his empty plate away, Randy wiped his hands on a paper napkin. His lips were pressed together in a thin line and his color was high. "I don't think we're going to agree on this. Maybe I should go."

"No, I should go. I have a lot of work to do."

"Proving Cal is guilty? Or innocent?"

Leaning down, Knox placed his hand on the table so they were face to face.

"You know what I love about law enforcement? Catching the bad guys?"

Randy shrugged. "I don't know. What?"

"The truth doesn't care how we feel. It doesn't care about my feelings or your feelings or what we want or hope for. The truth just is. It's neutral. *It's real.* It's not based on emotions, but on facts. That's what I love about my job." Straightening, he dug into his pocket and dropped a twenty on the table. "It was nice to see you, little brother."

With that, Knox turned and left the coffee shop. He'd known that the conversation wouldn't go well but he'd hoped for better. Ultimately, it didn't matter. Randy - and any of the rest of his family - wasn't going to stop him. If anything, he was more determined than ever.

He had a job to do. Find Lori. Discover the truth.

It was the only thing that mattered.

TOM WAS ALREADY in the kitchen eating eggs and toast when Jenna went downstairs the next morning, craving a cup of coffee. She wasn't in the best of moods. Knox had left to go see one of his brothers. He'd slipped a note under her bedroom door sometime early this morning. She'd wanted to go with him, of course, but he'd said in his note that he needed to speak to his family on his own.

She wasn't angry. Not really. She was frustrated, though, that he seemed to think that she was going to be nasty or accusatory with his siblings. He hadn't said so out loud or even in the note but she could see that he didn't quite trust her.

"The coffee's made," Tom said. He was sitting at the table in the breakfast nook, the newspaper spread out in front of him. "You can have the comic section."

Jenna had never been much of a morning paper person but she did like to read the funny pages. *Garfield* was her favorite.

"Thanks, I'm going to take you up on that." She poured

herself some coffee and added cream and sugar before joining him at the table. "I'm surprised to see you still here. I know you like to be in the office early."

"I have a meeting on this side of town," he explained. "It didn't make sense to go all the way to the office and then drive all the way back. I'll go into the office afterward."

He closed the paper and turned all of his attention on Jenna. "Actually, I was hoping you'd be up early. I wanted to talk to you while Michelle is still asleep."

Wrapping her hands around the warm mug, she braced herself for the coming conversation. Tom wasn't much of a talker. He was a quiet man who only spoke when he had something important to say.

"What did you want to talk about? Is...everything okay?"

His mouth turned down and he took an audible breath. "We need to talk, Jen. Really talk. I know that you have your friend here now to help find out what happened to Lori. This is what we've been waiting and hoping for. For someone to finally take us seriously and look into this. But..."

"But?"

He'd been looking down at his empty cup but now he looked up at her. His eyes were shiny with tears. "We have to be realistic. The chances of finding Lori...alive..."

He broke off, clearing his throat a few times. A large lump had taken up residence in Jenna's throat as well. Her stomach tightened painfully and she was glad she hadn't tried to eat anything yet.

"I know," she replied quietly. "I know the odds are against us."

"I know we don't talk about it," he said, his voice shaking. "We pretend that we just need someone to find her and that everything will all be okay again but Jen, I just don't think that's going to happen. I haven't said anything to Michelle. It would break her. She needs to believe, but I know that you're stronger.

Tougher. More realistic. You have to know that even if your friend finds Lori. She's..."

"Probably dead," Jenna finished for him. "I know. But I have hope. I have to have that or I think I'd go insane."

"I have hope too. I do. But with each passing day it's getting a little harder. You know? I just didn't want you to be heart-broken if this doesn't turn out exactly the way we hope it does."

"I'll be okay. But what about Michelle? She's going to be devastated."

He nodded in agreement, his expression somber. "She will be, and I wish I knew some way to spare her what she's going to go through but I just don't know. I've tried to talk to her before, bring it up, but she shuts me down right away. She doesn't want any negative thoughts. She says it's bad luck."

"We'll be here for her," Jenna vowed. "If the worst happens."

Tom reached across the table and placed his own hand on hers, giving her a weak smile. "We'll be here for each other. We're a family. Together we can get through this."

Her chest tight, Jenna gave him the best smile back that she could muster. "Family."

Clearing his throat again, Tom stood to refill his coffee mug. "Speaking of family, are you going to see Anita today?"

"Yes, I'm going this morning." She checked the clock on the wall. It was eight -thirty. If she hurried and showered, she could be there in an hour. "I was hoping I could borrow a car but if not, I can call a ride share or taxi."

"Take the Civic in the garage. The keys are on the peg next to the back door."

"Thanks, I may do that." Draining her coffee, she stood and placed her cup in the sink. "I better get dressed. Knox and I have a busy day ahead."

It was time to get to the truth. No matter how painful it might be.

11

"You really don't have to go in with me. I'll be fine on my own."

Jenna had repeated that statement at least three times in the last twenty minutes, but Knox wasn't deterred in the least. He'd shown up at the house just as she'd been about to leave to see Anita and had insisted on driving her there.

"I'd really like to meet and talk to her," he said. "Ask her about the last time she saw or spoke with Lori."

"She may not remember. Her memory isn't what it was."

"You never know," he replied, parking the SUV in a shady spot in front of the house. "It's the smallest details that can be the most help."

"I'll just warn you again that her memory isn't good. She gets confused easily. She has a nurse that lives in with her to make sure that she takes her medicines and eats every day."

Knox frowned. "Why doesn't she live in the family house with Tom and Michelle?"

"That's not our family home. That's Tom's house. He inherited it from his mother. Michelle moved in a few years ago when she sold her condo. It was going to be temporary but they got along well and they decided she would stay." Jenna pointed to the Tudor style dwelling. "This is the family home."

"I keep forgetting that Tom is from your father's first marriage." Knox paused on the walkway to the front door. "I was actually surprised to meet him. You don't talk about him much."

"He was so much older than us, I really didn't spend any time with him. He's always been nice though and it was clear that he loved Tom, his father."

"How did he and Anita get on?"

"Quite well, although it was rocky in the beginning from what Michelle and Lori said. Anita always said that she wouldn't try and replace his mother."

The front door opened and Anita stepped out onto the front step, her arms wide open and wearing a smile. Jenna didn't hesitate. She'd had very little affection in her life until she'd come into Tom and Anita's home, but now she realized that it was important to her. She flew into her adopted mother's arms and gave her a big hug and a kiss on the cheek. Her chest swelled with love and a few tears began to well up into her eyes. She needed to spend more time here. She'd been gone too often because of her career.

"I missed you," she said, hugging Anita again.

"I missed you too, sweetheart. It's good to see you." Anita looked over Jenna's shoulder. "And who do we have here?"

Jenna stepped back. "This is my friend, Knox."

"What an interesting name. Come in, Knox. Do you like iced tea?"

As usual, Anita didn't wait for an answer. Knox was going to get that iced tea whether he liked it or not. When they walked into the living room, the nurse had already set out a tray of cookies, a pitcher of tea, and two glasses.

"I'll have Mary get an extra glass," Anita said, sinking into her favorite chair by the front window. She liked to watch the neighborhood hustle and bustle.

"I'll get it," Jenna offered. Mary usually took the opportunity to run an errand or rest while one of Anita's children were there. "It will only take a minute."

"Your young man can tell me how he got such an interesting name while you're doing that."

To be honest, Jenna wouldn't mind hearing that story too. She dashed into the kitchen and grabbed an extra glass before hurrying back into the living room.

"I'm named after Fort Knox," he was explaining with a big smile. "My grandmother thought it sounded like a strong name since Fort Knox is supposed to be the most secure place ever."

Jenna poured everyone a glass of tea and then grabbed a cookie. She hadn't eaten any breakfast this morning. She also made a mental note to ask Knox about his grandmother. For once when speaking about his family, he actually looked happy.

Anita launched into a story about how she'd come up with names for Michelle and Lori. There was a wistful tone in her voice when she talked about Tom. It was clear that she still missed her late husband greatly.

"What about you two?" Anita's gaze went from Jenna to Knox and then back to Jenna. "Are you two a couple?"

Nope, and that's my fault.

"Just friends," Jenna replied quickly, not wanting to look directly at Knox. She had a bad feeling that her cheeks were bright red. "He's actually helping us with finding Lori."

Anita's smile immediately fell and her hands twisted together in her lap. "Lori will show up when she's ready. She just needs some time alone. That's what she said."

Except that Jenna didn't believe that Lori sent that text. Anita wasn't that great with technology and was convinced that they couldn't have received the text unless *Lori specifically* sent it. They couldn't seem to get her to understand that if someone had Lori's phone, they could send any message they wanted.

"It's been months, Anita," Jenna said, keeping her tone soft. "We want to be sure that she's okay."

"She's fine. She's an intelligent girl." Anita nodded and turned her attention to Knox. "Did you ever meet my daughter Lori? She's a smart one. Pretty too."

"I didn't have the pleasure but she sounds like she's a wonderful daughter, Mrs. Waters."

"Call me Anita. Everyone does."

Shifting on the sofa cushion, Knox pulled his phone from his pocket. "Before Lori left, did she ever visit you with a boyfriend named Callum? Cal?"

"I don't know. That name doesn't sound familiar."

Anita's voice was shaky and she was paler than only a few minutes before. She was getting tired and that strained her memory. This line of questioning was stressing her out.

Knox held out the phone. "Could you take a look at the photo, Anita? Did Lori ever come here with a man that looked like that? Did she ever say anything about Cal Owens?"

With a frown, Anita accepted the phone, studying the photo. "He doesn't look familiar. Should he? I don't think Lori ever mentioned him. Why would she? She already has a nice boyfriend, Will. They're planning to get married next year."

Tears burned in the back of Jenna's eyes. It had all been going so well. Then...bam. Reality reared its ugly head.

"Anita, Lori dated Will when they were in college. They broke up several years ago."

Anita scowled at Jenna. "Lori and Will were here at Easter."

"Not last Easter," Jenna explained as gently as possible. "Last Easter Michelle and I cooked dinner here for all of us. Tom Junior, too. We had ham and I made my famous macaroni and cheese."

Anita nodded slowly but Jenna could tell that she didn't

remember. She could easily remember little details from their school years but the more recent she didn't seem to retain as well.

"Where is Will then?"

"He's in the Army. He's stationed in North Carolina, last I heard."

"The Army," Anita repeated, her brow furrowed. "That's right. The Army."

"He might come home at Christmas. If he does, I'm sure he'll stop by to say hello."

Will had adored Anita and he did stop by when he was visiting his folks.

"Sometimes I forget things," Anita said to Knox. "My memory isn't what it used to be. Luckily, I have Mary here to help me. And my girls, of course. They take good care of me too."

"No need to apologize." Knox gave Anita one of his dazzling smiles that Jenna was sure had melted a thousand female hearts. Her adopted mother was no different, smiling back at his show of charm. "We all forget things from time to time."

They chatted about the weather for the next few minutes and then Mary came downstairs to remind Anita that it was time for her medication. And perhaps she might like to rest for awhile as well?

"I think that's a good idea," Anita said, rising from her chair. "I am a bit tired. Please excuse me, Knox. I hope you won't think me rude."

"Not at all," Knox replied, standing also. "It was very nice to meet you, ma'am."

"Come see me again and bring your friend. I like looking at handsome men," Anita whispered in Jenna's ear when they were hugging goodbye. "Are you sure he's just a friend? I think he could be more."

Thank heavens Knox didn't hear that. She didn't need him

to think that she was pining over him. Because she wasn't. If he didn't want to be a couple, that was fine. Just fine.

That charming rogue even gave Anita a peck on the cheek before they left. He knew exactly what he was doing. And to women of all ages. There ought to be a law or something.

"Proud of yourself?" Jenna asked when they climbed back in the SUV. "You've got Anita eating out of the palm of your hand."

"I was just being nice," he said with a laugh as they pulled out into traffic. "She's a lovely woman."

"Who thinks you're handsome."

He shrugged carelessly. "A gene pool accident. But she has good taste."

They were quiet for awhile before Jenna spoke again. "She has some memory issues. The doctors say it's early onset. She's only sixty-two."

"I'm sorry I didn't listen to you better before we went in. I apologize for that. Clearly, talking about her daughter upsets her."

Jenna picked at the hem of her shirt, her gaze on the floor. "Last time I saw her we talked about Lori and she was fine but...she's not getting better, you know? She's only going to get worse as time goes on. It gets bad when she's tired. She may not have slept well last night. She has good days and bad. Today wasn't great."

"I am sorry I brought it up. I should have listened to you."

"It's not the first time," she said without thinking. The words came out before she could stop them.

His gaze didn't stray from the road ahead. "Can we not talk about that? I don't want to argue with you today. We need to work together."

"I don't want to argue either. Just forget it."

"I already have."

"Good. It's no big deal. I get it. I'm a terrible person. Case closed."

It hurt. She couldn't deny it.

"You're not– Shit, can we just change the subject?"

"I already agreed to do that. Where are we going next?"

"To talk to the detective that looked into your sister's disappearance."

Jenna laughed but it wasn't with happiness. "I think I should warn you right now that the detective definitely thinks that I'm a terrible person. All because I asked him to do his damn job."

"Then let me do the talking."

"Gladly."

Knox was going to find out that this trip to the police station was a grand waste of time. No one had helped them and no one had cared that Lori had disappeared.

They were truly on their own.

12

————

Despite what Jenna might think, Knox had modest expectations regarding his meeting with Detective Bauer in Douglas. It was already established that the police had decided not to pursue the investigation after the text that Michelle had received from Lori's phone. As far as Knox was concerned, he had enough doubt not to be completely sure that Lori was the author of that text. All these months later she hadn't attempted to get in touch with her family? It didn't make much sense to him.

The town of Douglas was about an hour drive away. Knox loved to drive so he sat back in his leather seat and turned on the satellite radio to his favorite country station. His fingers tapped out the rhythm on the steering wheel as the tires ate up the miles to their destination.

Jenna didn't say much for most of the trip, seemingly content to watch out of the windows and enjoy the scenery. That was something that he liked about her from the very first. She didn't feel the need to fill in all the silences with talking. She spoke when she had something to say. That was it. She was a good listener too. She didn't interrupt him, instead listening intently and only chiming in when he was finished. Anita had been like that too, letting Knox finish his thoughts before she spoke.

"I noticed that you call your adopted mom by her first name."

It was really none of his business but for some reason he wanted to know more about Jenna and her family.

It's because of the investigation. I need to know all I can. It's not because I want to know more about her specifically.

"Yes, I do. Anita and Tom always said that I could call them Mom and Dad, but...I don't know. I just never did. I think that I have some negative connotations to those designations because of my parents. I should probably seek therapy about it or something before I have kids."

Jenna would be a good mother. She had patience and kindness.

"How did Michelle and Lori feel about you calling their parents Mom and Dad?"

Chuckling, Jenna shook her head. "Still trying to find the family issues? They always encouraged me to do it, but once I explained they backed off. Honestly, we're not dysfunctional. We all get along really well."

"I wouldn't know a thing about that. I spend as little time with my family as possible."

"But you basically did the same thing I did. You created your own family."

"I don't know what you mean. How did I create my own family?"

Turning in her seat, Jenna faced him. "The way you talk about your co-workers is like a family."

"I hate that shit," Knox replied. "That whole *this office is like a family* crap. I have a family. They just suck. Well, most of them do. My younger brother Randy is pretty normal."

Tilting her head, she tapped her chin. "If your family is

such a nightmare, how did you turn out so normal? Or at least almost-normal?"

"My grandmother. The one who named me. She was great."

She'd also passed on when Knox was a teenager. She'd made the best apple pies in the universe. He could still taste them in his mind.

"Did you spend a lot of time with her?"

"As much as I could, but she didn't live close by. What about you? Any grandparents, aunts, uncles, or cousins?"

"I'm sure that I have some but I'm not aware of where or who they are. My mom was an only child and my dad didn't talk to his family. Or rather, they didn't talk to him. For obvious reasons."

They arrived in Douglas, a small town that wasn't too small. It had a movie theatre, which was more than the little hamlet that Knox had grown up in. There hadn't been a damn thing to do on a weekend when he was a kid except go out to the woods and have bonfires with his friends. They'd drink beer and raise hell. Looking back, Knox hadn't been so much an asshole teenager as just unbelievably bored.

"Maybe I should just wait in the car," Jenna said when he pulled up in front of the sheriff's station. "I don't think the detective likes me."

"Did you do something that would make him dislike you?"

"Yes. I tried to make him do his job. He didn't like that."

Frankly, it would be easier for Knox to go in there by himself. Cop to former cop. Especially if Jenna and this guy already had a difficult history. He didn't want to ruffle the guy's feathers right out of the gate. It was usually a good idea to keep on the good side of local law enforcement.

"You don't have to go in if you don't want to." Knox pointed to a coffee shop across the street. "Why don't you go over there and wait for me? I shouldn't be too long."

"Sold. Good luck. You're going to need it."

Knox locked up the vehicle and headed inside while Jenna went to the coffee shop. The sheriff's station looked like so many that he'd visited. Desks crammed into a small space, the smell of burnt coffee, the low hum of telephone conversations.

"Can I help you?"

A young officer was sitting at the front counter and he barely looked old enough to drive.

Damn, I'm getting ancient. They're looking positively adolescent these days.

"I'm here to see Detective Bauer. I called yesterday. My name is Knox Owens."

"Uh, right, hold on," the deputy said before scurrying off to a set of double doors at the back of the room. Knox only waited a moment before the young man reappeared, motioning for him to follow. "Mike is back here."

Detective Mike Bauer was seated at a metal desk shoved into a corner. There was a second desk in the small room as well which Knox assumed was probably for a second investigator who wasn't in the office at the moment.

"Grab that chair and have a seat," the detective said. "Do you want some coffee?"

Having drank gallons of crappy coffee while a deputy and then a sheriff, Knox declined immediately. He needed to cut down on the caffeine anyway.

They shook hands and Knox introduced himself before taking a seat opposite the other man. Dressed in blue slacks and a white button-down shirt, Mike Bauer looked like he might be in his late twenties, early thirties at the most.

"Are you sure you don't want any coffee?" he asked, taking a drink of his own mug. "It's terrible but it's hot."

"Really, I'm good." Knox pulled out his phone and held up the photo of Lori that Jenna had sent him earlier. "I'm here about Lori Waters' disappearance. I'm told you were the detective on the case."

"I would hardly call it a case," Bauer laughed. "There really wasn't much to it. Lori Waters left her family and they were concerned. A few days later she sent them a text that she was fine and would be in touch. Case closed."

"Except that she never has contacted them again," Knox replied. "From what her family says, they were very close and talked or texted every single day."

"Maybe her family has a different view of how close they are. Maybe Lori Waters wasn't as thrilled with her family as they think she was. Hell, my relatives can drive me up a wall by two o'clock in the afternoon on Thanksgiving. There's no law against someone not wanting to keep in touch."

"That's true," Knox conceded. "But she didn't take her car. Or her luggage. Or anything from her home. You don't think that's weird?"

The younger man shifted uncomfortably in his chair as if he didn't like being questioned.

"Maybe she was in a hurry. Maybe she took a bus or a plane."

"That's a possibility." Knox tried a different angle. "Did you speak to her boyfriend Callum Owens?"

The detective's face split into a grin. "I did. Great guy. He answered all of my questions."

I just bet he did. Charming bastard.

Clearly, Mike Bauer hadn't put Knox's last name together with Cal's last name. Not yet anyway.

"He was supposed to meet her for coffee that day. He said he didn't see her but the coffee shop employees say that he did. That they talked and left the shop together."

Could it be the same shop that Jenna was sitting in right now? Shit, that hadn't even occurred to him. He needed to talk to those workers there. Being in the vehicle, right next to Jenna, was messing with his head. He needed to get in the game and keep his mind where it needed to be. Not on how lovely Jenna looked this morning.

And she did look good.

"Well...yeah," Bauer said, squirming in his chair again. "But after talking to them, they couldn't be completely confident that Lori Waters came in that exact day. Apparently, she came in almost every day so they could have easily gotten mixed up."

It was on the tip of Knox's tongue to ask if the baristas hadn't been confident or if Bauer himself hadn't been confident. Those were two different issues. He didn't ask it, however. He was beginning to see why Jenna had been so desperate. It was easy to see that no one here in law enforcement was going to help her. They'd been snowed by his brother.

"Do you have any traffic cameras that might have footage from that day?" Knox asked. "We can check that specific day and see if she was there."

Bauer shook his head. "We only keep the footage for about ten days."

Knox had known it was a long shot. Most municipalities kept video a very short time, some as little as twenty-four hours.

"What about the shops along the same street? Do any of them have security cameras?"

There was a small chance that a vendor might have accidentally picked Lori up on one of their cameras and that film was sitting in a database somewhere.

"Some of them do," Bauer confirmed. "We don't have a lot of crime in our town but we do get the occasional break-in or kids playing pranks."

"Did you check with any of them?"

Knox already knew the answer.

"No." Bauer cleared his throat and leaned forward. "Listen, I realize that you've been hired to look into this but I think you're going to find that there's nothing there. When I talked to Lori Waters' boyfriend, he said that she was a little flaky, kinda nuts.

That it wouldn't be out of character for her to just up and leave. You know the type...sexy but a little crazy?"

"I'm not sure that I do. Her sisters say that this wasn't something that she would do at all. Lori Waters had a responsible and professional job at a local marketing firm. She didn't even have a parking ticket from what I could find. I'm not seeing the flakiness that you are."

"I met one of her sisters. Jennie...Jennifer...not sure but it was something like that." Bauer's brows shot up. "She was a hot one. She sure as hell had a temper on her too. Probably just like her sister."

Misogyny was alive and well, living inside of Mike Bauer. It was all Knox could do not to lift the asshole out of his chair and shove him up against the wall. Maybe even try and talk some damn sense into him, but it would be a waste of time. Knox had worked with guys like this. They weren't going to change.

Knox stood, ready to leave. He wasn't going to learn anything useful here.

"I think I have all that I need. Thank you for your time, Detective Bauer."

After exiting the sheriff's station, he headed straight for the coffee shop across the street. She'd been right. He had wasted his time.

She'd been desperate for a good reason.

He owed Jenna an apology.

"ARE YOU OKAY? You're acting like someone spit in your food."

Jenna and Knox were walking along the sidewalk towards a second coffee shop. This one would be where Lori had met Cal that last day. On the way, however, Knox had barely said a word and had glowered the entire time. Clearly, his mood had gone downhill in the space of thirty minutes.

"That detective is a douchebag," Knox growled. "He was no help at all."

A better person would have simply agreed and moved on.

But when have I been the better person?

"I told you that he was a jerk. He treated me like garbage when I would go in there to talk to him. Smug asshole."

"I know exactly what you mean now," Knox replied. "It seems like he fell under my brother's spell. Cal can be charming as hell when he wants to be. It didn't help that Bauer was already a misogynistic piece of shit. I bet they were two peas in a pod laughing about how emotional and crazy women are. Fuck."

"He didn't tell you anything helpful at all?"

"After talking to Cal, he didn't think he needed to do much. Then when the text came in, he washed his hands of the entire investigation." Knox paused his steps, turning toward Jenna. "I'm sorry."

An apology. She hadn't expected that. For a moment, she wasn't quite sure how to respond.

"Thank you," she finally said. "It helps that you understand why I came to you."

"I remember Lori telling us that your family would brag about what a great cop you were. How you always caught the bad guy. There wasn't a case you couldn't solve. She also told us how you didn't take your father's side when he wanted to be paroled. That made me feel like you could be trusted to not take sides. At the very least, I thought you might be interested in proving that your brother didn't have anything to do with it."

"You could have hired any private investigator."

"We did hire one in the early days, right after the detective said that there was no case. The investigator looked into a few things, he worked for a couple of weeks, and then said that he agreed with the police. We were devastated and it colored our outlook for awhile. Looking back now, I should have hired another one immediately, but he sort of convinced us we were overreacting. Then as the weeks and months went by, I became more determined than ever that they were both wrong. We weren't overreacting at all."

"Do you know what he did?" Knox asked. "Did he give you a file of his results?"

"He said that he came up empty. He talked to everyone and he agreed that Lori left of her own free will."

"It sounds like he took your money and did nothing," Knox scoffed. "You should have been given any work products from his investigation."

All Jenna could remember from those first few months was an overwhelming feeling of fear. She hadn't slept or eaten well. She could barely think about anything but Lori. Perhaps if she had been thinking straight, she would have responded better.

"We haven't had good luck. I interviewed a new investigator that day that you came to see me. He was shady as hell."

"We're doing this now," he said. "We'll get to the bottom of it. Somewhere out there is the clue that we need. I always say that we need just one little break in the case. Just one."

"I hope you're right."

They'd arrived at the other coffee shop, and Knox opened the door for them. "I'm going to ask that you let me do most of the talking. I promise I'll give you a chance before we leave."

"You're the professional."

She didn't mind. She was kind of looking forward to seeing him in cop-slash-investigator mode. This was going to be fascinating.

The shop wasn't super busy, only a few tables occupied at this time of the day. Knox asked the young female barista how long she'd been working there and that started the conversation rolling. Within a few minutes, he had three of the workers there that remembered Lori.

"She was always really sweet and nice," the young man said,

nodding his head. "Never upset or short if there was a long wait. Always polite."

"She had the same order every day," the redhead told them. "We'd see her walk in and she'd wave, always wearing a big smile. She'd ask about us and always seemed to really care what was going on in our lives."

"How sure are you that Lori came in that exact date? You said she came in here pretty much every day," Knox said.

The other young woman who hadn't said much jumped in. "I know for a fact that it was that day. It was the day I had to take my cat to the vet because she was so sick. I thought she wasn't going to make it. She's okay now but I wouldn't forget a day like that. Lori was definitely here."

"Did you tell the detective that?" Knox asked.

The girl shook her head. "No, he never asked me. I never saw him."

"Kelly wasn't scheduled the day that the cop came to ask questions," the young man explained. "He said that he was going to come back to talk to Kelly but he never did."

"I left a message for him at his office," Kelly said. "I told whoever answered the phone what I just told you."

Jenna had already been frustrated with Detective Bauer but now she was just plain mad. He'd ignored an eyewitness. What an asshole.

Knox didn't look any happier than she felt. His lips were pressed together in a thin line and his blue eyes were icy cold.

"When Lori was here with her ex-boyfriend, did you hear what they were talking about?"

"No, but..." the young man's voice trailed off for a moment. "It looked like she didn't want to be here if you know what I mean. She wasn't her usual smiling self. She kept shaking her head no, over and over. Eventually, the two of them stood up and walked out. The guy kept trying to take Lori's hand but she kept shaking him off and pulling it away. That's the last time I saw her. Or him. He hasn't been in either."

This. Right here. This was why she suspected Cal Owens. A peek at Knox's expression didn't tell her what he was thinking, however. He wasn't giving anything away.

"Do you have any security cameras?" Knox asked, his gaze scanning the shop. "Inside or outside?"

"We do but they don't hold the footage for more than twenty-four hours," the redhead said. "The detective asked us that, too."

At least Bauer had done that much.

Knox pulled a business card from his shirt pocket. "If you think of anything else, even if it doesn't seem all that important, give me a call. Day or night. You never know what small details might mean to an investigation."

The baristas promised that they would get in contact if they thought of anything else before Jenna and Knox took their leave, walking back to their vehicle.

"I'm not sure what I expected, but I'm a little disappointed," Jenna confessed. "We didn't learn much of anything that we didn't know before."

"That's how this works. We have nothing and then hopefully we finally find something. Then we follow that something until we find something else."

"What happens if we don't find something else?"

Jenna was afraid to ask the question but she needed the answer.

"We'll find something." Knox's tone was upbeat. Determined. "I'm not going to give up easily."

Neither would she.

13

The words of the workers at the coffee shop kept echoing in Knox's head. His brother Cal had been there with Lori that day. Lori hadn't been happy, had kept saying no, and Cal, as usual, had been trying to talk her into something. He'd probably been pissed off that he couldn't charm her anymore. She'd finally figured out Cal's game and wasn't falling for it again.

But she had walked out with him. Shit. Had Cal offered to walk her to her car? Had she tried to get rid of him but he'd insisted? Damn, Knox didn't like this. After hearing their stories, Jenna had to be thinking the same thing as well.

Cal had a hell of a lot of explaining to do. Knox wasn't going to be nearly as nice as Detective Bauer had been. His brother may have been the last person to see Lori Waters alive and well. Even if he didn't do anything wrong, he still might have important information that could help the investigation.

"I know, I know. Let you do the talking and asking questions," Jenna said with an eye roll when they entered Lori's former workplace. Knox wanted to talk to her co-workers and see what they knew about her life, friends, and yes, Cal.

"It doesn't mean you can't say anything. You're allowed to ask questions too."

Jenna wasn't one that absolutely had to say something though. She was more of a listener.

That would be good because later they could discuss everything they'd learned today.

The people on Lori's "team" at the marketing firm had agreed to sit down with Jenna and Knox and answer questions. According to Jenna, Lori had been well-liked at her workplace and everyone was upset about her disappearance. They wanted to help if they could.

Jenna, Knox, and the four other members of Lori's team gathered in a conference room at the back of the building that overlooked a lake.

"I feel like an animal in the zoo," Jenna said as they walked through the busy office.

Knox had the same feeling. All the activity had come to a halt and the room was hushed, several sets of eyes watching them intently. He wondered if they had many visitors or if they knew exactly why he was here.

They settled around the oval table and Knox didn't waste any time. There were two males and two females, all of them somewhere between twenty-five and forty. In fact, from what he'd seen in the office, the demographics definitely skewed young. Not a gray hair in sight.

"I have some questions about Lori Waters," he began, placing his phone on the table between them. "Are you okay with me recording this? I have a terrible memory."

He didn't but he wanted to be able to remember their conversations in detail. He'd neglected to do the same at the coffee shop as the place had been loud and they'd had more than a few disruptions. The conference room, on the other hand, was quiet.

"How about we start with the other co-workers here? I'm

told that there was someone that had an interest in Lori, but maybe she didn't return their feelings. Does any of this sound familiar?"

A woman, possibly the youngest in the group, raised her hand shyly. "I think I know who you are referring to."

"Good. Go ahead."

She looked at her co-workers before continuing. "We've all been feeling guilty. We feel like we should have said something before now, but we didn't want to get anyone in trouble."

Jenna stiffened in the chair next to him. He could almost feel her holding her breath.

"You won't get anyone in trouble if they haven't done anything," he assured the young woman. "What's your name, by the way?"

Her cheeks turned pink and she giggled. "Oops, sorry. I'm Sherry. Sherry Lytell."

"Okay, Sherry. How long have you worked here? Did you work closely with Lori?"

"I've been here three years and Lori and I shared an office for over a year before she went to remote work."

Bingo. Sherry might have been privy to private conversations that Lori would have had on the phone. Knox's own co-workers knew a hell of a lot about his own personal life just because they sat a few feet away. It was inevitable.

"So go ahead and tell your story," he urged. "I'll try not to interrupt you but I may have a few questions as we go along, okay?"

She nodded and once again glanced at her teammates. "Okay, here goes. We all noticed it. We should have said something before now but we didn't want to get Brett in trouble or anything. He's a nice person."

"Brett works here?" Knox asked.

"He used to," Sherry said. "He doesn't anymore."

"He works at a local law firm now. He's an accountant," one of the men said. "He's still friends with Sam, though."

"Sam works here?" Knox asked.

"Yes," Sherry said. "He still works in accounting."

They'd need to talk to Sam too. Knox quickly glanced over at Jenna to see her expression. Did the names ring any bells? Had Lori ever mentioned her former co-worker?

"So tell me about Brett and Lori."

Michelle had been correct. The co-worker's name did start with a B.

"It was clear that he had a crush on Lori," Sherry replied. "He'd sort of follow her around and he'd get this really weird look on his face whenever she was in the same room. Whenever he would grab a coffee in the break room, he'd make one for her too. But he didn't for any of the rest of us. When he'd get lunch, he'd always bring something back for her. Like a slice of cake or donut or something. He'd hang around her desk and there were a few times that she'd find little gifts there. We're sure they were from Brett because he'd ask her all sorts of questions about them, but mostly he wanted to be sure that she liked them."

One of the men who looked to be the oldest in the group leaned forward. "I actually pulled Brett aside once and told him that he should back off. Lori had a boyfriend. I told him that it was disrespectful, but he said I didn't understand."

"Did Lori realize that it was Brett?" Knox asked. "Did she ever talk to him about it?"

Sherry nodded her head. "She knew, but she ignored it. She said it would all blow over and he'd find someone else."

"Did he?"

"We don't know," the other man said. "He quit a few weeks after Lori disappeared."

"That's not suspicious at all," Jenna muttered under her breath.

Knox was happy to see that she was open to other suspects than his brother Cal. Speaking of which...

"Did you ever meet her boyfriend Cal?"

They all nodded but Sherry appeared to be the spokesperson for the group.

"We did. He was...okay."

Normally, people adored Cal. At least until they really got to know him.

"You don't seem all that enthused by him. Care to elaborate?"

Sherry shrugged. "He was fine. Friendly. But we could hear her on the phone with him and they argued a lot. When we'd all go out for drinks after work, he'd find reasons to join us. He was sort of a know-it-all, and really possessive with Lori. It was kind of cringeworthy, to be honest."

Knox couldn't stop himself from asking, "Did you meet Cal before or after you heard Lori arguing with him on the phone?"

"After. I guess you could say we already had a bad impression of him before we met him. Maybe we weren't all that fair to him. To her credit, Lori never said anything bad about him even after they broke up, but we got that she was frustrated."

That explained it. Cal never had the chance to turn on the charm machine.

"Did he bother her after the break-up?"

"He called all the time. Mostly, she'd just send the calls to voicemail."

Knox was going to kick his brother's ass the next time he saw him. Cal was acting like a toddler and he needed someone to check his behavior. No one had ever even tried during their childhood, and clearly, he was out of hand and acting like a douchebag.

"Listen," Sherry said urgently, leaning forward in her chair. "We all knew Lori. She never would have just bugged out in the middle of a big project. She was the team lead. She was far too responsible to chuck it all and head out to some destination without telling anyone. It wasn't who she was. And she was really happy those last few weeks. She'd ended things with Cal and she was back to her old self, smiling and laughing. It doesn't make any sense to us."

"Did you tell the detective all of this?" Knox asked.

"We didn't tell him about Brett," the other man said, his cheeks a ruddy shade. "We should have but we didn't want him to get in trouble. That was our mistake. We did tell him that Lori wasn't the type to run off like that. She wouldn't just disappear and not tell anyone."

Knox turned to Jenna, his brows raised in question. If she had questions, this was her chance. She shook her head no.

Now they needed to talk to Sam. Brett, too.

They were finally making progress. This was the break that Knox had been hoping for.

THE MEETING with Sam didn't turn out to be all that helpful. He said that Brett and Lori went on a few dates, which surprised the hell out of Jenna. Her sister had never mentioned Brett at all, let alone that she'd gone to a movie and dinner with him. When questioned, Sam admitted that he'd never actually seen them together but Brett had told him about the dates in question. They'd been careful in the office because they didn't want anyone to know.

"It sounds like horseshit to me," Jenna said as they settled into a booth at a local cafe. They were both starving. "Lori never mentioned anyone named Brett and we knew about every guy she dated. And she definitely would have told us about him when we were encouraging her to dump Cal. There's no way they dated. Brett is full of it."

Knox was studying the menu and stroking his chin. Was he contemplating what she'd said or his lunch order?

She tapped on his plastic menu with her finger. "Are you listening to me?"

"I am."

"Do you have thoughts?"

"All the time."

Sighing, she picked up her own menu. He was going to be a shit until he ate. He was hungry all the time and, like herself, he could get a little testy when he was like that. He didn't answer until they'd both ordered and the waitress had disappeared into the kitchen.

"I agree."

"You agree? You think Brett was lying too?" she asked.

"Yes. I think he told Sam that to either make himself feel better or he said it because he truly believed it. There's a small percentage of people out in the world who unfortunately don't deal with reality all that well. This Brett may be one of them. I suppose we'll figure out which one he is when we talk to him."

"His friend Sam is going to get to him first," Jenna warned. "I bet he was on the phone with Brett before we hit the parking lot."

"I think you're right but that's fine. If he's the delusional type then warning him won't help anyway."

"And if he's just your garden variety liar?"

Knox chuckled. "We'll find out that too."

"You seem very confident."

"I've been doing this a long time."

She had to admit that she'd been impressed so far. He had a way of making people feel comfortable while talking. She wouldn't call it charm; that was way too superficial, but somehow he made people feel calm - as if everything was simply great.

They were halfway through their lunch when Knox's phone buzzed. He checked it and sent the call to voicemail.

"Not important?"

"It's my dad. Again. He's not getting the hint that I'm not going to call back."

"You could just block the number."

Knox shrugged. "I just ignore him. My younger brother Randy is trying to convince me to give my father a second chance. He says he's *changed.*"

It didn't appear that Knox agreed with that sentiment.

"And you don't think that he has?"

"I can't even imagine how that would look. And as for giving him a second chance, fuck that. I've given him dozens of chances and he's blown every single one. He's a mess of a human being and I don't think he'll ever change. I don't honestly think that he wants to. What he really wants is for *us* to change. He wants us to forgive and forget whenever he gives us one of his lame ass apologies."

With her own background, Jenna didn't blame Knox. A child - even as an adult - could only take so much. At some point they had to drop the rope if only for their own sanity.

"I think you should do whatever it is you want to. Your brother can't make your decisions for you."

Knox's brow quirked. "You don't think I should give my dad another chance? Everyone else thinks I should."

"Only if you want to."

"Would you give your father another chance?"

"Doubtful. But to be fair, he's never proclaimed that he's changed. In fact, he's rather proud of being an asshole. He thinks he's just fine and everyone else around him is in the wrong." She hesitated for a moment, not sure if she should continue. But why not? She'd already told Knox deeply intimate things about herself. What was a few more? "I used to think that there was something wrong with me. After all, if my own dad couldn't love me then I must not be lovable, right? I just couldn't understand what I'd done wrong. Tom and Anita eventually sent me to a therapist who helped me understand that I hadn't done anything. It was him. I was lovable and loved. It was a huge revelation for me."

He gave her a lopsided grin. "Are you worried that I don't think I'm lovable, Jenna? That I think that there's something wrong with me? Never fear, I don't. I've known for a very long time that my family is fucking dysfunctional and that my parents suck. And I didn't need to talk to a therapist to come to that conclusion."

Whenever she got too close, he'd lash out. Even if he did it with a smile.

"Are you saying that therapy is dumb? Because I think it can help a lot of people. It might help you."

"How? What help do I need?"

She sat back in the booth, her fingers idly playing with her fork. "For one thing, you seem to think that having a shitty family is an important part of your identity. It seems to define who you are and I also think that you don't like having to share that. You want only you to have had a crappy childhood. That's why you minimize my childhood."

He was already shaking his head before she'd finished speaking. "I don't minimize it. You do. You admit that you were basically saved by Tom and Anita. You had an escape hatch to a better life. I didn't. I only had me to depend on."

"So that makes you better?"

"I'm not falling for that."

She laughed and shook her head. "You're just not saying it out loud, but I'd bet that I'm right about what you're thinking about inside."

"You don't know what I think about. All I'm saying is that I don't think you can truly understand my life."

Gobsmacked. It was the only word that she could think of that summed up this situation as well as it did.

"What an incredibly sad, lonely, and assholish thing to say," Jenna shot back. She wasn't angry with Knox. He hadn't hurt her by what he'd said. If anything, he was only hurting himself by not letting people in. "This is actually quite fascinating in a psychological way. For some people, having crappy parents makes them doubt themselves. In your case, it's made you an arrogant douchebag because you think you've survived something that no one else has. News flash. You're deluding yourself. But don't listen to me. After all, I could never understand."

Knox threw up his hands in frustration. "What is it that you want from me? You want me to be sad and have shitty self-esteem? Because it sounds like it. I just don't let my craptastic family get to me. I see them as little as possible and live my life. End of story."

"Fine. End of story. Let's drop the subject."

He sighed, rubbing the back of his neck. "Don't get that way, okay? We just look at the situation differently. That's it."

Jenna stared down at the table, her appetite completely gone. "I just wanted you to know that you're not alone."

"I don't mind being alone. I like it. I prefer it."

She looked up at him then, tears burning the backs of her eyes. He appeared to be confident in what he was saying. He believed it. So she needed to as well.

"I promise I won't intrude on that then. I'll leave you to it."

"Listen, we're not a couple–"

She held up her hand. "You're right. We're not, and it's probably for the best."

"I think that it is."

"Fine."

"Good."

But it was still sort of sad. She didn't like to think of Knox all alone. He said that he wanted it that way.

Was he sure? She'd have to take his word for it.

Stop reaching out. Stop letting him into her heart.

He wasn't interested. And that wasn't going to change. She should feel glad that she'd figured it out before falling completely head over heels for him.

Why do I feel so crappy then?

14

The rest of their lunch was awkward. Knox had changed the subject and was trying to pretend that their conversation had never happened. Jenna wasn't the type to sweep disagreements under the rug. She would have preferred to talk it out but he clearly didn't want to so instead she shut her mouth, only giving him the bare minimum of responses. He might be over it but it was going to take her a little longer.

She was beginning to think that perhaps her feelings for Knox ran deeper than she'd originally believed. They hadn't known each other long. Not really. But there was something about him that drew her in, like a moth to a flame.

It wasn't his dazzling looks, although that didn't hurt. It wasn't that he was a fantastic conversationalist or brilliant or amazingly funny. It wasn't that he was the best of the best at any of those things. He wasn't. He was sweet and kind, sharp-witted and he made her giggle. He made her want to spend more time with him, to ask him questions about what he liked and didn't like. She wanted to know his favorite ice cream and whether he liked classic rock. She was fascinated by how a man who dumped copious amounts of ketchup on his scrambled eggs could say there was too much gravy on his mashed potatoes.

He was laid back but his mind was working every moment. She'd become one of those horrible women who wanted to know what their man was thinking all of the time. Hoping, of course, that he was thinking about her. She wasn't delusional enough for that, though. She knew good and well he wasn't thinking about her.

Knox pulled up in front of Lori's townhouse. "You said that you haven't changed anything? Everything is the same as when she left it?"

"Everything," Jenna assured him. "Except we cleaned out the refrigerator. We didn't want to harbor spoiled food. Luckily, Lori wasn't much of a cook so there wasn't much there."

It was stupid, keeping Lori's townhouse. But their hope had truly never died. Even now, knowing the odds were stacked mightily against them, they held onto it, keeping it just as she left it.

Lori's home was in a newly constructed townhouse development on the edge of Douglas. All the exteriors were exactly alike, painted beige with white trim, up and down the street. Jenna remembered that she'd teased her sister that she needed to put up a colorful flag or paint the mailbox red otherwise she'd drive right past her own house. Michelle and Jenna had come over the next weekend and helped plant colorful flowers in decorative pots for the front porch.

They approached the front door and if Jenna hadn't been paying attention she would have run right into Knox's back. He'd come to an abrupt halt.

"What–"

He placed his hand over her mouth, shaking his head. His head jerked toward the townhouse and then he pointed to his ear.

It was when she was quiet that she heard it. Sounds coming from inside the house. There shouldn't be anyone in there. Her heart lurched and then accelerated, the adrenaline beginning to pump through her veins.

Someone was in Lori's house.

"Would your sister or brother be in the house?" he asked, his voice so low she almost didn't hear him.

She held up the key. "No, we only have the one spare. If I have it, they don't."

"Stay here."

Before her brain could register his movements, he'd gone back to the SUV to retrieve something and was standing back on the front porch again.

He was holding a gun. *A gun.*

Now her heart was pounding even harder and faster. Real fear was crawling at her insides, pressing against her lungs and making it difficult to take a deep breath. Knox thought that whoever was inside the house was dangerous. Was that person armed too?

Gently pushing her back, he plucked the key from her hand and slowly unlocked the front door.

"Stay here," he said again, pushing his shoulder against the door and entering the house.

Jenna didn't like staying behind but she didn't want to go inside either. She was frozen to her spot on the porch, her feet immovable objects. Her brain wasn't in charge at the moment.

She heard a flurry of activity, some curse words, and then the sound of a door and footsteps. Hurrying to the edge of the house, she caught a glimpse of Knox running through the backyard, dodging lawn furniture and leaping over a flowerbed before disappearing between two houses.

Now what?

She didn't have to be a genius to realize that Knox was chasing someone. The "someone" who had been in Lori's house. Had he or she been alone? Was there anyone else still in there?

Should I go check? Should I get in the car and try and help Knox?

She then realized that she didn't have the keys to his vehicle. She was stuck here.

Glancing back at the front door, she took a few tentative steps toward it but then stopped. He'd said to stay put. He was the former cop, after all. If she walked into the house and there was still someone in there it would be her own damn fault if she ended up hurt or dead. He'd warned her when they started this investigation that if she was going to follow him around, she had to do everything he told her to do. No exceptions. He wasn't going to take any chances with her safety.

Even if there wasn't anyone in the house, if she went in there while he was gone he might get pissed off about it. She didn't want to give him a reason to exclude her from the investigation. She was in this for the long haul, wanting to find her sister. Nothing was going to stop her now that she had Knox on the case.

So I'll just stand here, I guess. Feeling like an idiot.

Jenna kept her eyes peeled in case she saw anyone suspicious running through the neighborhood but it was quiet, almost serene. If one didn't include a former law enforcement officer chasing a home intruder around the block.

"You listened. I'm surprised."

Whirling around, her heart in her throat, Knox was striding up the opposite side of the building. His face was sweaty and he looked mad. Very mad.

"You mean about staying? I did, although I admit that I was tempted. What happened?"

Bounding up the porch stairs, Knox held out his arm, gun still in his hand. "I lost him about a street over. I think he might have parked there and walked here because he seemed to just disappear."

"It was a he? What was he doing?"

"I actually don't know if it was a male. They were dressed in dark pants and a hoodie, with the hood up. I didn't see their face, but the figure was bulky. I'm assuming it was a male but it could have been a female wearing oversized clothing."

"What were they doing?"

Jenna was beginning to calm down with Knox so near, her heart rate beginning to return to normal. He seemed to have a good handle on what was happening.

"If you look inside, you'll see. I think they were searching for something." He beckoned to her. "I'm going to go in and make sure the house is clear. Wait here for me, this won't take long. Then you can enter."

True to his word, he wasn't gone long before returning for her. He was also correct when he said that she'd see what he was talking about. The house was a shambles. Drawers open, contents strewn all over. Couch and chair cushions cut open, the stuffing ripped out. The kitchen cabinets had been opened and their contents thrown around.

"I'm afraid to look at the rest of the house."

"It doesn't get any better," Knox warned. "Unless your sister is a total slob, they tore apart her bedroom and office too."

It looked like a bomb had gone off. Repeatedly.

The mattress was pulled off the frame and cut open. Every single drawer had been dumped onto the floor, the contents strewn around the room. She couldn't take a single clear step. The curtains had been torn down and all the clothes in the closet had been thrown out, along with dozens of pairs of shoes and purses. Lori adored buying handbags and she'd had a large collection.

The office was no better; in fact, it was worse. Lamps had been overturned, file cabinets emptied. It appeared that every single solitary piece of paper had been thrown into the air, landing willy-nilly on the floor. It would take days to put this place back together.

"What on earth were they looking for?" Jenna asked, picking up a lamp and setting it on the desk. "Lori wasn't a government spy, for heaven's sake. She didn't have any secrets."

Hands on hips, Knox was scowling at the mess. "What about a diary or a journal? Did she keep one of those?"

"I have no idea. She had a journal when we were teenagers but I don't know if she kept it up." Her gaze ran over the rubble. "Is that what you think they were looking for?"

"Maybe. I don't know."

"But why now?" Jenna asked. "It doesn't make any sense. After all this time, they're just looking now?"

"Because we're looking into Lori's disappearance. Before they didn't have any worries."

"You sound almost happy," Jenna said with a frown. "They've just destroyed my sister's home."

"Because we've shaken them up. Good. Now is when they'll start making mistakes. We need to keep them off balance. Keep up the pressure. They're starting to get scared after being complacent for months."

That did sound like good news. But...

"I'm happy but I still have a huge mess to clean up here."

Knox peered into the open filing drawers. "You said that you and Michelle checked this place and nothing was missing, right?"

"Yes, except for Lori's purse and phone."

Knox rubbed the back of his neck and grimaced. "Did anything look out of place? Maybe a man's belongings? A tie or something like that? Even a coffee mug that didn't look familiar?"

"I don't remember anything like that but I have to be honest—that's not what we were looking for. We were looking for her possessions that we knew she would never leave without." Jenna sat on the edge of the desk. "So what happens now? Do we call the police? I'm sure Detective Bauer is going to love this."

"Maybe this will finally convince him that there is more to this case than just a young woman running away from her life," Knox replied in a grim tone, pulling his phone from his pocket. "But I doubt it. He doesn't seem the type to change his mind easily."

Jenna had real doubts that Detective Bauer would change his tune. He wouldn't want to admit that he might have been wrong.

They were on their own.

Just the two of them...and whomever had ripped the townhouse apart.

DETECTIVE BAUER HAD BEEN ONLY SLIGHTLY MORE helpful in the afternoon than he'd been earlier. He did admit that it was a weird coincidence that Lori's townhouse was broken into and torn apart just one day into Knox's investigation, but he wasn't *convinced* that the two events were related.

"Correlation doesn't equal causation," he'd said, taking notes while the other officer he'd brought along had photographed the scene. "Could just be a strange coincidence. Let's not jump to any conclusions."

Knox, on the other hand, didn't give a shit what Detective Bauer thought. He didn't seem the type that wanted to truly work on...anything. In fact, Knox was puzzled as to why this guy was even a police officer, let alone a detective. Mysteries didn't seem to excite him, nor did doing actual investigative activities such as questioning suspects. Bauer mostly wanted Knox and Jenna to drop the subject and go away.

Plus, Bauer wouldn't even talk to Jenna at all. He'd only

speak to Knox, which was total bullshit. He might think Jenna was uptight or difficult but that wasn't an excuse for completely freezing her out of any discussion. This was her sister's home and she knew a hell of a lot more about it than Knox did. Yet, the detective still didn't want to talk to Jenna. He'd avoided her the entire time. If this wasn't an active investigation, Knox would have been quite amused by how Bauer practically raced around the townhouse trying to stay out of Jenna's orbit.

"He's a douchebag," Jenna said when the cops were gone. "I wouldn't trust him to get my cat out of a tree."

"He didn't seem all that engaged," Knox agreed. They were locking up the townhouse and heading back to Tom and Michelle's home. "But he did say that he'd check with the neighbors to see if they have any security camera footage."

"I'll be shocked if he actually follows through."

"I think he'll do it. He said he would."

"So cops can't be assholes?"

Knox chuckled and opened her car door. "I would imagine the percentage of assholes in cops is about the same as the percentage in the overall population. There are always going to be a few. But Bauer specifically said he was going to check for security footage so I think he actually will. I just kind of get the feeling that he doesn't love his job."

"Did you love your job?" Jenna asked after Knox settled into the driver's seat. "Do you love it now?"

"The quick answer is yes and yes. I didn't love every single day of being a cop but I loved the job overall. Do you love your job? Are you anxious to get back to it?"

Tapping her chin, she considered his question. "I love parts of my job. But I have to admit that I'm not as fond of the traveling as much as I used to be. I used to think it was kind of exciting to see different states but now I would rather curl up in my own bed at night. I guess I'm just getting older."

"So you won't sign on to another campaign?"

"I probably will," she admitted. "Eventually. It's what I do and I think I do it well. I have thought about going back to school to get my doctorate. Right now I'm simply concentrating on Lori. Later I can think about my own situation."

A question had been in the back of his mind since meeting her family.

"If you stopped traveling would you live with Tom and Michelle?"

Laughing, she shook her head. "I can tell that you think that living with a sibling is weird. But the answer is no, I wouldn't live with them. I like having my own space and I'm mostly an introvert."

"I can't imagine living with any of my siblings. Not even the ones I get along with. I couldn't wait to get my own place. I don't like sharing things."

"Like the bathroom?"

"The bathroom, the kitchen, the couch, the television. You name it, I don't want to share it. I love living alone. I can do whatever the hell I want without anyone there to tell me I'm not doing it right."

Her brows shot up. "Wow, your family really did a number on you, didn't they? Did they often tell you that you were doing things wrong? Because they brag a lot about you being a super cop."

She didn't even realize how loaded her question was.

"Every damn day. Now we need to talk about next steps. Obviously, we need to talk to that Brett guy and find out where he was this afternoon. He's my top suspect for the break-in. We'll need to talk to Sam again too. I'm guessing he called his friend but I'd like for him to admit it."

Jenna's finger tapped on the door armrest. "What about your brother Cal? You haven't talked to him yet. When are you planning to do that?"

Soon. Knox had wanted to get as much information as possible before he did it.

"I need to call him and schedule something but he doesn't yet know that I'm investigating Lori's disappearance."

Jenna didn't reply but Knox wasn't an idiot. The tension between them had gone from zero to a billion in about thirty seconds. She hadn't liked his answer. He could almost physically feel the resentment radiating from her.

"You're pissed. Care to tell me what I did this time?"

Glancing quickly at him, she turned to stare out of the car window. "You always sound so sure of yourself. Do you ever have doubts? At all? For example, you said that Cal doesn't know that you're doing this investigation. But how can you be so certain? Didn't you talk to your brother this morning? He could have told Cal."

Knox opened his mouth to say that Randy wouldn't do that but then snapped it shut. Because he didn't know that for sure. His brother had talked a hell of a lot about *loyalty* in that conversation. Fuck.

"You're right. I'm going to have to call Randy and find out if he told Cal. If he did, then yes, I agree that Cal would also be a suspect in the break-in."

"So you'll talk to him?"

"I was always going to talk to him," Knox assured her. "I just wanted to have my ducks in a row before I did."

"That's good. Ducks and rows are good."

"I think we need to talk about you and Lori."

Her head jerked around, her brow furrowed. "What do you mean?"

"My firm is going to be sending me Lori's financial records, credit cards and all of that sort of stuff. This is the part of the investigation where we might find out things that you wouldn't want to know normally. Things that our family and friends don't show us. It's the hard part of looking into cases like this.

People have secrets, Jenna. Even nice, normal people have secrets that they don't let the world know. Maybe they sleep with a dozen stuffed animals, maybe they watch kinky porn. Maybe somewhere in between. But either way, what we find out can alter your perception of that person. Are you ready for that?"

"You make it sound ominous. Like I'm going to find out that Lori was a secret spy for some paramilitary group."

"You may just find out that she really, really liked Care Bears and spent hundreds of dollars every month on them, but you still need to be ready for your view of her to be changed. It would be the same if we were looking into you or me. Most people's lives look different when we dig deeply into them."

A slow, mischievous smile spread across Jenna's face. "I wonder what your secrets are. I bet they're a doozy."

In his opinion, he lived the most boring life on the planet. He didn't think anything he did was all that exciting.

"I doubt you'd find them that interesting."

"And you'll never find out my secrets either."

It was a perfectly normal reply. Jenna hadn't said it in a mean tone or anything. She'd sounded like she was teasing, to be honest.

But she had a point. They weren't a couple anymore and he wasn't going to be learning any of her secrets. He wasn't going to find out more about life unless it was something he learned through this investigation. She wasn't going to be telling him about her hopes and dreams. Or whether she liked Christmas more than Halloween. Did she do turkey or ham on Thanksgiving?

And he wanted to know those things. He wanted to know more and more about Jenna with every passing day. This wasn't going how he'd planned.

He could say that he didn't want to be her man.

He just wasn't sure he was telling the truth.

15

Later in the evening, Jenna was starting to fix dinner when Knox joined her in the kitchen. He'd been holed up in his bedroom for over an hour combing through Lori's credit card statements. Jenna had wanted to help but Knox had said it was a one-person job.

"Where are Tom and Michelle?" he asked, leaning a hip against the kitchen counter. Knox was dressed casually in jeans and a white button-down shirt. Nothing special. Yet somehow, he managed to look incredibly handsome even with his hair slightly askew. Jenna knew that it was from him scraping his fingers through his hair when he was thinking or concentrating. He probably didn't even realize he was doing it.

His jaw was covered with a shadow of whiskers after their long day and there was a tiredness around his eyes. She was impressed with his work ethic when on a case. He'd already said he planned to stay up tonight to go through all of the files that his firm had sent. She'd offer to help again, of course. Maybe this time he'd take her up on it.

"Tom had a business meeting tonight in Billings so he'll be home quite late. Michelle has a nasty migraine so she took some medicine and went to bed early. We're on our own for dinner."

Leaning over the pan on the stove, Knox gave the simmering food a sniff. "If you'd let me know, I would have come down to help."

Despite Knox's overprotective instincts, he wasn't the type that got stuck into gender roles. She liked that about him.

Stop. I don't want to admire or like anything more about him.

I want to find things I don't like about him.

"It's not a big deal. I'm making some skillet lasagna. It's easy to whip up. You said you liked Italian food."

"I do," he confirmed. "Is there anything I can help with?'

Jenna nodded toward the refrigerator. "You can do the salad. It's just one of those bagged Caesars. When this is done, I've also got garlic bread to go in the oven for a few minutes. I need to mix up the butter and garlic."

"I can help with that too."

His help would be fine but that meant that he was moving around the room, often brushing up against her or accidentally making contact when reaching for a utensil or bowl. She'd never realized just how small this kitchen could be with two people in it. She, Michelle, and Lori had prepared meals a thousand times in here but she'd never been as hyperaware of another human being in her life. She could smell his body wash or aftershave, a clean citrus scent. When he reached over her head to grab a large salad bowl from the cabinet, she could even feel the heat of his body.

I am such a wuss.

She was weak and it was pathetic. He was only a man. Yet, he had her practically following him around with her tongue hanging out. She'd never cared like this before. She'd gone *much* longer without sex and it hadn't fazed her in the least. Hell, when she was working on a campaign, she might go months. It had never been a big deal but tonight this man had her literally sweating.

"I can do this."

Now she sounded frustrated and pissed off. Which she was. But she didn't want Knox to know that he had her tied in knots. He didn't look like he was even aware that she was in the same room.

Asshole.

Knox paused tossing the salad, his expression perplexed. "You don't want me to help?"

She couldn't explain it. Not to him.

"You can help," she finally said with a sigh. "But you don't have to if you don't want to."

"I want to."

She placed the lid on the skillet and set the timer for twenty minutes so the broken lasagna noodles could soften in the meat sauce. The kitchen was filled with the delicious aromas of tomatoes, garlic, and oregano. She adored Italian food and this was one of her favorites. They'd have leftovers for sure. If Michelle got hungry in the middle of the night, she could have some or they could eat it for lunch the next day.

Determined to ignore Knox, she retrieved the cheeses she needed from the refrigerator and set them on the counter. She grabbed a large spoon from the drawer and then opened the cabinet next to the stove for a bowl. The size she needed was on the top shelf and she stretched her arm up, going up on her tiptoes but she was still a few inches too short. She'd need a step stool. Before she could move, another arm came over hers, his big body pressed up against her back.

"Let me get that for you."

His voice was close to her ear, his breath tickling her cheek. She accepted the bowl that he held out, their hands brushing together. Her skin tingled where they had touched, her heart pounding against her ribs. She was surprised that he couldn't hear its deafening noise.

She'd turned around to face him, her gaze level with his shoulders before wandering up to his face. He was looking down at her, watching intently, scanning her for...what? She didn't know what he was looking for. She didn't even know what *she* was looking for.

That was a lie. She did know.

She was looking for him to look at her. That way. She had a terrible feeling that she was looking that exact same way at him. Like she wanted him. And she wanted him to want her.

Their gazes locked, his blue eyes almost black from the pupils blown wide. Jenna could almost feel herself being pulled into his orbit, a force far too great for her to be able to fight. Not that she was planning to.

What happened next was inevitable. They'd been dancing around it for days. His face came closer to her own, their lips mere millimeters apart. She could feel his warm breath, smell his heady scent. At that moment, she couldn't have said what day it was or where she was standing. Her world had narrowed down to the two of them and she could happily be like this, blocking out the universe. Reality was overrated.

She didn't know which one of them made the first move. Did it matter? Not much. Their lips touched briefly, a soft brush like the wings of a butterfly. Then more, her lips parting to allow his own to plunder and conquer. Her limbs were heavy and she had to hold onto his broad shoulders to keep her knees from turning to water and falling into a heap on the floor.

This man knew how to kiss.

She'd been in his arms before, of course. This wasn't their first embrace, but it shook her far more than the previous ones had. Maybe because she knew Knox so much better now. It meant more because they were more. Except that...they weren't.

He'd made his position clear more than once. He didn't

want to be a couple. He didn't want to be in a relationship with her because he said he couldn't trust her anymore. She'd apologized but it wasn't enough. Now they were kissing. Not a friendly peck on the lips, either. This was a three-alarm inferno they had going here but had he changed his mind? Did he want her after all? Only hours ago he'd been adamant that they were only friends.

Of their own accord, her palms flattened against his chest, pushing him backwards. It certainly wasn't her heart initiating that action, so it could only be her brain. Or maybe it was some primitive self-survival instinct that had kicked in when under stress. Whatever it was, he immediately stepped back, his arms falling to his sides. His shoulders fell and rose rapidly with his breath and his color was high. He was as aroused as she was. If he was going to deny it, he was a lying liar who lied. She could easily see that their kiss had affected him. Now she needed to know what it meant.

"You can't do this."

Her voice came out hoarse and ragged, like broken glass on gravel. She had to suck oxygen into her lungs to be able to speak. With one kiss, he'd taken her breath away.

"You can't do this," she repeated, taking her own step away, putting more space between them. "You can't say that you only want to be friends and then kiss me when we're making dinner. It's not fair to me."

"I was only–"

She held up her hands and angrily shook her head. Now that her mind was clearing, she was beginning to get a little pissed off. Who the hell did he think he was?

"Have you changed your mind?"

Her tone was aggressive but she wasn't going to play games with him. She was far from in the mood.

He didn't reply right away; instead his head dropped so he

was looking at the floor. She had her answer then. He didn't need to say anything.

"You haven't changed your mind," she said, wanting to reach out and give him a shove, or maybe kick his shin. Something to make him feel a quarter of the pain she was feeling at the moment. Her heart was breaking into tiny little shards that was currently slicing her guts into a million painful pieces. "But you kissed me anyway. That's bullshit, Knox. You don't get to use me that way–"

"I wasn't using you," he replied, straightening his shoulders. "I got carried away. I admit that. But I wasn't using you. I wouldn't do that."

She pointed at his chest, right where his cold heart resided. "You don't get to be carried away. You made these rules, and you have to stick to them. Unless you're ready to blow away the rules. Are you? Are you, Knox? I'll go out on a limb here. Why not? I'll say that I don't want these rules. Can you say it?"

She was literally shaking like a leaf, her entire body trembling with emotion. There was anger, for sure. Fear, as well. Terror that he didn't feel the same when she knew deep inside that he felt...something. Was it only lust? She'd seen that plenty of times in her life but this didn't feel the same. This felt like something she'd never experienced before. He had to be feeling it too. She'd seen it in his face.

He whirled on his heel and strode a few paces away before turning back.

"I don't know how this even happened," he said, scraping his fingers through his hair so it was almost standing on end. "We were having a perfectly normal conversation and fixing dinner. And you took that–"

"Don't you even go there," she said quietly. "I'm not taking the fall for this all on my own. We both wanted this. I didn't jump your bones or make you do anything that you weren't all on board for.

Hell, Knox, if I hadn't stopped you, I have a feeling we'd be doing more than just kissing right now. This was a mutual decision. You don't get to wash your hands of it because it's inconvenient."

"I don't want to talk about this. You're not being reasonable."

"Because I won't let you blame me? Fuck you, Knox Owens."

He didn't say anything else, his jaw tight and his lips pressed together in a thin line. After a long moment, he turned and walked out of the kitchen, leaving Jenna standing there all alone. Just as she'd been less than thirty minutes ago. So much had changed in that small window of time.

All these emotions had been simmering between them and the moment they allowed the heat to turn up, they'd exploded. All over the place making a big, damn mess. She hadn't wanted this tonight, but she couldn't say that she was sorry either.

Her anger draining away, she leaned against the counter, letting her heart rate and breathing go back to normal. The realization of what had happened was penetrating her brain. This was a cluster fuck of gigantic proportions. She'd thought she'd been so clever, pushing her feelings aside and pretending that they didn't exist. She couldn't, however, deny them any longer. Where did that leave them? They had work to do still.

The next time she saw Knox could she act as if nothing had happened?

She wasn't sure she was that good of an actress. And she was tired of lying to herself.

She wanted Knox. Did he want her?

16

After leaving the kitchen, Knox had gone upstairs to his room to lie down. He couldn't rest; he was far too agitated for that, so he ended up staring at the ceiling and replaying his conversation with Jenna over and over in his head.

Not a pretty picture.

Knox wasn't feeling all that proud of himself. In fact, he was ashamed of his behavior with Jenna. She'd called him out and for good reason. His actions weren't matching his words and he was acting like a giant hypocrite. And if there was one thing that he hated, that was a hypocritical person. He'd grown up with that shit so he didn't have any patience or pity for himself when he displayed that sort of crap. There wasn't any excuse that was good enough. He'd acted like a jerk and she'd rightly given him a big *fuck you*.

He'd walked out on her not because he thought she was being unreasonable. Far from it. He didn't have an argument in defense. Guilty as charged. He shouldn't have been kissing Jenna. He'd been the one that had put the rules in place and then first chance he'd broken them.

He should have had more control. But...he couldn't deny the heat that shimmered between them whenever they were together. He was attracted to Jenna. Fuck it, he really liked her as well. As a person. She was genuine and fun to be around. She was smart and witty and she made him laugh.

He'd been sure that he wanted to end their relationship. There hadn't been any doubt in his mind at the time. He'd been angry and hurt, disappointed too. But now that he was ass deep in this investigation, he understood how desperate Jenna had been. She'd been at the end of her rope, willing to do just about any outlandish thing to find out what happened to her sister. Plus, he could tell that she wasn't a bad person. She didn't go around pretending and lying about shit. He trusted her.

So where did that leave him? And them? She'd kissed him back. She'd said that she had feelings, although she might not anymore after he'd walked out. If she was angry, he couldn't blame her. Neither of them had acted well since the beginning. What they needed was a fresh start. Put all of the past well and truly behind them. He'd say he was sorry. He'd tell her that he had feelings too.

Which was scary as hell because he didn't go around telling women that he had feelings for them. The last one had been a long time ago. Years, actually. He'd thought he'd been in love. Perhaps he had been but he'd been so young then. He hadn't really known what it meant. He was older, hopefully more mature, and love meant a shitload more now than it did then.

I might just be in love. Why aren't I scared? Why haven't I run? Because I don't want to.

It was a sobering realization. He'd been avoiding "feelings" for a damn long time. He'd become a master at it. In and out of relationships without a second thought. He was always up front with the female about avoiding commitments - and he'd told Jenna the same - but now he wasn't trying to dodge anything. It had all happened while he was paying attention elsewhere, sneaking up on him from behind. Jenna was important to him. How much he couldn't say, but there was something there. He couldn't walk away from it, or from her.

His stomach growled with hunger, reminding him that he'd walked out on dinner before it had even been put on the table. He needed food and to apologize. He wasn't a man that enjoyed apologizing all that much. In fact, he kind of hated it, admitting that he was wrong. But it had to be done. He might as well cowboy up and do it. Then he and Jenna could move forward. If she still wanted to.

Taking a deep breath, he went downstairs and into the kitchen, following his nose. The delicious aroma of tomatoes and garlic filled the air making his stomach growl even louder than before. He found Jenna in the kitchen, sitting at the island with a plate of food in front of her. She turned when she heard him walk in.

"Are you done pouting?"

Inwardly, he chuckled at her greeting. She wasn't going to take any shit from him. Good for her. He liked that she didn't back down from a challenge.

"Yes, I am. I came down here to apologize and then hope that you'd take pity on me and feed me. I'm sorry about how I acted earlier."

No sense beating around the bush. Get that apology right out there first thing.

She was surprised. He could tell by the way her brows went up and her eyes went round. But then she tried to cover it up, acting all cool as if she'd expected him to apologize the entire time.

"Apology accepted. And yes, there's plenty of dinner. I can fill you a plate."

There was already a second plate on the counter and he assumed it was for him.

"I've got it. You go ahead and keep eating."

Knox made his plate and sat next to Jenna, both of them eating silently until their bellies were full and their plates were empty. She set her fork on the edge of hers and dabbed at the corners of her mouth with a napkin.

"Just a quick question. What exactly are you apologizing for? Kissing me? Or walking out when I asked you a question? Not that it matters because I've accepted the apology already."

"I am not apologizing for kissing you. I don't want to take that back. I am sorry that I acted like an ass afterwards. You were right. I made the rules and I was the first to break them."

"They were dumb rules," she replied with a roll of her eyes. "We both knew we were going to break them eventually. Or we should have known."

"I can't argue that fact. I'm sorry that I put us both in that position. Let's just say I was still angry about what you did."

She turned in her chair so they were eye to eye. "Are you mad now?"

"Only at myself. I get it. I really do. I see why you misled me."

She gave him a sideways look. "And you're not going to throw this back in my face down the road when we argue about something?"

"Are we going to fight?"

"Probably," she sighed. "We're both hard-headed and convinced we're right. And you're stubborn as hell."

"Pot...this is kettle..."

"Okay, I'm stubborn too. What I'm saying here is that I think we're going to butt heads from time to time."

He waggled his eyebrows. "Can we kiss when we make up afterward?"

A smile tugged at her lips. "Yes, but that's not always going to get around me. Sometimes, I'm going to be mad because you deserve it."

"Can we kiss and make up right now? We did have an argument, after all."

Knox had leaned closer so that their breath mingled together. He didn't want to fight the urge inside of him that was screaming to kiss this woman.

"I suppose a kiss wouldn't hurt."

It would feel amazing. He already knew how good it could be and he was going to get to experience it again and again.

The first touch of their lips was tentative but it didn't stay that way for long. He slid out of his chair, pressing their bodies together and feeling the heat of her skin through his clothes. Her lips parted sweetly and he deepened the kiss, the heat in his body building along with the tempo of his heart. His fingers tangled in her honey-colored locks, loving the silky feel between his fingers. Her palms skimmed down his spine and it was all he could do not to sweep her up into his arms and carry her upstairs to ravish her some more.

We're in her family's home. This is not the time or place.

Reluctantly, he pulled away watching as her eyelids fluttered open. Her pupils were blown wide and he was relieved to see that she was as affected as he was. The desire and passion was mutual.

"I'm going to admit that I tend to walk away when I'm angry or frustrated," he found himself confessing softly, taking a step back. He needed to cool off. It was getting far too heated. "Arguing in my house growing up wasn't productive and no one listened to me anyway."

"I'll listen."

Two simple words. They'd punched him squarely in the gut so he had to concentrate to breathe in.

"I believe you."

Knox didn't know what else to say. He did believe her, but he wasn't ready to talk about maybe falling in love. Not yet.

Jenna slid off her chair and picked up both their empty

plates. "After cleaning up, should we take a look at the files your firm sent?"

"We can. There's about two years of credit card data plus a year of Lori's phone records. Are you sure you're up for this?"

"Let's do it."

"Then I'll help with the dishes," he offered. "The sooner we start, the sooner we'll be done."

He could only hope that her financial records held a clue that would eventually lead to some answers.

IT WAS ALMOST four in the morning when Tom arrived back home. Jenna and Knox were heads down in the living room over the electronic files that had been sent over. She'd learned a great deal about her missing sister in the last few hours, not the least of which was that Lori had been spending a lot of money. Then it had abruptly stopped a few weeks before she'd disappeared. It didn't take a genius to figure out that she'd been spending that money on Callum Owens. There'd been expensive dinners, clothes, and trips.

Tom looked exhausted, the lines around his eyes deeper than they had been this morning.

"You look like you're ready to fall over," she said. "Did the meeting go well?"

"It did but I'm tired as hell. It seemed to go on forever. I'll probably fall asleep the moment my head hits the pillow," he declared with a grimace, stretching his arms over his head. "Of course, I still need to be up early tomorrow. We're in delicate negotiations right now."

"Then go ahead and go to bed," Jenna urged, elbowing Knox. "We'll be quiet down here."

Tom looked longingly up the stairs. "A bomb could go off

and I'd sleep through it. Are you sure though? You two look like you're busy. I can help if you like."

"It's fine," Knox assured him. "We've got this. Honestly, we'll be done soon. Probably another half hour should do it."

"I'm not even going to argue," Tom said with a tired smile. "I'm just going to be grateful and go upstairs to bed."

"We'll see you in the morning," Jenna said to her brother's retreating figure. He grinned and waved before heading upstairs. "Tom works all the time but he loves it."

"If you're going to be working long hours, it helps to love what you do," Knox replied with a yawn. "Damn, hitting the sack sounds good. How much do you have left?"

"I'm done with the phone records. Are you finished with her finances?"

Knox had insisted on taking the more difficult records, saying that he was used to it.

"I have a few more months to go but as we've already talked about, the patterns are clear. She spent a whole lot of money after meeting Cal and then stopped when they broke up. I swear the next time I see my brother I'm going to punch him in the mouth. He's such a loser. He makes a decent living. There's no reason for this shit."

This was the second time that Knox had said he wanted to punch his brother. She was beginning to think that he just might do it too. At this point, she'd cheer him on.

"When are you going to talk to him?"

It was a loaded question. She'd asked it before but they'd found out quite a bit since then.

"Right after we talk to that Brett guy from Lori's work. Right now Cal and Brett are on my suspect list."

"I'm glad you're finally going to talk to him. I'm anxious to hear what he has to say for himself."

Knox tapped Jenna's iPad. "From what Lori's phone records tell us, he wouldn't leave her the fuck alone even after she ended things. Cal's never liked it when other people make decisions. He likes to control everything around him. When I ask him about it, he's just going to whine about how life isn't fair. That's his usual go-to."

"You'd think by now he would have realized that life usually isn't fair."

"Life has been more than fair to Cal," Knox ground out, his teeth gritted together. "He leaves messes in his wake and expects others to clean up after him."

It was beginning to dawn on Jenna that Knox had issues with his older brother. Not just little ones but really big ones.

"You don't like him at all, do you?"

He didn't reply at once, instead jumping up from the floor where they were sprawled out on a bunch of cushions.

"I don't hate him..."

"But you don't like him."

"No, I don't like him." Knox sighed, rubbing the back of his neck. "Sometimes I just can't believe I'm part of the same family. Randy and I are pretty normal, but my brothers and sisters... Shit, and don't get me started on my parents."

"Is your dad still contacting you?"

"Yes, and I keep avoiding him."

"Maybe you should just talk to him. Get it over with."

"You're starting to sound like my brother Randy. Why should I give him five minutes of my day?"

"Not for him, but for you. Tell him once and for all that you're done."

"I don't care to even spend that much time with him. I've given him too many chances as it is."

Jenna never had the chance to respond. Before she could open her mouth, there was the sound of breaking glass. Knox pushed her to the carpet and behind the couch, telling her to stay down. Crouching behind the sofa, her heart racing a mile a minute, she peered around the edge of the cushion and watched as Knox ran out of the house.

Toward the danger.

Maybe it was nothing. A tree branch falling or something like that.

That was it. It was probably nothing at all. Everything was fine. Knox would check it out and calmly come back in the house and tell her that all was well. He'd been overly cautious but it was all good outside.

Except that he'd left the front door open and the slight smell of smoke was beginning to waft through the living room.

Fire?

17

The sun was peeking over the horizon by the time the local fire department put out the flames completely. An acrid scent filled Knox's nostrils and hung in the air along with the wisps of smoke from the smoldering building.

When he had exited the house, he'd seen the orange and yellow flames jumping on the detached garage's roof. The wooden structure went up like tinder, the fire eating at the building until there was only a skeleton and some rubble left behind. The firefighters had done all they could, but in the end their valiant efforts simply weren't enough. The flames had been far too aggressive, and luckily, not deadly.

To Knox, it wasn't a coincidence. He'd definitely heard breaking glass. Had someone given them a warning by starting a fire in the garage? It was a possibility. Right now, the fire marshal was combing through what was left of the dripping and sodden structure to find the cause.

Jenna, Michelle, and Tom, along with Knox had watched in ever growing horror as the scene played out. They were totally helpless to stop the carnage.

All three of the siblings were huddled together, their faces pale and tear-streaked. Jenna looked so shocked and hollow that it was all Knox could do not to pull her into his arms and tell her that everything would be okay. He'd take care of her. He wanted to protect her from the ravages of the world. That's how much he felt for this woman. He'd been slow to put a name to his emotions but clearly, they were strong. Stronger than anything he'd ever felt.

Yet, he had to stand there and do nothing which wasn't in his nature in the least. He wanted to do *something*, but what? He didn't know except that he wanted to carry Jenna off somewhere where no one could ever hurt her.

But he wasn't a part of their world. They were drawing strength from one another, a close and loving family. And if there was one thing that Knox didn't know shit about that was family. He couldn't intrude on their bond, but he could damn well be there for them if they needed it.

"I guess we were lucky," Michelle murmured, wrapping her cardigan more tightly around her body. "The fire could have jumped over to the house if the wind had been blowing in a different direction."

"I don't feel very lucky," Jenna replied, her voice low. The whole scene seemed eerily quiet now that the firefighting part was done. Only one fire truck remained and there were a few people milling around. A news truck had arrived much earlier and taken video when the flames were at their zenith, but then left shortly after. "Although I suppose that we are."

Tom placed an arm around each of their shoulders, pulling them closer. "We are lucky. We're alive. It could have been so much worse. We only lost the garage and the vehicles inside. We have insurance. It will be fine."

Knox's SUV had been parked in the front of the house and was undamaged, as was Michelle's sedan. Tom's car, on the other hand, and his truck that he liked to drive on the weekend were incinerated. A complete loss.

Tom had already called his insurance company and the adjuster would be arriving at any moment. But Knox had yet to call Detective Bauer. He wanted to hear what the fire marshal had to say first. If the fire was set intentionally, then Bauer needed to know.

My money is on that this was no accident.

If this was some crazy accident, Knox and Jenna would go back to working the case as if nothing had happened. If it wasn't an accident...

He needed to put this family under protection immediately. This might have been a warning, but it didn't mean that the next time would be. And there would be a next time. Someone wasn't going to go to the trouble of burning down a building and then giving up. Whomever had done this wanted Knox and the Waters family to be scared. They wanted them to back off.

Not going to do that.

Even now, Knox found himself striding back and forth around the grounds, his gaze darting from one corner to the other, looking for anyone or anything that seemed out of place. He had that prickle on the back of his neck, the sign that told him that something wasn't right and he needed to pay close attention.

Eventually, the fire marshal walked out of the burned-out structure and stood in front of the family.

"My preliminary findings are that the fire was set intentionally with an accelerant."

That would explain why the garage went up so quickly. They hadn't had a chance to stop it.

"Who would do something like this?" Michelle asked, her voice choked and broken. "Why would someone do this?"

Knox didn't say anything out loud but he and Jenna exchanged a quick glance. She was thinking the same thing that he was. They'd stirred up a hornet's nest by asking questions about Lori's disappearance.

"Has anyone at your work made any threats, Mr. Waters?" the fire marshal asked. "Have you let anyone go from the company recently that might harbor a grudge?"

Tom shook his head. "No, nothing like that."

Michelle tugged at her brother's arm. "What about Miles Clark? You let him go last week. He wasn't happy about it."

"He wasn't happy but he didn't threaten to burn our house down," Tom replied. "I doubt Miles did this."

The fire marshal was already making notes. "Miles Clark? We'll need to check him out. Just to be sure. Is there anyone else?"

Jenna glanced at Knox again, her brows raised.

"There might be," Knox said. "I'm here investigating Lori Waters' disappearance. I think we may have ruffled a few feathers."

The fire marshal appeared confused so Knox quickly explained the situation including the break-in at Lori's townhouse.

"So you have suspects for the break-in?" the fire marshal queried. "Then you think that they may also be suspects in this case? The police are going to want to talk to them after I turn all of my evidence over to them."

Would Detective Bauer finally take this case seriously? It really didn't matter one way or the other. Knox was already planning to have a serious conversation with his brother Cal. It was time for Knox's older brother to face the consequences of his actions. Even if he wasn't responsible for Lori's death - and Knox truly didn't think that he was - he had a great deal to answer for when it came to their relationship. Cal was a total douchebag but he wasn't a killer.

Knox stepped away from the group and beckoned Jenna to

follow him. They walked around to the far side of the wrap around porch.

"I'm going to call Logan and let him know what's going on," Knox said to Jenna. "We're going to need to get you all to a safe house as soon as possible."

At first, she didn't react but then her eyes widened in surprise. "Wait...you think...that they might hurt us? They burned the garage, Knox. They easily could have set fire to the house but they didn't."

"What if that was just a warning? Their opening salvo. We can't take those sorts of chances with your life. You, and your family by extension, need to be protected. Right now this house isn't safe."

Jenna's gaze ran over the house and then over the smoldering remains of the garage.

"Are you sure? Do you think they would come after us?"

"I think it's better to overreact and be safe. The good news is that we've clearly upset someone with our investigation. We just need to keep the pressure on."

The fire marshal climbed the porch stairs and waved to get their attention.

"Uh, there's something you might want to see," he said, shifting from foot to foot nervously. "My guys didn't see it until the sun came up and one of our trucks was moved."

"I'll follow you," Knox said. He was getting that feeling again, watching how uncomfortable the fire marshal looked. This wasn't going to be good.

The three of them walked down the long driveway almost to the street where Tom and Michelle were already standing. The fire marshal pointed to something written in spray paint at the end of the drive. Knox had to step around it to be able to read the scrawl. His blood ran cold when he saw the message their arsonist had left.

You're next.

18

It all happened so fast. One minute she'd been standing in the driveway taking in the threat scrawled in spray paint on the concrete, the next Knox had her packing a bag while he dealt with Detective Bauer who had shown up a few minutes later.

The cop was grouchier than normal, clearly not happy about the turn of events. Once again, he wouldn't even make eye contact with Jenna, talking only to Knox and the fire inspector. He took pictures of the driveway and asked about any security video that they might have. She was surprised he was actually doing his job - albeit not very happy about it. Unfortunately, Tom had never installed any security cameras or alarm. Their area wasn't dangerous and he hadn't thought it necessary. Her brother was now regretting that decision.

"We're going to drive to Tremont," Knox said, entering her room. His hair looked like he'd been scraping his fingers through it again - standing on end. "Are you almost ready to go?"

"What's in Tremont?"

It was on the opposite side of Douglas so they would still be able to work on the case.

Wait...we are still working the case, right?

"A safe house," he replied. "It's actually a home that belongs in the Anderson family which is my boss Jason. Apparently, it's all set up with security, plus Logan is sending the new guy at the office to help out."

If they were sending more help, then they were still investigating.

"Well, thank you to your boss then. They're okay with us staying there?"

"They're fine about it. They've been renting it out but it's currently between occupants. It's in a good location in town, not too remote. I think you'll be safe there."

"What about Michelle and Tom?"

She'd heard Tom and Knox going back and forth about leaving this house, and the safety of staying. Tom didn't want to let anyone scare him from his own home. He was digging in his heels and stubbornly saying that he wasn't going to leave.

Knox sighed and shrugged his shoulders. "I can't convince your brother to go. He already told me that nothing I say is going to change his mind. He did agree to have an alarm system installed along with some cameras. My firm is working on getting someone out here to do that, hopefully today."

"And Michelle?" Jenna asked. "Please tell me she's going with us."

Michelle, although frightened, hadn't liked the idea of leaving Tom all alone in their home. Jenna didn't like it either but Knox was going to drag her out of there if she tried to stay. Frankly, she thought her brother was crazy to want to stay here after the fire this morning.

"Tom agreed to send your sister to Miami for a business trip. I think she'll be safe there."

Jenna sunk down onto the mattress, sighing in relief. She'd been afraid that Michelle was going to be as stubborn as Tom.

"Thank goodness. Now I only have to worry about my brother being burned alive."

"You won't have to worry about that either if we can get the security system set up here."

Knox sat down next to her, reaching over to hold her hand. Their fingers laced together and she instantly felt better just knowing he was with her. He wasn't going to let anything bad happen if he could help it.

"Did Detective Bauer leave?" she asked, cushioning her head on his shoulder while he wrapped an arm around her waist. It felt good to have someone to lean on when everything seemed out of control. "He was certainly in a mood, wasn't he?"

"I'm getting the distinct feeling that he hates his job. A whole lot. At this point, I wouldn't take it personally. I think he simply doesn't like police work."

"Then he should find another job."

"Probably, and he may be doing that for all we know. In the meantime, I'll deal with him plus the police from the local jurisdiction. He seems happy to let me do whatever the hell I want so I'm not going to complain too much."

"And after we set up house in Tremont? What happens then?"

"We talk to that Brett guy, plus I need to talk to my brother, of course. They're both going to need alibis for this morning."

"And for the break-in at Lori's home."

"That too. Basically, I'm going to crawl so far up my brother's ass he's going to wish he was an only child. Hell, he probably already does. We've never seen eye to eye on anything."

"When was the last time you saw him?"

"That day at the prison for my dad. We barely spoke because he pisses me off by simply existing. I swear every time he opens his mouth he says something that grinds my gears."

"Because he's like your dad."

Jenna didn't make it sound like a question because she was pretty sure of the answer.

"He's far too like our father. Sadly, he doesn't see anything wrong with that."

"Do you think he'll tell you the truth?"

"Eventually, but he won't be happy about it. I can tell when he's lying, which is why he avoids me as much as I avoid him."

She ran her hand up Knox's arm, squeezing his shoulder. "You know...you know that I don't *want* it to be your brother? I don't. Not really. It's just...he's the one that I knew about."

Knox nodded, his expression grim. "I get it. He looks suspicious. If he wasn't my brother, and I didn't know him the way that I do, I'd believe that he was guilty too. I don't think that he had anything to do with Lori's disappearance. I've said that before. But I do think he might know more than he's letting on about that last day. That I would believe."

"I know you'll find out who did this. I know you'll find Lori."

She didn't say the last part of the sentence out loud. Dead or alive. At this point, Jenna was aware that the odds weren't in their favor.

Knox turned toward her so she could look up into his blue eyes that were dark with emotion. Her heart drummed against her ribs, so loud she was sure that they could hear her downstairs.

"I will. And I'll protect you. I promise you that."

Leaning closer, he brushed her lips with his own. She reached up and pulled him down to her, their kiss soft, sweet, and long. Despite all the chaos around them, she was falling for this man. She wasn't scared or nervous about it. It seemed right and natural.

Knox Owens just might be her future. It was certainly something to look forward to when all of this horror was finally over.

AFTER HUGGING her brother and sister goodbye, Jenna had climbed into Knox's SUV and they'd driven directly to Tremont. The ride had been uneventful and she'd found herself dozing off at one point, her head lolling against the window. She'd woken when the vehicle came to a stop.

"You needed the rest," Knox said, leaning over and dropping a kiss on her temple. "I'm glad you were able to sleep.'

Stretching in her seat, she yawned widely, her hand over her mouth. "I can't believe I actually slept. I thought it would be the last thing I would be able to do."

He smiled, pushing open the driver's door. "Maybe you felt so safe with me, you were able to relax."

That might be it. She hadn't been scared with him next to her. She didn't think a big truck was going to come out of nowhere and run them off of the road.

"But you didn't get to sleep, and you have to be just as tired. Now I feel bad because I should have helped drive."

"I'm fine. I'm used to living on little sleep. Not as little as my buddy Ryan, but almost. He's unreal. Sometimes I'm not sure he's even human."

He hopped out and pulled the bags from the back before unlocking the front door. The house was charming and obviously well-maintained. It was white with dark blue trim, with window boxes filled with multi-colored blooms. The whole property had a welcoming vibe that Jenna instantly liked. There was a warmth in this home that she desperately needed at the moment.

"I'll put the car in the garage after we unload," Knox said. "Apparently, they just returned it to being used as a garage. It was being used as an art studio for a long time."

An artist had lived in this house. That explained the riot of colors that greeted them when they walked inside the living room. Far from being unsettling, the color scheme actually made the interior more relaxing and warm with its mix of blues and golds, with a few splashes of red.

"This is lovely," Jenna said, peeking into the light blue kitchen with white cabinets and dark granite countertops. "Just beautiful."

"Think you could be happy here while we investigate?"

"I'm sure I can." She hesitated before asking the question that had been bugging her since this morning. Did she even really want the answer? "How long do you think we'll be here?"

His expression softened and he set the bags down and pulled her into his arms. He was warm and solid, and she could hear his heartbeat under her cheek. This...right here. This is what she'd needed all day.

"Hopefully, not long. Whomever is doing this is getting brash and arrogant. That's when people get caught. They're getting nervous and scared."

That made two of them.

"You've said that before. I hope that it's true. Michelle can't stay in Miami forever, and I'm worried about Tom all alone in that house."

"The alarm system and cameras are going in as we speak, plus he knows how to use a gun."

That was news to Jenna. She'd never seen her brother with a firearm.

"I didn't know that. Does he own a gun?"

"He does," Knox confirmed. "He showed it to me before we left and he says he knows how to use it. Why are you so surprised? This is Montana."

"My family had guns, but Tom and Anita never showed any interest."

"They probably had them but didn't say anything to you."

"You're probably right." She looked around the home they'd be living in. Together. If her life had to be in danger, there was no one she'd rather be with than Knox. "So what happens now?"

"We unpack and then head to Douglas. There's still time to talk to Lori's stalker friend Brett. Then later I'm going to talk to Cal."

"Just you?"

"Just me. By that time, Eli will be here and he can watch over you while I'm gone."

I never thought that as an adult I'd need to be watched over. How...strange.

"You don't want me there when you talk to your brother."

"It's not that I don't want you there. It's just that it will be better if I'm on my own. I know Cal well and I'm on to his tricks. He might try a few new ones, though, and I need to be on my toes and focused. Don't worry, I'll tell you every word when I get back."

"Do you think he'll lie?"

"Without a doubt. He lies all the time."

"But you know when he's lying?"

Knox leaned down, rubbing his nose against hers. "I'm talented like that."

"I believe it."

"You betcha. Now let's get unpacked and get on the road. We have a lot of work to do today."

No fire was going to stop this investigation. That would be giving them what they wanted.

Back to work. If Knox was right, they were getting closer to the truth.

They just had to stay alive long enough to find it.

19

Knox had only received a small amount of background information on Brett Hedgcock so far. Jared was still digging but he'd sent over that Brett was an only child, thirty-three years old, and worked in the accounting department at a local company. He bought a lot of takeout food and liked to read historical biographies. He'd never been married or engaged. He had no pets.

He had a mortgage on a modest home, a midsize sedan paid off, and very little other debt. He seemed like a regular guy who spent his weekends cutting the grass and watching television. But serial killers probably mowed the lawn too.

Pulling up in front of Brett Hedgcock's home, Knox paused before getting out of the vehicle.

"Okay, we're going to go in there and just be friendly. We're talking to all of Lori's friends and hoping that he might be able to shed light on the last few days before she disappeared. I'm hoping to keep the conversation light and casual, if possible."

"And if that doesn't work?"

"Then we'll go to Plan B."

"What's Plan B?"

"I don't know but I will by then."

As Logan always said, sometimes a man just had to depend on what his gut was telling him. Knox's brain sure as shit didn't have any ideas so his gut was up on deck.

The administrative assistant had called ahead, so Hedgcock must have been looking out the window waiting for them because the door opened as they were walking up the path. Brett was pretty much as he had been described by his former co-workers - medium weight, medium height, brown hair and eyes. Nothing about him stood out. He could have blended into any crowd without a doubt.

"You must be Knox Owens," Brett said pushing his front door open even farther. "And of course, I know you, Jenna. Lori talks about you constantly. I can't believe we've never met."

To her credit, Jenna didn't skip a beat. "I know. That's so weird. But it's nice to finally meet you, Brett. Thank you for talking to us."

"I'm happy to. Come on in. I just brewed a fresh pot of coffee."

Knox didn't usually drink coffee after ten in the morning but if it loosened Brett's tongue, he'd drink gallons of it. They entered into the home which had an open floor plan with a kitchen and living room combination. The steaming coffee pot sat on the rectangular island that "separated" the two rooms, along with three mugs and some cream and sugar.

"Let me pour you a cup," Brett said, a wide smile on his boyish face. "Now let me guess, Jenna. Lori takes hers with lots of cream and a little sugar. Do you do the same?"

"Uh no, I take mine with lots of sugar, just a little cream."

Brett quickly made up three mugs and invited them to relax on the sofa. He sat on a chair to Knox's right while Jenna sat to the left, also on the couch. Clearing his throat, Knox decided to jump right in and see how Brett would react.

"I'm investigating Lori's disappearance and we were hoping

you would be able to help us. I'm told that you and Lori worked together at Atwater Marketing, and that you moved on to a new job a few weeks after she went missing."

Knox had been hoping that the man might react to the second part of his statement - about getting a job right after Lori disappeared, but he was disappointed. Hedgcock focused on Knox's first sentence.

"I'd love to be able to help in any way that I can," Brett exclaimed, the smile falling from his face. "You do think she's okay, right? She said she'd be back soon."

"We don't know if she's okay," Knox replied, keeping his tone even and his gaze intent on Hedgcock. He wanted to watch for any nervous tics or other body language. "We're concerned for her safety and we're trying to find out what happened. Can you tell me a little bit about your relationship with Lori? Did you know her well?"

Color crept into Hedgcock's cheeks, and he squirmed in his chair.

"I know Lori very well. I mean, we're practically engaged."

Knox could feel Jenna stiffen next to him and he pressed his leg against hers, hoping she'd understand the message. She was dying to ask a question, but Knox needed her to back off just for a few minutes. He wanted Brett to run with this topic.

"Wow, engaged. That's fantastic. Congratulations. So all of this must be terrible for you, wondering and worrying when all you want to do is plan your wedding."

"It's awful. Some days it's all I can think of. But then I remember how much we love each other and how great our life is going to be and I figure that I can be a little bit patient while she works out whatever she needs to. We have our whole lives ahead of us, after all."

Knox was getting that feeling again...the one in his gut that was telling him that Brett might have a reality problem. In that, he wasn't participating in it.

"So you and Lori met at work?"

Brett smiled excitedly, placing his cup on the coffee table so he could clasp his hands together. "It was love at first sight for both of us. We just sort of knew that we'd found our person. It was really magical. Of course, we didn't let many people know since we worked together. They had rules about co-workers dating so we kept it quiet for awhile. That's why I was looking for another job. So we could be open about our relationship. Especially after we started talking about marriage and kids."

"Kids?" Jenna asked, her voice choked. "You were talking about kids?"

"We want three or four. We'll need a bigger house, of course, but this one will be okay for the first two."

Jenna's leg pressed hard against his. She desperately wanted to speak but, thank goodness, she was going to let Brett keep going.

Knox leaned forward so he could look directly into Hedgcock's eyes. "I don't want to make this awkward, but did you two break up at all during your time together? I ask because we know for a fact that she dated Cal for awhile."

Brett was already shaking his head before Knox even finished speaking.

"No, that was just Lori being nice. They were only friends. She was in love with me." Hedgcock jumped up from his chair. "Let me show you some pictures of us together. You'll see that we are in love."

Hedgcock ran down a hallway and then came back, two large picture frames in his arms.

"Sorry, but I had to get one of them down from the wall. I keep this one on the table next to my bed."

This one was a gold-framed photo of Brett and Lori sitting next to one another at a conference table. The same conference table that Knox and Jenna had sat across from Lori's co-workers at the marketing company. Lori was smiling but looking away from Brett. He, on the other hand, was looking directly at her.

Hedgcock had a point. They did look happy, but for completely different reasons. When he looked at this photo, he had to see something that Knox didn't. This was a photo of two co-workers, not two people in love.

The other photo in a dark frame was a picture of Brett and Lori standing outdoors, smiling and laughing on a sunny day. Lori was holding a flower and looking at Brett. Except that Lori's shadow didn't match Brett's. The picture had been doctored.

Well, that's creepy as hell.

Knox wasn't going to bring it up, however. Clearly, Hedgcock was quite delusional about his relationship with Lori. Yet, he was obviously functioning as an adult at some level, keeping a job, paying his bills, and appearing to lead a normal life. Unfortunately, it looked like his personal life was mostly fantasy. He'd stuck on Lori and couldn't seem to move forward. He needed professional help.

Knox cleared his throat again. "Did you ever meet Cal Owens? Talk to him?"

A look of distaste crossed Hedgcock's features. "He came to the office a few times. I can't say that I liked him much. He seemed rather arrogant if you ask me. Lori didn't like that about him. In fact, no one in the office liked him much."

"When was the last time you saw Lori or talked to her?"

Hedgcock rubbed his chin in thought. "I guess it was a few weeks ago. Right before she left on her trip."

A few weeks?

"Can you remember the exact time? It's really important."

Jenna had reached out, her fingers curling around Knox's forearm. She was biting her lip, her face pale of color. Knox now regretted even bringing her here with him. This had to be fucking upsetting to hear. But if he'd tried to leave her at home, he knew he would have had an argument on his hands. Fuck, this was shit.

"She was here on my birthday," Hedgcock said. "June third. That's for sure. We rented a cabin by a lake for the weekend. She made steaks and baked potatoes for my birthday dinner. She got me a tie, too. Do you want to see it?"

"That's okay," Knox said. "So she was here at the beginning of June. Did you see her after your birthday?"

"Of course, she's my girlfriend. It was two weeks later that she left. She told me she had some work to do, and she'd be back."

"Do you have any emails or text messages from Lori?"

The other man shook his head. "She doesn't like phones. She liked talking face to face."

They weren't going to get anywhere here. Brett Hedgcock's world only resembled the real one. What they needed was probable cause for a search warrant. Knox would love to see what the man had hidden around his home and yard.

"I think that's all I have," Knox said, turning his attention to Jenna. "Do you have anything?"

She shook her head, looking almost nauseous. "No. Nothing."

They'd need to have a long talk when they left here. This meeting hadn't been good for her at all. He'd buy her a strong drink and let her lean on him for as long as she needed to.

They stood to exit but Jenna stopped when they were at the door, frowning at the coat tree near the entrance.

"Is that Lori's cardigan?"

Brett smiled and plucked it from the tree. "It is. It will be here for her when she gets back. I know that it's one of her favorites."

Jenna grabbed onto Knox's arm again, her nails digging into the flesh. "I bought that for her for Christmas a few years ago. Lavender is her favorite color."

The way Hedgcock was clutching the sweater there was no way he was going to hand it over peacefully. Jenna looked like she wanted to grab it from him, but she didn't, simply bidding goodbye and hurrying out of the door. Knox thanked Hedgcock again and said that they'd be in touch if they had any more questions. When he walked outside, she was already in the vehicle waiting for him.

"I think I might be sick," she said when he pulled out into traffic. "Like really, really sick. That was...shit, I don't even know how to describe that. Was it even real? Did I imagine all of that? Because it was fucking weird. It was weird, right?"

"That was very weird," he replied, his tone grim. "Completely strange. I think we can safely say that Brett Hedgcock might need some professional help."

"He had a photo of them together," Jenna said, her voice going up. "But I've seen that picture of Lori before, Knox. Michelle took it one day when we were having a picnic and he wasn't there. He wasn't in that picture. It was me and Lori."

"It was doctored," Knox said, reaching across so he could hold her hand. Her fingers were icy and he lifted them to his lips to press a kiss on the knuckles. "He put himself in that photo. Shit, he probably stole it off her desk at work or something."

"They couldn't have talked about having kids," Jenna went on as if he hadn't spoken. "Lori couldn't have children. She had a hysterectomy about five years ago due to lots of medical issues. She was always in pain. She was okay with it, though, because she wasn't sure she even wanted kids."

Knox navigated into an empty parking lot and put the vehicle into park before turning to Jenna. Unclipping his seat belt, he scooted as close as the truck console would allow him to, smoothing her golden hair back from her pale face. She was shaking in his arms, her skin ashen.

"It doesn't matter what Hedgcock says. All of that wasn't

reality, honey. That was all his fantasies. We know that Lori and Cal dated. For real. You also say that Lori told you about all her boyfriends and she never mentioned Brett. Not even in passing or a casual remark. This is something that he's built up in his head. It's not real."

Tears spilled from her eyes, her lashes spiky and wet. "He has her sweater. It doesn't belong to him. What else does he have? Did he stalk her? Does he have some sort of shrine to her in his house that we didn't see? My God, does he–"

Jenna broke off as she began to sob but Knox had a decent idea what she was about to say.

Does he have her body buried somewhere?

Hedgcock was a strong suspect. From what Knox could see, the sweater could be a "trophy" that helped Hedgcock relive Lori's death over and over.

Or it could be part of an elaborate fantasy on his part but it wasn't violent or deadly. It might be completely creepy but also innocent.

Knox was determined to find out which. In the meantime, he needed to be there for Jenna. All of this was simply too much. She'd been strong for so long. He picked her up and lifted her onto his lap, running his hand down her back in a soothing motion while she cried, her body wracked with sobs.

"Just let it all out, baby. Just cry all you want. You'll feel better afterward."

He wasn't the greatest at comforting a person. It wasn't his strong suit. But there was something that he was good at...something that might make her feel better.

Find the son of a bitch responsible. He could do that.

And he would. For Jenna.

20

Ａfter arriving back at the safe house and meeting up with his teammate Eli, Knox excused himself and went out into the backyard to call Logan. The whole meeting with Hedgcock had been creepy as shit and Knox had some serious concerns.

"First and foremost, we need to somehow get a search warrant for his home and property," Knox said to Logan. "I have visions of Lori Waters being held against her will in a shed in the backyard, for fuck's sake. If I'm thinking it, then I bet Jenna is too. It's a grisly thought. Just as bad would be that he hid her body on the property, buried her under a flowerbed or something like that. This guy isn't dealing with any sort of reality at all."

"I'll talk to Jason," Logan assured him. "He can talk to his brother West and see if he knows the sheriff or chief of police in that town. If not, we can always do some covert operations of our own. We can at least make sure that there are no other heat signatures on the property."

If they couldn't get a warrant, it would have to do. It would at least confirm that Hedgcock wasn't holding Lori Waters at his home. But that's all it did.

"We'll dig into his background and see if he has any other properties," Logan said. "We'll also try and look into his family a little more. See if they've had any problems with his rejection of reality. We'll check the towns he's lived in, including where he went to school. See if they had an issue with disappearing girls or if he had any run-ins with the local police."

"I doubt this is his first fantasy about a female."

"It probably isn't but this could be the first time he's taken it to these extremes. Lori's disappearance could have sent him spiraling."

"I've got a bad feeling about him."

"Don't worry, we'll find out everything about him, including what laundry detergent he uses." There was a long pause before Logan continued. "We had an interesting phone call yesterday. I didn't mention it until now because so much was going on. A man saying he was your father called the office. He asked to leave a message."

Fuck. Knox had never thought his dad would call his workplace.

"What was the message?"

"He asked if you could call him back. He left a phone number, but I have a feeling that you already have it. Am I right?"

"You are," Knox confirmed. "He's left me several texts and voicemails. I've honestly been avoiding them. I'm sorry that he bothered you at the office."

"It's not a problem. He talked to Carrie and she took the message. I just wondered if everything was okay."

Was it okay? The answer was complicated.

"I don't have any desire to talk to him. He's told my siblings that he's changed."

"And you doubt that."

It wasn't phrased as a question.

"I can't even imagine him changing. Why would he?"

"He was in prison. That might change a man."

"If he wanted to change."

"That's true. I find that few people truly have it in them to make great changes. Small ones? Maybe. Big ones that require work and sacrifice? Rare as hen's teeth."

"I am sorry that he called the office," Knox apologized again. "He shouldn't have done that."

"Like I said, it's not an issue. I just wanted to make sure that you knew."

Knox couldn't seem to stop himself from asking the next question. It was stupid, but he respected Logan's opinion. The man had more family shit to deal with than anyone else Knox knew.

"Do you think I should talk to him?"

Logan chuckled, and Knox could almost see his boss shake his head. "I don't have an opinion here. It's not my dad and it wasn't my childhood."

"You've had family issues too."

"True. What I think you need to do is ask yourself if talking to your father is something that you want to do. Is it? Because you don't have to no matter what your brothers and sisters say. They can't make that decision for you. A lot of people will tell you that he's getting old and he might not be alive for much longer. That you need to make your peace with him before he passes. I'm not sure that I'm a big proponent of that type of thinking. Because you can never make peace with someone that wants chaos."

Chaos. That was an excellent word to describe what followed Ben Owens through his life. By his own doing, of course.

"Those are some wise words."

He'd made Logan laugh even harder. "Shit, I don't have any

wisdom. I'm just talking out of my ass most of the time. Just ask my wife, she'll tell you. Just...listen to me, Knox. Don't let anyone pressure you either way. This is your decision. Frankly, I trust your judgment. You'll do fine."

That was a huge statement. Logan Wright trusted Knox's judgment. Big, big stuff.

"I appreciate that."

"Let us know whatever you need. This case has become a priority since the fire this morning. You keep your girl safe."

Had it only been this morning? It seemed as if it was days ago. So much had happened in that short span of time.

One thing was for sure. No one was getting near Jenna.

JENNA HAD ALLOWED Knox to hold and comfort her while she cried and sobbed, haunted by what she'd experienced in Brett Hedgcock's house. She couldn't stop the horrifying images of Lori with Brett, possibly begging for her life or even worse, being held captive by him to live out one of his sick fantasies. Even now that she'd somewhat pulled herself together and they'd arrived back at the safe house, she couldn't shake the feeling that Hedgcock was responsible for Lori's disappearance.

Knox had been wonderful, even holding her hand while he drove back, and never letting her think that he wasn't there for her. She was sure that she wouldn't have been able to deal with any of this without him. Funny, how she'd come to depend on him so quickly. She'd always been a little standoffish about being comforted or showing too much emotion around others. She liked thinking that she could deal with whatever the world threw her on her own. Today that image had been crushed.

"Do you want me to make you a drink?" Knox asked, his hand on a kitchen cabinet handle. "I saw a few bottles up here when I was looking around earlier."

She wouldn't mind a shot of whiskey to steady her nerves but she didn't want Eli Hammond to think that she had a drinking problem. She'd only met the former lawman and new co-worker of Knox's about ten minutes ago. He seemed like a nice man, perhaps closer to forty than thirty. He had a calm way about him when he shook her hand warmly, introducing himself. He could easily see the traces of tears on her cheeks but he didn't say anything, simply offering to pour her a glass of iced tea which she gratefully accepted. Crying so much had certainly left her dehydrated.

"I'm good." She held up her glass of tea. "Maybe later."

Eli sidled closer to the back door. "I think I'm going to go outside and check around the perimeter. Let me know if you need anything."

The other man slipped out of the door leaving Knox and Jenna alone.

"I think he's trying to give us privacy," Jenna said. "He seems like a nice guy."

"He is," Knox confirmed with a nod. "I don't know him super well. He's new and helped Luke on a case before he came here. But he seems to know what he's doing and I have to say that so far, my bosses have made good hires for the most part. There's been a few that couldn't hack it but we figured that out damn quick. There's nowhere to hide in our job. If you don't know what the hell you're doing, it's going to show."

She looked up at the clock. "When are you going to talk to Cal?"

Even if Knox left right away, he wouldn't be back until late in the evening.

Grimacing, he followed her gaze. "I need to leave as soon as possible, but I don't like the idea of leaving you here when you're so upset."

"That's sweet but you need to do this. I'll be fine," she assured him, giving him her best smile. "I got upset, that's true, but I'm not going to fall apart. You need to talk to your brother. I'll be okay here with Eli."

She didn't have the luxury of continuing to be upset. They had an investigation to do. She could fall apart later when it was all over. In fact, she was going to set aside some time to do just that.

Knox went outside to talk to Eli and then came back to kiss her goodbye. He told them not to wait dinner on him but he'd try and be home for it if he could. Jenna stood at the window watching him drive away, wishing she could go with him. Not this time, though. She'd been lucky so far that he'd brought her into his work.

"I'm a poor substitute for Knox but would you like to play a board game or cards? Maybe watch some television? It might help pass the time and get your mind off of things," Eli said. "Or I can just keep quiet and sit in the corner."

The idea of Eli sitting in the living room like a garden gnome had her smiling. Which she was sure was what he was hoping for when he said it.

"I wouldn't mind a game of cards. What did you have in mind? Gin rummy? Poker?"

Eli's face lit up. "You play poker?"

"I'll take all your money and have you crying to your mama."

"Lady, I am in. Let's do this."

Two hours later, Jenna had a huge pile of pretzels and cookies in front of her while Eli's pile was rapidly dwindling. Because they'd wanted to stay friends, they'd decided to forgo betting actual cash money and used the snacks in the cupboards instead. Pretzels were a dollar and cookies were two dollars. While she was having a good time, she had a feeling that this man was perhaps letting her win. He didn't seem the type to bet recklessly but he had more than a few times.

"I think you're letting me win," she finally said, raking in another pot. He'd bet on a loser hand that he should have folded right away. "You don't have to do that. I'm not going to wither away and cry if I don't win. I promise. Maybe we should play blackjack. It's harder to throw that game."

Eli bit into one of his remaining cookies. "These aren't too bad. You can't go wrong with chocolate chip."

"I'm more of a snickerdoodle kind of gal but I do like chocolate chip. And oatmeal."

"Oatmeal is good. But not with raisins."

"I hate raisins too."

They'd pretty much exhausted the topic of cookies. Eli was trying to be kind to her, which she appreciated, but he didn't have to walk on eggshells. If he was going to help with the investigation, she didn't want him feeling like he couldn't speak freely.

"I'm okay now," Jenna said. "I was upset before but I'm good. I'm guessing that Knox filled you in on our visit to Brett Hedgcock. It was so incredibly strange. It messed with my head a bit."

"And your heart, I would imagine," Eli replied with a gentle smile. "Having your sister disappear one day and then wondering what happened all these months cannot have been easy for you or your family. You're obviously a strong person, Jenna."

"I'm trying to be." She paused not sure if she could put her feelings into words. "It was all just so surreal. He talked about Lori like...she's still alive. And I hope that she is, but..."

"But you're losing hope?"

"Yes, I'm losing hope."

It was hard to admit. She'd said it out loud before but always in the back of her mind was a pinprick of hope. Did she even still have it? To be honest, she'd been thinking about Lori as passed on for awhile now. She wanted to believe, be optimistic. But she also didn't want to be a fool, living in an unreality. It would only make things worse down the line.

"It's hard to lose our hope," Eli said, his expression changing. "Sometimes hope is all that keeps us going, getting us out of bed every day. Even when all we want to do is pull the covers over our heads and go back to sleep. Because when we're asleep we can pretend that all of it isn't happening."

"You sound like you know this from experience."

Leaning his elbows on the table, he bit into another cookie. "My wife Debra passed away several years ago. Cancer. Some days hope was all I had to keep me going."

Shit, she shouldn't have asked. That was...personal.

"I'm so sorry. I shouldn't have said anything. I'm so sorry," she repeated, her cheeks growing warm.

He shook his head. "You didn't ask. I told you. It's not a huge secret or anything. I don't talk about it much, but I'm at a point where I can. This job, actually, is supposed to be my new start in life. New job, new surroundings. But I'll never forget Debra, and you won't forget Lori either. She'll always be alive inside of you."

He touched his chest right over his heart. Jenna's throat tightened painfully as new tears burned the back of her eyes.

"I don't want to forget her but sometimes...sometimes I get busy and life happens and then I realize I haven't thought about her in a whole day or even two days. Then I feel like shit because she's my sister and I love her. How can I possibly forget about her? I must be a terrible person."

Eli reached across the table and patted her hand. "You're not even remotely a bad person. It's okay to not think about Lori every second of every day. I don't know anything about your sister, but I'm going to go out on a limb and tell you that she wouldn't want you to put your life on hold for her. I know that's what Debra would have said. In fact, she told me that if I just laid around the house mourning for her she'd be really disappointed in me. She said that I had to live my life or it would all be a waste. She was wise like that. She always knew things that I didn't know."

"She sounds like a smart woman."

He chuckled and shrugged his shoulders. "Now that might be debatable considering she ended up marrying me, but I always thought she was a smart one. Pretty too. Maybe she just took pity on me. I had to ask her twice to marry me before she said yes. The first time she said that we should think about it because we were so young."

"How old were you?"

"Nineteen. She was eighteen. I was going into the military and I didn't want to leave her behind. She eventually said yes but I had to do some begging. Don't regret it, though. It was worth it. There's nothing better than marriage when it's to the right person."

"And if it's the wrong one?"

"I would imagine there's nothing more hellish," Eli replied, popping a pretzel into his mouth. "Now how about you and I start thinking about dinner? Knox is going to be hungry when he gets home."

That was an excellent suggestion. She needed to keep moving forward. Sitting around was only allowing her to wallow in all the crap that had happened to her family. Despite everything that had happened today, the most important thing hadn't changed.

Finding the truth about Lori.

21

"What the hell was that for?"

Callum Owens was lying on his ass and rubbing his sore jaw where Knox had punched him.

The entire drive here Knox's anger and frustration with his brother had grown. Cal had been treating everyone around him like shit since he was a kid and Knox was tired of it. Exhausted, actually, of dealing with the bullshit. Their parents hadn't done a damn thing to rein in Cal, and while Knox and his siblings had made an effort over the years, it was simply easier not to be around him at all. More peaceful, too.

By the time Cal opened his front door, Knox had built up quite a head of steam. He might not have done anything to Lori to cause her to go missing, but he'd treated her - and all his other girlfriends - like shit. If Lori was anything at all like Jenna, she hadn't deserved that.

So Knox had punched him. It wasn't the first time, and it wouldn't be the last, either. That he was sure of. Cal had punched Knox as well many times over the years. Since Cal didn't like to *talk things over*, they'd usually end up arguing the old-fashioned way - with their fists. When they were younger, they'd been more evenly matched, but as time had marched on Cal had let himself go a bit and now Knox could cream him if he wanted to.

"Because you deserved it," Knox stated, stepping farther inside Cal's home and slamming the door behind him. "In fact, someone should punch you in the face every fucking day until you straighten the hell up."

"It's nice to see you too, little brother," Cal mocked, a wide grin appearing on his face as he hopped up from the floor. Knox should have hit him harder. "So glad you could stop by."

"This isn't a visit for tea and cookies," Knox snarled. "We need to talk."

"So talk. I'm listening."

Knowing Cal, though, he wasn't. He didn't listen to anyone because he didn't think anyone had anything interesting to say other than himself.

"I'm here to talk about Lori Waters."

Cal shrugged, leaning a hip against the back of a chair. "And? Randy told me all about your little investigation. I'm not sure why you need to talk to me about it."

"You were the last person to see Lori Waters alive."

Cal shook his head. "No, I wasn't. I think you're mistaken."

"I'm not making any mistakes. I know that you met Lori at the coffee shop that day. *That day.* Not another day. One of the baristas remembered the exact date, douchebag, so stop lying your ass off and tell me the goddamn truth. You saw Lori at the coffee shop and whined and moaned trying to get her back. Luckily, she'd finally seen through your act and saw you for the piece of shit that you actually are and dumped your pathetic ass for good."

It was just a ghost of a change, almost a whisper, but Cal's expression fell for a single second. No one else would have noticed it, but Knox had spent most of his formative years learning to read his self-absorbed older brother. Then it was gone and that arrogant smirk was back on Cal's face.

"You think you know everything. If you're so smart, why do you need to talk to me anyway? According to you, I'll just lie about it. Isn't that what you said to Randy? You called me a big liar."

The usual defense from Cal was to complain that he was a victim.

"Because you are a liar. You lie about everything." Knox stepped forward, bearing down on his big brother so they were almost nose to nose. "But today you're finally going to stop being a pathetic waste and tell the truth, even if it's only for a few minutes. And do you know why? Because we're talking about a human fucking life here, Cal. This isn't about making yourself look successful for a woman or telling Mom and Dad that you're the best son. This is about an actual human being who might be dead. So I'm not going to cut you any slack today. Start fucking talking. Tell me about that day and don't try to lie to me because I know when you're lying."

There was a fine sheen of sweat on Cal's upper lip but no other outward sign that he might be concerned or nervous. He'd been hiding his true self for so long Knox wasn't sure if his brother was even aware of the truth anymore. In a way, he and Brett Hedgcock had much in common. Neither of them was fond of reality.

Cal stepped back, a ruddy tone in his cheeks. "So what if I saw her that day? It doesn't mean I killed her or anything. I saw her. We talked. That's it. End of story."

"That's not the end of the story. You walked with her out of the coffee shop. You two were arguing."

"It doesn't mean I killed her. Jesus, I'm not a murderer, for fuck's sake. I walked her to her car and she drove away. I never saw her again, but she was very much alive that day."

"Then why did you lie?" Knox asked, his tone aggressive. He

didn't have the patience for his brother's shit. "Why didn't you just say that?"

"Because I didn't want the hassle," Cal yelled, his expression a twisted grimace. "I didn't want to deal with all the shit that was coming from it. I knew that Lori was alive when I left her so why should I have to deal with it? It wasn't my problem. None of this is my problem."

"Did you even care about Lori at all? Did you? Because if one of my ex-girlfriends disappeared off the face of the earth, I'd do anything I could to help the police find her. All you had to do was tell the truth."

"You're such a Boy Scout," Cal jeered, his lip curled in a sneer. "You just love to lord over us regular mortals how perfect you fucking are. Whatever, brother. I stayed out of it because it wasn't mine to deal with. I didn't hurt Lori."

"Not physically. But you did hurt her. Just like you hurt all your other girlfriends. You were a total asshole to her. She paid for everything and don't fucking deny it because I saw her financials. Christ, you aren't even man enough to pick up a fucking dinner check. All you did was use that poor woman. You're just like Dad."

Cal was instantly in Knox's face, his finger stabbing into his younger brother's chest. "Fuck you. Just fuck you. She wanted to pay for those things. She wanted to buy me things and take me on trips. It made her happy. So I let her."

"Bullshit," Knox said between gritted teeth, knocking his brother's hand away. "You did it for yourself. Just like you do everything. You're a piece of shit and everyone knows it. You're pathetic. Here you are standing in front me lying about a woman that's probably dead. Do you have any feelings at all?"

Cal shrugged and walked over to the window, staring out at the road.

"I'll take that as a no," Knox said. "You don't feel anything, do you?"

"Why?" Cal shot back. "Why should I? So I can be like you? You feel every goddamn thing and it clearly hasn't made you happy. I didn't hurt Lori, so back off. Why would I kill her? It doesn't make any sense."

"Because if you couldn't have her, then no one could."

"I didn't care one way or the other."

"Really? Like the time that Stacey Bailey broke up with you in high school and you told everyone that she gave you an STD so no one would date her? Is that how you didn't care?"

Cal shrugged again and shook his head. "I have no memory of that happening. If there was a rumor then it wasn't started by me."

"You really are a piece of work. How do you sleep at night?"

"I sleep just fine, thanks for asking. Is there anything else you need to talk about? Because I'm rapidly losing interest in this conversation."

"I'm surprised. It's about you and I know that you love that."

"Fuck you."

"As a matter of fact, I do have a few more questions. Where were you yesterday afternoon between one and three, and also four and five this morning?"

"Work and home. You can check with my boss and my new girlfriend. Now, are we done here?"

Knox wasn't going to get anything more out of Cal. He probably should have been nicer or more patient. Cal might have opened up more, but he simply didn't have that much self-control. He wasn't a saint and his older brother sure as hell wasn't one either. They'd just as soon kick each other's ass than talk and hang out.

"I doubt you did have anything to do with Lori's disappearance. You couldn't work up the energy or the initiative. But if you did," Knox said, moving closer to his brother and giving him the most menacing look he could manage, "I will make sure you spend the rest of your life behind bars. Do you understand me?"

"You're not an Owens," Cal snorted. "You're a traitor to the family. I know it. Randy knows it. And Dad knows it, too."

"Good. I'd rather be a traitor than the pathetic asshole that you are. If I need anything else, I'll be in touch."

"I'm so looking forward to that," Cal laughed as Knox stomped out the door. "Have a nice day, little brother. It's always so nice to see you."

That was a complete waste of time. But then I knew it would be.

It hadn't been a pleasant visit, but Knox had walked away with more information than he'd started with.

He didn't think that Cal was responsible for Lori's disappearance. His older brother was a jerk of the highest order, but he wasn't a killer. At least not this time. Hedgcock, on the other hand, was looking like the number one suspect.

They needed a warrant for the house and grounds. Was Lori there? Dead or alive, he was going to find her.

THERE WAS something about good food and friends that made even an especially ugly day much more tolerable. It turned out Eli loved to cook so both he and Jenna worked side by side in the kitchen preparing dinner. Since it had been a trying day Eli had suggested comfort food, telling her that his mother's meatloaf recipe was life-changing. She'd enthusiastically agreed and they'd chatted while he prepared the entree and she peeled the potatoes that would hopefully become a creamy, garlicy side dish.

They'd planned to eat late in the hopes of Knox being able to join them and they'd timed it almost perfectly. The delicious-smelling meatloaf was just being taken out of the oven when he turned in to the driveway.

They all sat down for dinner, although Jenna was dying to hear what Knox had to say about questioning Cal. While she felt that Hedgcock was the number one suspect, Cal still had been the last one to see Lori alive as far as anyone knew. He might have information that could help if he stopped lying about seeing her that day.

"So I punched him."

They were halfway through their meal when Knox made the announcement. Eli was trying to hide his laughter, and Jenna wanted to hear more.

But she was kind of glad that Knox had punched his brother. Violence was never the answer but Cal Owens didn't sound like a good person at all. Not from Lori, and certainly not from his own sibling.

"Before or after you talked to him?" she asked.

"Before. He opened the door and I was really pissed...so I just punched him. It was a sucker punch and I don't feel all that good about that. I should have given him a warning before I did it. Don't get me wrong. I'm glad I did it, and I'd do it again, but I should have told him I was going to do it. That would have been fair."

Eli's brow quirked. "Would he have been fair to you?"

"No," Knox admitted. "He fights dirty. Always has. But I'd like to think that I'm better than him. I'm probably not, but I like to think that way."

"I think that you're probably head and shoulders above your brother," she replied.

"You might be biased," he said with a playful wink.

"Not that biased."

"What happened after you punched him?" Eli asked, getting the conversation back on track. "Did he hit you back?"

"No, but only because he knew I'd pound him into the ground. He's really let himself go these last few years. There was a time in our lives when we were evenly matched."

She adored Knox, but he was taking too long to get to the meat of the story.

"So what did he say? Did he admit that he saw Lori that day?"

"He did. He also said that he walked her to her car and she drove away. That's the last he saw of her. He also says that he has an alibi for yesterday and early this morning. I haven't had a chance to check those out yet but I will."

Jenna exchanged a glance with Eli. "And do you believe him?"

Knox took his time answering, wiping his mouth with a napkin and taking a drink from his glass. "I do. And not because he's my brother. Because I think he was telling the truth. I don't think he had anything to do with Lori's disappearance. He was nervous but not because of that. He wasn't sure what I was going to do and that kept him off balance."

Eli sat back in his chair, patting his stomach. "You're thinking that Hedgcock is our best bet?"

"Let's just say that he definitely has my attention. Logan and Jason are trying to get law enforcement to issue a warrant for the house and grounds. In the meantime, we're going to make sure that there aren't any additional heat signatures on the property that can't be accounted for."

Jenna's heart lurched in her chest and her fingers wrapped around her napkin until the knuckles turned white. "You think Lori could be alive? A prisoner?"

It had crossed her mind briefly but Knox hadn't mentioned it, so she'd put it out of her head. She didn't want to think about it. It was far too horrifying.

Knox reached out and placed his hand over hers. "I think it's a small possibility but we need to make sure."

Jenna wasn't sure she could finish her dinner now. The thought of her sister being held all these months was too awful to comprehend.

But she'd be alive.

When Jenna had held out hope that her sister was alive, she hadn't really thought through the details. She'd sort of assumed that Lori would have actually gone off somewhere, although that would have a remote chance of happening.

"That would explain the text I received while we were cooking dinner," Eli said with a short laugh. "A few of Jason's old buddies from the DEA are going to meet me a few blocks from Hedgcock's house tonight. We'll check the property out and report back."

"Wouldn't that be illegal?" Jenna asked.

"Are you planning to tell on me?" Eli said, a wicked smile on his face. "With the tools that the DEA have we won't even have to go onto his property. No laws will be broken tonight. I promise."

"It's all a little much to take in," Jenna said. "Of course, I want Lori to be alive..."

Knox squeezed her hand, their fingers tangling together. "Don't let your imagination run away with you. We don't know anything for sure."

Already images were crowding her brain and none of them were good. She'd always had a vivid imagination and she'd thought it was a good thing. Maybe not so much this time.

"I just wish this were all over."

She couldn't stop the words from tumbling out of her mouth, but it was the bare truth. When she'd pictured having a real investigation done, she hadn't thought about what it would mean. Knox had said he would find the truth, no matter what it was. He was fulfilling that promise. Yet, she wasn't sure she was ready for it. He had warned her.

"We're getting closer," Knox replied. "I can feel it. People are getting shaken up, secrets are going to be revealed. I think we're on to something."

"I hope so."

"If this is too much for you, I completely understand. We can put you on a plane back to Seattle while Eli and I continue on here. This is a hell of a lot to put yourself through, Jenna, and you don't have to. No one will think less of you if you want to go home."

Home. A funny word. Seattle wasn't home. She had a temporary rental there. She didn't really have much of a home. Her job didn't lend itself to putting down roots in one place for very long. Her time with Knox was the most "at home" she'd felt in a long time, even when they were staying in a house belonging to his boss.

She didn't need to think about the offer very long. She'd long ago made her decision. She would see this through. Her temporary discomfort didn't outweigh her need to find out the truth about Lori. It just hurt, but she could endure it.

"I'm going to stay. It's disturbing, but I need to do this. I'll be okay, I promise. I won't faint on you or anything like that."

Knox didn't get a chance to reply. Jenna's phone started buzzing with an incoming text. She'd left her phone on the kitchen counter so she quickly excused herself to check it. She'd sent an earlier message to Michelle to see how she was doing and she was hoping for a reply. Her sister was in meetings all day, but it was evening now and she should be done with work.

Thumbing to her messages, she scanned the text and the sender. Her knees almost gave way underneath her and she had to grab onto the granite counter to keep from falling into a heap on the floor. Her dinner was threatening to make a second appearance as her stomach tumbled in her abdomen.

Knox shot up from the table and wrapped his arm around her waist to steady her.

"Honey, are you alright? You're white as a sheet. Are you sick?"

Her entire body was shaking as she handed him her telephone, showing him what had brought about this reaction. He frowned, looking down at the phone, at her, then back at the phone again. The message was straight and to the point.

Stop digging or you'll regret it. I can see what you're doing and I know where you are. You can't hide from me. You have protection but eventually it won't be enough. Back off.

And the sender of the text?

It was from Lori's missing cell phone.

22

K nox didn't have the opportunity to feel triumphant. Jenna was intensely shaken by the text from Lori's phone, clearly upset by the blatant threat. He needed to be there for her even though he didn't think he was a particularly comforting human being. But he'd do his best.

Inside, however, he was doing fist pumps in the air. They were making waves with the investigation and someone was scared and panicking. As he'd told Jenna a few times, this was good news. Panic made people make mistakes. It also meant that they were getting closer, otherwise their quarry wouldn't be troubled in the least.

He'd sent the message off to Logan, who was going to get Jared to try and triangulate the location of Lori's cell phone, if at all possible. Wherever Lori's phone was, surely the responsible party was also.

Eli had offered to stay behind but Knox had assured him that he needed to go check out Hedgcock's house. That needed to be done sooner rather than later. Knox didn't think that anyone would try anything at the safe house but they had plenty of security, just in case.

"When we're done there, I can do the night shift if you like," Eli offered. "I slept on the plane on the way out here, and I don't need much sleep anyway."

"You sound like Ryan. He's practically a robot. He lives on caffeine and chocolate donuts."

"Sounds like my kind of guy. Seriously, you stay with Jenna. I'll keep watch over things."

"I should argue but I'm not going to. But if you need me, let me know."

"Hopefully, it will be a boring night."

That was Knox's hope as well. After Eli left to meet the former DEA guys, Knox went to find Jenna and see how she was doing. She'd gone to lie down after dinner, but he didn't want to leave her alone too long. He had a feeling her mind was making up ever-worsening stories in her head and she needed to stop torturing herself.

She wasn't lying down, however. There was a strip of light underneath the bathroom door and he tentatively knocked, only wanting to be sure that she was okay.

"Honey, do you need anything?"

"No, I'm good. I decided to take a soak in the bathtub."

Knox wasn't a saint. He was only a flesh and blood man. And currently that blood was rushing into places south of his belly button. He shouldn't even be having these thoughts. Jenna was in a vulnerable place and here he was thinking with his dick about how she might look in the bathtub.

I'm a bad man.

"Oh, okay. I'll–"

"You can come in. It's okay."

No, it wasn't. This wasn't fine at all. He was a horn dog. No, he was King of the Horn Dogs. He should be ashamed of himself. He really should.

He opened the door anyway.

His hand wasn't taking orders from his addled brain right now.

Jenna was in the bathtub covered in a sea of bubbles. Christ on a pogo stick, it was sexy as fuck. The foam was playing a particularly sadistic game of peek-a-boo with her legs, arms, and upper torso sticking out but covering all the delicious parts. A stubborn cluster of bubbles stuck to her pink cheek.

"Uh..."

Knox couldn't remember the last time he'd been this tongue-tied around a woman. Maybe when he was a teenager? His normally smooth demeanor was gone, and he was acting like he'd never seen the female form when he most certainly had. More times than he could count, although for the life of him he couldn't even begin to conjure up the face of even one of those other women at the moment. They'd all faded away until there was only Jenna.

"You can come in and sit down. I'm guessing you want to talk. I'm really okay. I'm not going to cry or anything, I promise."

He didn't even make a conscious decision. His legs just walked into the bathroom all on their own. Settling on the edge of the tub, he trained his gaze on a spot just to the left of her head. Not down where the bubbles were beginning to dissolve in the heat.

"I was just worried about you. I don't think that Lori is at Hedgcock's home, but we have to check every box. I'd be remiss in my job if I didn't make sure."

"I know. It's just the reality of this is hitting home. I let it get to me."

"You shouldn't beat yourself up about it. It would get to anyone. You're only human."

Her fingers played with a mound of bubbles. "I know. I guess I thought that this investigation would make me happy somehow. Michelle, Tom, and I have been living in this sort of limbo-like state where nothing seemed real. Now everything is almost...too real. I don't know if I'm explaining it right."

"You are. I see it a lot in my line of work. You think that finding the truth and getting to a conclusion will solve all your problems. It does solve some, but then it creates other issues that you'll have to deal with."

He didn't say out loud that she'd need to mourn her sister. He had a feeling that she and her family had been delaying, holding on to hope that Lori was alive. He had hope too, but not much. Sadly, the odds were stacked against them.

She moved around in the bathtub, bubbles and water sloshing the sides. "Give me a minute and I'll get out and get dressed. I think I could use that drink right about now. Care to join me?"

"I'll pour two shots."

He left the steamy bathroom and went into the kitchen, retrieving the whiskey bottle from the top shelf. By the time he'd poured their drinks, Jenna had joined him. Her hair was still piled on top of her head in a messy bun, and she'd put on a pair of baggy pajama pants and an oversized t-shirt.

She was absolutely the most gorgeous woman he'd ever seen in his entire life. It wasn't even close. She was a knockout. Naturally beautiful and sexy, and she almost brought him to his knees just standing there. She had no idea, either.

He was falling and for the first time in his life, he welcomed it. He was ready. If she was the one, then bring it on.

He handed her one of the glasses filled with the amber liquid. "Maybe this will help."

"At this point, it can't hurt." She lifted the glass as if in toast. "Should we drink to something? I'm not sure what, though."

Lifting his own glass, he said, "I had a friend in basic that always used this one. May you be in heaven half an hour before the devil knows you're dead."

"I'll drink to that."

They both knocked back their shots and then placed the glasses on the countertop. Jenna sighed, her shoulders slumped.

"That didn't make me feel any better. But my guts are on fire."

"Give it time. Whiskey doesn't work in seconds."

Knox's phone beeped and he pulled it from his pocket, reading the text message.

"It's Eli. There's no sign of any additional heat signatures anywhere on Hedgcock's property."

Jenna didn't respond at once, but then her eyes closed and she leaned her elbow on the countertop. He immediately moved forward, wrapping his arms around her in case her legs gave way. She was shaking and a few silvery tears had made their way down her cheeks.

"I'm relieved and sad at the same time."

He didn't say anything, simply held her more tightly, running his hand up and down her back in what he hoped was a soothing way. He wanted so desperately to take away the pain she was feeling inside. If only he could lift it from her slim shoulders, he'd gladly bear it. She was too good of a person for this. But hadn't he seen horrible things done to decent people in his career? So often he'd met a person on the worst day of their lives. They were victims but he knew if he said that word to Jenna, she'd deny it vehemently. She didn't think of herself that way and she wouldn't want him to think that, either.

Leaning her cheek against his chest, she snuggled closer, close enough that he could smell the scent of the bubbles she'd used in the bath. Lavender, maybe? He wasn't an expert.

"So what happens now? What do we do?"

"We get a good night's sleep," Knox replied. "One of my co-workers is digging deeply into Hedgcock's background. We should know more before morning. They're also working on getting a warrant for the property."

He didn't say out loud that a warrant was a long shot. They didn't have much evidence. But he'd seen warrants issued for far less many times. It simply depended on the judge. Would this go in their favor?

"And the texts?"

"Jared will try and get the phone's location. It was a mistake for them to use it. They must be getting desperate."

Straightening, she blew out a breath. Jenna was wearing a frown. No, scratch that. She was wearing a frown directed *at him.*

"Can I say that I'm getting a little tired of you constantly saying how scared and desperate they are and how they're making all of these mistakes? So far, I haven't seen it. When do we get that big break in the case from one of those supposed mistakes?"

It was good that she was still feisty, still pushing forward.

"It's not like on television, babe. It often happens slowly. It's like we're untangling a knot and we pull a string here, and another there, and we keep pulling strings and unwrapping them until finally we find one that loosens it all. Then we follow it."

"Are you saying Brett Hedgcock is a loose string?"

"For want of a better analogy? Yes."

She held up her glass. "I think I'm going to need another drink."

"You've got it."

He poured each of them another shot, but not a full one. Although she might want to get drunk, he didn't think it was a good idea. Not for her, and definitely not for him, although two shots weren't enough for him to even get tipsy. He could hold his liquor.

"What about Eli? Is he coming back?"

Knox threw back the shot and slapped the glass down on the counter, enjoying the burn all the way to his belly.

"He says that he's wide awake so he's taking the night shift watching the house."

"I'm not sure what that means."

"It means he's in the garage, watching all the camera feeds from around the home. From there he can also see if there are any cars driving by, maybe slowing down to take a look."

"Should we take him a snack?"

"I will definitely take him drinks and food before we go to bed. He's not the only one out there, by the way. We have a few guys patrolling the neighborhood. No one is going to get close to you."

"I didn't mean for all of this to blow up so seriously. I didn't want to put anyone in danger."

"You didn't do this. The person that's responsible for Lori's disappearance did this. It's on them."

"I still don't want anyone to get hurt."

"We're not planning to get ourselves - or you - hurt. Trust us."

"I do trust you."

His chest squeezed tightly at her words, far more powerful than she knew. It meant far more than it should to hear that she trusted him.

She rinsed out their glasses and placed them next to the sink. "I'm going to be honest. I don't think I'm going to be able to sleep."

"We can watch television," he suggested. "I think I saw some board games and a few jigsaw puzzles in the entertainment center."

"I haven't done a jigsaw puzzle since I was a kid."

"It's been about that long for me too. Want to give it a go?"

"Why not? It's better than lying in bed staring at the ceiling."

He had one mission tonight. Distract Jenna.

Tomorrow they'd dig deeper into Brett Hedgcock.

23

Jenna tapped at Knox's knuckles. "You have to do the border first. You don't get to do the fun part until the hard work of separating the border is done. Don't you know the rules?"

Knox snickered and popped another fluffy piece of buttered popcorn in his mouth. They'd settled in at the coffee table to work on the puzzle. Knox had pulled the cushions from the couch down to the floor so they could be comfortable. They lounged next to one another their backs against the sofa, the table in front of them, and a giant bowl of popcorn in between their bodies.

"There are jigsaw puzzle rules? I didn't see any rules in the box."

"They're unwritten rules but everyone knows them. You do the border first. That's how it's done."

"Yes, ma'am. I didn't realize that putting together this hot air balloon could involve such a faux pas."

"You separate the border, put it together, and then you separate the pieces by color family. Then maybe by shape, if you want to."

Knox's brows were almost at his hairline. "For someone that hasn't done a puzzle in years, you certainly take this seriously. You're one of those list makers, aren't you?"

Guilty as charged. She liked her lists. And her planner. Her job was often hectic and it helped her keep everything straight.

"So what if I am? You might want to try it. It's very freeing."

"It's freeing to write up a list?"

"Yes, then you can sit back and relax by not having to worry about remembering things."

Knox grinned, his blue eyes twinkling mischievously. "I like to challenge myself by making grocery lists, leaving them on the counter, and then trying to remember what was on them while I'm at the store."

"Then make them on your phone. I know you always have it."

She'd reached over to tap his phone and he placed his hand over hers, rubbing his thumb against the palm.

Yikes.

He'd barely touched her and yet he'd sent a lightning bolt of energy down her spine, settling in her lower abdomen. Their gazes clashed and if she didn't know better, she would have thought the temperature in the room climbed about twenty degrees in ten seconds.

It couldn't do that. Could it?

His thumb continued to stroke her palm while his other hand reached up and caught a stray strand of her hair, tucking it behind her ear. His fingertips tickled her cheek softly, barely glancing the skin but leaving behind a trail of heat in their wake. A delicious tension had built between them, bouncing back and forth and raising the energy in the room. She was so aware of him she could feel his every breath.

She didn't remember making any conscious decision but she found herself moving the bowl of popcorn situated between them to the table, knocking puzzle pieces to the floor.

Pressing her body against his, she kissed his lips, tasting the butter and salt on his tongue. He must not have minded her sneak attack because instead of pulling away he laughed and tangled his fingers in her hair, gently tugging her even closer until they were lying on the cushions.

He lifted his head and dropped kisses on her nose and cheeks. "I like a woman who knows what she wants."

Jenna wasn't fooling anyone. She wanted Knox. He wanted her too. She could feel how hard he was against her hip.

"I hope I'm not alone here."

"Are you kidding? I've been grappling with myself to keep my hands off of you. I didn't want to take advantage of you when you were so upset. I don't want you to do anything that you'll regret later."

"You wouldn't be taking advantage of me, Knox. I'm a grown woman and I make my own decisions."

His smile grew wider and a frisson of awareness flew through her veins. Damn, this man was far too gorgeous for his own good.

"Am I one of your grown woman decisions?"

Denying it would be a lie.

"You are, but don't let it go to your head."

He threw back his head and laughed. "I like your style, Jenna. Take no prisoners. But maybe we should take this into the bedroom. We don't want to shock Eli should he need to use the bathroom."

Her eyes widened at the thought. "Didn't think of that. Yes, let's take this behind closed doors."

Giggling like two teenagers, they jogged into his room, falling down onto the bed and pushing the covers back after they'd locked the door. She slid her hands down his back, exploring the dips and planes she found there, and loving how hard and solid he was in contrast to her own softness. He nuzzled at her neck, finding that sensitive spot that had her eyes rolling back in her head and leaving her gasping for air. His fingers played delicately along her ribcage under her shirt, stroking the skin until she thought she might lose her mind. She needed to be closer, as close as she could get.

"Knox," she breathed as his lips ghosted over her collarbone. She could feel his chuckle against the sensitive flesh where her t-shirt had been pushed aside. "Knox."

"I love it when you say my name like that. Say it again."

Saying no to any of his requests had never crossed her mind.

"Knox," she said again, the word coming out breathless and needy.

Her fingers had curled into his thick hair, and she arched her back as he nipped at her skin then soothed it with his tongue. Her hands moved to his chest, fumbling with the buttons on his shirt. They were simply in the way.

He helped her impatient fingers when she would have ripped the offending material to get rid of it, tossing his shirt aside before going to work on the button fly of his jeans. In mere seconds he was gloriously naked. Knox was a beautiful man, his body almost carved from marble.

"You're wearing far too many clothes," Knox said, capturing her lips for another soul-searing kiss. "Let's see what we can do about that."

His hands skimmed up her sides and then down to the hem of her shirt, pulling it over her head with smooth expertise. He pressed his lips to every single newly exposed inch of flesh until she was a writhing mess, whispering his name under her breath. A bar of arousal building in her abdomen, and a liquid heat winding its way through her veins.

"You seem to know how to undress a lady."

She felt his smile against her skin. "I can do buttons all by myself. I can tie my shoes too."

"Then get to it."

"Yes, ma'am."

He took his ever-loving sweet time, making sure to kiss, caress, and worship her body as it was exposed to him. By the time she was naked, she was hot and needy, wanting him inside of her now. He dropped butterfly kisses on her belly, his fingers tickling her rib cage.

"You're making me crazy," she moaned as he pressed open-mouthed kisses on her hip bone. She closed her eyes and savored the simmering heat, letting it wash over her like the tide.

"Honey, that's the point."

He pushed her thighs apart and began to trace patterns on her inner thigh with his tongue, almost sending her into the stars. She didn't know whether to giggle from being ticklish or scream from the sheer pleasure. Before she was able to decide, he'd placed his mouth exactly where she needed it most, his devilishly talented tongue flicking around the pearl and sending her skyrocketing into the stars. Her thighs clamped onto his head and her nails dug into his shoulders.

By the time she came back to earth he was hovering above her, their foreheads pressed together. His weight on top of her was delicious, and she wrapped her arms around his to pull him closer. She could feel his hard length pressing into the softness of her belly.

"Are you ready for me?"

"I was ready ten minutes ago."

Chuckling, he kissed her again. "Do I need to–"

"I'm healthy and I'm on the pill. Are you okay?"

"I'm good, but I have a condom if you'd be more comfortable."

It didn't seem weird to have this intimate conversation with Knox. He was his usual caring and protective self even at a moment like this when he could have been selfish.

"I trust you."

Those weren't words she used easily. Or often, to be honest. She did trust this man, with her life.

He pressed forward, his lips and tongue playing with a pebbled nipple while he entered her slowly, giving her ample time to get used to his size or to even say stop. Not that she was planning to do anything of the kind. If anything, she wanted to urge him to go faster. And she would have too if he hadn't completely taken her breath away. She couldn't have formed sentences if her life depended on it.

Once he was into the hilt, he stayed there for a long moment, his eyes closed, as if he was savoring the sensation. He began to move, pulling out and then thrusting in, slowly and gently at first, but then building up speed. With each clever stroke, he rubbed that spot inside of her that sent her into the clouds. It was as if they were hovering in the sky, zipping from star to star, making circles around the moon. The world had come down to only the two of them and the pleasure they created together.

Running her hands down his spine, she wrapped her legs around his trim waist. "More, Knox. I need...more."

It wasn't the most articulate of pleas but Knox seemed to understand, stroking that spot inside of her faster while using those talented fingers on her clit. She was close to exploding, her body bowed and her toes curled. At any moment, the world might shatter and break into pieces. Their damp flesh slapped together lewdly and the air was filled with the smell of sex and their breathy moans. They'd found the perfect rhythm and they would ride it over the edge.

When her orgasm hit, heat poured through her body like rivers of fiery hot lava. Throwing her head back, she whispered Knox's name as he, too, fell over the edge. She had to force her eyes to stay open so she could watch him, his expression one of agony and ecstasy all at the same time.

Eventually they collapsed, their damp limbs tangled

together. Knox pulled the sheet over their rapidly cooling bodies as he tucked her into his side. Jenna wanted to say something, but she didn't have the words. How did she express what she was feeling when she barely understood it herself? It was so much more than anything she'd experienced before. Honestly, Knox was more than she'd ever expected. She'd grown weary and pessimistic these past few years regarding relationships, wondering if they were even worth the effort.

"Do you need anything, babe? Are you warm enough?"

She snuggled closer to him, his body heat keeping her cozy.

"I have everything I need."

Tomorrow they'd have to face the world, but tonight she'd pretend that they were the only two people left on earth. Just Knox, Jenna, and their love.

24

During the drive to Randy's house the next day, Knox changed his mind about a dozen times about even going there. He had to keep himself from turning around and heading back to Tremont and the safe house. He didn't fucking want to go to this stupid birthday party, but he did want to be there for his nephew's big day. Dylan was turning ten and the first double-digit birthday was always an event in a kid's life.

Randy had assured him that their dad was going to show up later in the day, which meant that Knox was going to be early to the damn party. Early to show up, and early to leave. It was a plan. But just because his dad wasn't going to be there didn't mean that Knox was anxious to deal with any of his other family members. By now, they all had to know that he'd questioned Cal about Lori's disappearance.

"We don't have to go. You can call them and tell them I got sick or something. You can blame it on me."

Bless his sweet Jenna. She was willing to be thrown under the bus so he didn't have to spend any time with his dysfunctional family.

"It wouldn't matter because they wouldn't believe me. I've avoided far too many family get-togethers for them to buy any story. The last few years I just stopped telling any story at all except that I didn't want to be there. That was the truth, after all. They didn't like it, but they couldn't argue except to tell me that we were family. For some bullshit reason that I'm still not clear on, a person is apparently supposed to put up with anything short of murder if it's from a human that you might share some DNA with. I'm perplexed about the whole thing but they seem quite sure about this rule. It's almost all they talk about. That and what a disappointment I am to the family."

Shit, he hadn't wanted to say that much. He sounded bitter and he really wasn't. He'd grown used to his relatives being crappy.

"I can't imagine how they could say that you're a disappointment. You're successful. And they do talk about that. What a great cop you are and all."

"They don't care about my job. They think being a cop is terrible. They only care about loyalty."

"They sound like the mafia."

Laughing, he couldn't disagree. "They would have made the Corleones proud. But enough about how I don't want to go. I'm guessing you don't want to go, either. This isn't going to be any fun for you. You probably should have stayed home with Eli."

"I couldn't let you do this alone." She stuck out her lower lip playfully. "What kind of girlfriend would I be to let you walk into this without anyone by your side?"

"A smart one. This isn't going to be pretty, babe. Don't say I didn't warn you."

"I've been warned and I ignored it of my own free will. Feel better now?"

"Not particularly. I won't be in a good mood until we're done and on our way back."

"You are the biggest pessimist. Maybe they'll ignore you and corner me. You know, question me to see if I'm good enough for you."

"They'll question you but not because they think you're not good enough."

She placed her hand on his thigh, giving it a squeeze. "Listen, if it starts getting bad just give me a signal and I'll do something loud and outrageous. Start dancing and stripping or something like that. Start whooping it up and calling everyone an asshole. I'll take all the focus off of you and put it in myself."

"Stripping?"

"I'd totally do it." She held out her hand, pinky finger extended. "Pinky swear."

"You don't need to swear, and you don't need to rescue me. I can handle my family. But it is nice that you'd want to help. Even strip. But my family doesn't deserve it. Just ignore them like I do."

"I've got your back. Just know that."

He didn't deserve this woman. But he sure as hell wasn't going to let her go. It felt like they were more than a couple. They were a team.

"And I've got yours. Always know that."

Knox parked on the street a few houses down from his brother's home. There were cars all along the street due to the party. He recognized a few as his sister's and also his older brother Roman's. Carrying the present he and Jenna had shopped for and wrapped this morning, he rang the doorbell.

"This is going to be a shitshow. Just let me know if you want to leave and we will."

The door swung open and Randy stood there, grinning ear to ear like he'd won the lottery. Dylan ran up behind him and squealed Knox's name in such a high pitch it almost made his ears ring.

"Is that for me?" the brand new ten-year old asked, jumping up and down. "Is it the Legos I wanted?"

Knox handed over the gift to his excited nephew. "You'll have to open it to find out."

"You won't open it now. You can wait until later," a stern voice said from somewhere behind Randy. It could only be Randy's wife Julia. "Put it on the table with the rest of the gifts."

"Aw, Mom," Dylan whined, but ran off to do as he was told.

Julia peeked around Randy's shoulder and then tugged him back. "Let them inside, for heaven's sake. They don't want to stand around on our front porch all afternoon."

Actually, Knox might prefer it but Julia wasn't going to allow it. He gave her a hug and then stepped back to introduce Jenna.

Julia's eyes were wide and her brows were almost up to her hairline. "It's certainly nice to meet you, Jenna. I don't think we've met any of Knox's girlfriends before. In fact, I'm sure I haven't."

Knox placed his hand on the small of Jenna's back. "Then she must be special."

Randy grinned and rubbed at his chin. "I guess she must be. Come on in. Get yourself a drink. There's pizza in the kitchen as well."

Like all of the Owens family get-togethers, it was a casual party. The food was first come, first serve in the kitchen and the guests mingled in the living room or out back if the weather was cooperating. Today was warm and sunny so there was a group of men in the backyard while the women congregated inside, pushing the kids outdoors so they wouldn't make a mess in the house. Randy's kids, especially, were high energy pretty much every single hour of the day and Knox didn't know how they did it. He was exhausted just watching them. Maybe he should go on a diet of peanut butter, chicken nuggets, and pizza.

"Your brother and his wife seem nice."

Knox was filling two red plastic cups with soda. "Randy is a good guy and Julia is great too. They're the normal ones. Don't get too comfy because I see my brother Roman heading right for us. He doesn't look happy."

Not that Roman ever did. He was perpetually angry about something. He seemed to always be grumpy about the state of the world in general and his life in particular.

"We need to talk," Roman said, getting into Knox's personal space. His older brother smelled like beer so this probably wasn't going to end well. "I heard about you accusing Cal of being a killer."

Sliding an arm in front of Jenna, he nudged her behind him.

"That's not what I did, but I'm sure Cal made the story sound a hell of a lot more dramatic than it actually was. I asked him about a woman he'd been dating and about the last time he saw her. Which he lied about to the police, by the way. Not that you give a shit about that, I'm sure."

"What do you care about some girl anyway? She probably ran off with a guy and is holed up in a motel room with some tequila. Get real."

He could feel Jenna stiffen against him, shocked at his brother's words. Knox stepped aside and placed his arm around her waist.

"Roman, I'd like you to meet Jenna Waters, the sister of that girl that maybe ran off with another guy and is holed up in a motel with some tequila. Jenna, this is my halfwit brother Roman who talks way too much for his own good."

To Knox's brother's credit, he flushed a deep shade of crimson. Roman opened his mouth to speak but only a few sounds of gibberish came out before he snapped it shut again.

Sighing, Jenna shook her head. "You did warn me."

"Told you so."

Randy elbowed Roman out of the way. "Christ, I can't leave you alone for a second. Ms. Waters, I'm so sorry about my big brother. He often talks without actually engaging his brain first. We're used to it but you're a guest. Please accept our apologies."

"It's fine. And please call me Jenna."

Roman finally found his voice.

"I'm really sorry. I didn't mean to make it sound like your sister...I mean...I'm sure your sister is...what I'm saying–"

"What are you saying?" Knox said, cutting off his brother. "Because you're not helping yourself here."

"Roman, your wife is looking for you," a deep voice said from outside the kitchen area. Knox recognized it immediately. Cal. He joined them in the kitchen and gave his brother a glare that had Roman turning on his heel and muttering under his breath as he walked away.

"Ms. Waters," Cal said, turning his attention to Jenna. "It's nice to see you again. Maybe it's time for you and I to talk. What do you think?"

Knox didn't know what Jenna was going to say but he thought it was shitty idea. Cal was going to try and charm his way out of this. Fuck that.

"I think that's a good idea," Jenna replied before Knox could tell his brother to go pound sand.

"Jenna, you don't have to–"

"I want to." She placed her hand on his arm and looked up at him. Her expression was serene and composed but there was a look in her eyes that he couldn't ignore. She wanted him to trust her. He did. He just didn't trust Cal. "We won't be long. If I need you, I'll call for you. I promise."

With a kitchen full of people staring at him he could only give in gracefully, nodding his grudging agreement. Leaning down, he pressed a quick kiss to her cheek and whispered in her ear.

"Don't take any of his shit."

She gave him a cheeky grin. "That's the plan."

"You can use my office," Randy said. "If you'd like to. Lots of privacy. No one will bother you there."

Randy led Jenna and Cal out of the kitchen leaving Knox, Roman, and Julia.

"I guess I'll go check on the kids," Julia said far too brightly. "If I leave, can you promise that you won't come to blows? This is a family party."

It wouldn't be the first time fists were thrown at an Owens family get-together, but Knox wasn't going to be the one to do it today. Unless someone else threw the first punch. Then all bets were off.

"We're okay," Roman said. "In fact, how about we go outside and get some fresh air? It might do us both some good."

"I could go for some fresh air," Knox agreed, following his brother through the garage and out to the back deck. There were some kids playing soccer in the yard and a group of men gathered around the picnic table. Almost magically, the crowd of about eight or so parted to reveal the one person that Knox didn't want to see.

Benjamin Owens.

And he was walking toward Knox.

Unless Knox was planning to run away, it looked like he and his dad were going to have that talk after all. Roman had known exactly what he was doing. So had Randy.

25

"I didn't have anything to do with Lori's disappearance. I liked your sister. She was a nice person."

Cal had opened the conversation pretty much as Jenna had expected. He'd smiled at her as if he had nothing in the world to hide. And that might be true. She didn't know for sure. But that's why Knox was working on this investigation. She needed to find out the truth.

"That's not what you told the Douglas police detective. You told him that Lori was kind of crazy and was capable of doing weird things."

She wasn't planning to make it easy for him. Knox had warned her that his brother had at most a *casual* relationship with the truth, and Lori had talked quite a bit about her troublesome boyfriend. Michelle hadn't anything good to say either.

Cal's throat bobbed and he squirmed in his seat. He'd tried to take the "power position" behind the desk but she'd been immediately on to him, and instead suggested that they sit on the small loveseat against the wall. From there she could watch his expressions and body language closely. She was a psychology major and had learned a thing or two about how a person reacts when telling a big fat lie. She'd be watching for those tells.

"I don't remember saying that," Cal finally replied after a long pause. "I think maybe the cop was taking what I said out of context."

"He said you used the word *crazy* to describe Lori. How could that be taken out of context?"

"I just don't know that I even used that word. Maybe that's his interpretation. He seemed kind of cynical if you know what I mean." Cal leaned forward, his gaze on Jenna's face. "You look so much like your sister. It's uncanny. She was always the most beautiful woman I'd ever seen. Absolutely gorgeous."

So if Jenna looked like Lori, then she was beautiful too? She had a feeling that Cal didn't get called on his shit very often. He probably sailed through life fairly smoothly, making people feel special. In the beginning, he'd made Lori feel special too.

"I was adopted into the family," Jenna replied, watching his expression. "There's no blood relation between Lori and I."

And absolutely no resemblance either. Jenna didn't look a bit like her sister.

Cal's face fell, just for the briefest of moments, but then he was smiling again. He'd realized Jenna wasn't going to be a pushover.

"I know you must be in so much pain, missing your sister. I cannot imagine what you've been going through–"

"You lied to the police about seeing Lori that last day. Why?"

Jenna simply didn't have the patience. When she looked at this man, she could see his resemblance to Knox but it was only superficial. She didn't get the same vibes from him - integrity, security, honesty. If anything, she felt a little dirty just sitting next to him on the couch.

"I'm sure you can understand my position. I knew that I wouldn't be any help in finding her–"

"How could you possibly know that?" Jenna broke in, irritated as hell. "It looks like you lied because you didn't care if anything had happened to her."

"Did Knox tell you that? Because that's not what I said."

Cal wasn't bothering to keep up the facade. He didn't look happy, handsome, or charming at the moment.

"I'm telling you how it looks from my perspective. It looks like you were protecting your own ass. Like maybe you had something to do with it and you didn't want anyone to find out."

"I didn't have anything to do with Lori disappearing," Cal protested, hopping to his feet. His red cheeks indicated his displeasure with her words. "I cared about Lori. I would never have hurt her. She disappeared, but it wasn't me."

"Then who was it?" Jenna asked, keeping her tone even. She didn't want to get too emotional. Cal would surely point that out. "Did you ever see anyone bothering her? Did she complain about a friend or co-worker? That last day did you see anyone on the street watching you?"

Cal shook his head. "No. No, I didn't. There were a few people but no one stood out. As for people she complained about there was this one guy at work. Hell, I don't even remember his name but she said that he had a creepy crush on her. She was always trying to avoid him without hurting his feelings."

Now Jenna was simply plain mad. Angry. Furious.

"And you didn't think to tell any of that to the police? Not once did it cross your mind that this person might be important? That maybe he had something to do with Lori's disappearance? You just didn't think it was worth telling the police?" Jenna stood, her legs eating up the space between herself and Cal. He was far taller but she got as close as she dared, poking her finger into his chest. "We now know about that guy and we're investigating him. But damn, it sure would have been nice to know about him months ago. Then maybe there might be a chance of finding my sister alive. But hey, you don't really care, do you?"

So much for not getting emotional. Too late. She was pissed as hell and Cal Owens was one of the reasons. Just one of them, though. She was also angry about the unfairness of the world. Lori should be living a long and happy life right now. It wasn't right that her life had probably been cut short like this. Lori was a good person and she'd deserved a hell of a lot better.

Cal threw up his hands, his frustration evident. "There was nothing I could do to help. Why can't you see that?"

"Because I don't believe it," Jenna stated firmly. "Maybe you could have helped, maybe not. But you didn't care to find out. You just wanted to sweep everything about Lori under the rug like it didn't happen. Let me ask you a question...does it still bother you that Lori dumped you? That she dug through all the bullshit and saw you for what you really are?"

It looked like Cal wanted to say a whole lot to Jenna, but he didn't. Instead, he swept past her and stomped out of the room.

That went well.

Cal had asked to talk to her thinking that he could lay on some smarmy charm and get her to think that everything he said was true. Frankly, she'd seen his type more times than she could count. She worked in politics, after all. They weren't known for being the most truthful and transparent people. She'd worked with men and women far worse than Cal Owens.

Knox was probably right that his brother didn't have anything to do with Lori's disappearance. But he was definitely guilty of being a jerk. How he and Knox shared DNA she didn't know. Other than the same coloring, they shared nothing else.

So they were back to Brett Hedgcock. Hopefully, they'd get that warrant to search his home. If they didn't? Jenna didn't know what Plan B was, but she was sure that Knox did.

"It's good to see you, son. You look well."

Knox bit back a retort. It was not good to see Ben Owens. He could have gone the rest of his life peacefully and serenely, never missing his father.

"Thanks. I didn't know you were going to be here."

Ben gave Knox a smug smile. "If you did, you wouldn't have come."

Why deny what was absolutely true?

"Yes, Randy told me you were coming later."

"And you were planning to be gone by then."

"I was. But I have a feeling that what Randy told me might not be the truth."

"I asked him for a favor." Ben shrugged as if it wasn't important. He always just wanted to get his own way and to hell with everyone else. "You and I need to have a talk and your brother understood."

Knox was planning to chew Randy a new asshole. His baby brother didn't get to make his decisions for him.

Strangely, the group of people and children that had been outside had disappeared, leaving Knox and his father all alone. Yep, this was definitely a setup.

"So let me get this straight. You decided that we needed to talk, and even though I've said no, you once again decided to get my brother to lie to me. Do I have it right? It appears that you haven't changed a bit, Ben. You're exactly the same as you always were."

It always pissed his father off when Knox called him by his first name. He'd been doing it since he was an adult. Ben had never been much of a parent to begin with.

There it is.

Ben's expression had changed...just for a millisecond. It was a momentary flash of irritation and anger, so fleeting that no one else would have noticed it except for someone that had lived with Ben's crazy mood swings all those years. Back then

Knox had learned quickly and early that he needed to be attuned to his father's every emotion. When Benjamin Owens wasn't happy, Knox had made sure that he was out of his dad's way, not wanting to listen to his father rant and rave about how life wasn't fair and they were all idiots.

That was a long time ago, however. Now? Knox didn't give a shit if his father didn't think that life was fair or whatever his complaint of the fucking day was. Making Ben Owens happy was impossible, so he'd given up years ago.

Checking his watch, Knox sighed loudly, wanting his father to hear his impatience.

"You've got five minutes. Make it fast."

"Only five minutes for your own—"

"Time's ticking away," Knox said, tapping the crystal on his watch. "And you're wasting most of it. Trust me when I say that I'm going to walk away in four minutes and forty-five seconds and I really don't think there's anyone here that's strong enough to stop me."

Ben slapped his bottle of beer down on the edge of the deck railing. "Fine. We need to talk."

"You keep saying that but you haven't said anything yet."

"I had a lot of time to think when I was inside and I knew that I had to make some changes in my life. I'd like my son to recognize that I'm a different person now. I've changed."

Ah, Ben wanted applause. He wanted to be praised.

"Before I congratulate you, I need to know how you've changed."

"If you were around at all, I wouldn't have to tell you. You'd just see it," Ben groused, his expression stormy. "You'd know."

"Well, I haven't been around, I've been working. So humor me and tell me all the wonderful changes you've made. Hey, let's start with Patty. It didn't take you long to replace her with a younger model. But wait...that can't be a change because that's what you've always done. Do you have a job? Because that would be a change from letting everyone else take care of you like you're royalty. Have you started paying child support for all the kids you've fathered that are running around? Because that would be a huge change. Have you done any of that? Because those are the changes that I would be most interested in."

Knox had called out Ben many times since becoming an adult but the man didn't seem to be getting used to it at all. Every time they met up, his father seemed to think that he could somehow talk his way into his son's good graces and that Knox would fall for his lies like he did when he was a little kid.

When I wanted to believe.

"You're not listening–"

"When you say something worth listening to I will, but if all you're going to do is keep making the same old tired promises from my childhood...I'm out. I'm not interested anymore. If you had truly changed, I don't think you'd be dancing around trying to get everyone to celebrate you. You'd have just changed and waited for all of us to notice. But no, it's still all about you. You, you, you. As if you're the fucking center of the goddamn universe. I'm too old to believe in your stories, and I'm definitely too old to believe in your lies. Tell them to someone who still cares. I don't."

His father's demeanor changed completely, his body stiff and his eyes narrow and cold. This...right here. This was the real Benjamin Owens, although he didn't often reveal himself. But maybe this time he'd finally got it through his thick skull that he didn't have to put up the front anymore. Knox wasn't buying whatever it was that he was selling.

"I'm your father. You're supposed to care about me."

That almost made Knox laugh out loud.

"That's hilarious coming from you. I'm your son and you're supposed to care about me. Do you? Let me ask you a question. When's my birthday, Dad? I won't even ask the day, just the month. When is it?"

Ben had no answer, which Knox expected. Knox waved toward the house and the people who had gathered at the window to watch them talk. Could they hear? Knox didn't care if they could. He wasn't about to censure himself. His only regret was that a child might hear his curse-laden replies.

"Why don't you concentrate on the people that still believe in you or at least want to believe in you? They want to. They've fooled themselves into thinking that you give a shit about someone else besides yourself. But you and me, we both know that it's not true. There is no one you love more in this world than yourself. You'd throw me or any of them under the bus to save your miserable hide. In a heartbeat. You wouldn't even debate about it. Just own it, Ben. I'd honestly have more respect for you if you did."

"You take after your mother," Ben snarled, his blue eyes an icy gray color. "Stubborn and ignorant."

"Not so charming now, are you?" Knox replied with a chuckle. "I think our five minutes have passed and even if they haven't, I've grown bored talking to you. You probably won't believe this but I do wish for you to change someday. I hope that you can because you have kids out there that could use a decent father. It's too late for me but it's not for them. They need you."

"You're not going to lecture me about growing old and ending up alone? That's usually your favorite."

"I'm surprised that you actually listened."

Ben waved his finger in front of Knox's nose. "I know you, boy. You like to put on that you're perfect, but you aren't. That pretty girl in the house is going to realize that eventually."

"I've let her know that I am about as far from perfect as one human can get. I admit that I have issues. But the difference between me and you, Ben, is that I can actually put another person before myself. I can care and feel love."

"If you love her then you'd better let her go. You'll just mess up her life like you did your own."

"You might want to take your own advice. I'm done with you."

With that, Knox turned on his heel and strode back inside the house, looking for Jenna. He wanted to leave. Immediately. He had words for Randy as well but he needed to cool down before delivering them.

Ben Owens hadn't changed. Would he ever? Probably not, but even if he did Knox had been through far too much chaos with his father to ever want a ticket on that ride ever again. He was walking away and there was no looking back, no regrets. Jenna had been right - as usual. Knox had created his own family of friends, people he trusted and had chosen. They were people he could count on with his very life if the situation called for it. He'd be there for them too.

And maybe Jenna could be part of that created family.

Because he'd told his father he could feel love. Love for Jenna.

He should tell her. Would she say it back?

26

Knox was uncharacteristically quiet on the drive back to Tremont. His brother Randy, who Knox said was a decent guy, had been extra proud of himself at the party. He'd told Jenna that he'd managed to get Knox outside to talk to their father. Knox might like his younger brother, but in Jenna's short acquaintance she thought Randy was a douchebag for doing that.

"He can't avoid Dad forever," Randy had said with a big proud grin on his face.

"Actually, he can," Jenna had replied and walked away. She had much more to say but it would probably be better not to speak any more than she already had.

She couldn't say Knox hadn't warned her about his family. He had, and she'd believed him. Honestly, he'd been kind. From the crap that she heard from his own brothers while he was out back talking to Ben Owens, she wanted to drop kick them in the balls.

"Do you want to talk about it?"

They were almost halfway back to the house and the silence had stretched on for longer than Jenna was comfortable with. If he didn't want to talk about it, that was fine, but she needed to make the offer. They were a team now, so his problems were her problems too.

"Did you want to talk about my conversation with my dad or your conversation with my brother? We both probably wish we could get that wasted time back in our lives."

"How about we start with you and your dad and work from there?"

"Fine with me. I'll make it short. He said he'd changed and I challenged that. Then he dropped the facade and showed me that he hadn't changed a bit. I told him to pound sand. End of story. How did your meeting go? Any better than mine?"

Jenna wasn't quite ready to move on yet. She had questions.

"What do you mean when you say that he dropped the facade?"

"He stopped pretending to love me and be charming and friendly. He turned cold and nasty. He said that I should break up with you so I won't ruin your life like I've ruined my own. I guess he thinks that regular employment and paying my own bills is a bad thing."

"You weren't actually going to do that, were you?" she asked, more than a little scandalized. She might have lost Knox because his dad was a jerk. "I wouldn't have let you anyway."

Knox threw back his head and laughed. "That's what I love about you, babe. Even if I wanted to break up - which I don't - you'd just tell me no and to go sit down and stop complaining."

She leaned in closer to Knox, feeling the warmth of his body through the thin cotton of her blouse. "You love that about me, huh? What else do you love?"

He looked at her then, a quick glance because he was driving, but his blue eyes had turned dark with emotion. A zip of awareness ran up her spine and she wished they were already back at the house.

"Pretty much every damn thing about you."

His words washed over her like waves on the beach on a hot summer's day. She was finding out that she pretty much loved every damn thing about Knox too. She wasn't mad about it. In fact, she was happy. She was falling in love with a man that she liked. What could be better?

"Why did you talk to him?" she asked. "You could have just walked away and we would have left."

The one thing she'd learned about Knox Owens is that he rarely did anything he didn't want to.

"I've been asking myself that same question since we left," he confessed. "I'm more than a little ashamed to say that there was a little pinprick of hope in my mind. That eight-year-old boy inside of me that wanted to have a cool dad that loved me and spent time with me. I think that's why I did it, as pathetic as that sounds. I guess I thought that if anything would change Ben it would be a stint in prison. It didn't work, though."

"It's not pathetic to want your parents to love you."

"It's pathetic to still have any hope at my age. I should fucking know better by now."

"We all have that little kid living inside of us. We all want our parents to love us."

"Do you still want that? Do you have hope that your dad will change?"

Good question. It was one she didn't allow herself to ponder.

"Like you, I think that I have that small part of me, that optimistic and naive child that still believes that pots of gold were at the ends of rainbows, hopes that my father will sober up and become the person that I always wanted him to be. The vast majority of me knows that he'll never change but if he called me and said that he'd stopped drinking...yes, I'd probably give him a chance. Even after all the shit he put me through. I don't think that makes us pathetic, Knox. I think it makes us human. Humans have hope even when it doesn't always make sense."

"You're a wise woman, Jenna Waters."

"Keep going," she said with a giggle. "I love hearing effusive compliments about myself."

"How about I think you're beautiful? Oh, and funny, even when you aren't trying to be. Now you tell me how great I am. I want some of these compliments too."

She could sing his praises for hours but she definitely knew the item that was top of the list.

"You're the kind of man that would help a woman find her sister even when his own brother was a suspect."

"Aw, baby. There isn't anything I wouldn't do for you."

His phone beeped in his pocket and he retrieved it, handing it to her. "Can you read the text coming in? I don't want to pull over."

She opened the message and her heart dropped to her stomach. Maybe this day wasn't a total loss after all.

"It's from Eli. The request for a warrant to search Hedgcock's home was approved. It will be executed in the morning."

Jenna dug her phone out of her purse. "That's amazing news. I'm going to call Tom and Michelle. They'll be so happy."

Finally, progress. Things were really looking up.

WHEN THEY ARRIVED BACK at the safe house, Eli was awake and rested after his long night. He was in the kitchen fixing a sandwich and was surprised to see them back so early.

"Was the party a bust? I didn't expect you two for hours."

"The party was indeed a bust," Knox replied with a laugh. "Or maybe I was just a big party pooper. Either way, we're home. Did you get some sleep?"

"I did. Now I'm starved. How about you? Did you get a chance to eat at the shindig?"

"We did not," Jenna said. "I'm starving too."

"There's some rare roast beef and some grilled chicken," Eli said, pushing the bread closer to Jenna. "We also have chips and some fruit salad in the fridge."

"I'm on it," Jenna said. "Knox, what do you want?"

"You don't have to make me a sandwich. I'm not a misogynistic jerk."

Jenna waved away his concern. "You would be a chauvinist jerk if you asked me to make you a sandwich for you alone. It's not being a jerk when I'm making one for myself. Besides, I asked you. You didn't ask me. It's okay. I'm not going to suddenly become a 1950s housewife and greet you at the door with a martini and slippers."

The thought of Jenna doing any of that had Knox cracking up. More likely, she'd shove those slippers down his throat after a long day and drink the martini herself.

"Then I'll have roast beef. Thank you. Next time I'll make the sandwiches."

"You're welcome, and you will."

"Jared wants you to give him a call when you have a chance," Eli said, dumping some chips on his plate. "He thought it would be much later this afternoon but you can probably try him now."

"Did you talk to him?"

"Briefly. He wanted to make sure that I was okay to stay here and back you up. If not, he could send out Ryan. He just wrapped up the case he was working on and could be on a plane tonight."

"What did you say?"

Eli grinned and settled at a spot at the small kitchen table. "I said I was fine either way. I'm the new guy, remember? I'm going with the flow. What about you? Would you prefer Ryan? Because I totally get it if you do. You know him better than you know me. I won't take it personally."

It was true that Knox knew Ryan much better. They'd

worked together before and they hadn't had any issues. Ryan was a good guy and a true professional. But honestly, Eli seemed to be that as well. Knox wasn't having any problems and the sooner they got to know one another the better. They'd be working together at some point in the future without a doubt.

"Naw, I'm good. Ryan could use a few days off anyway."

"I doubt he's going to get one," Eli said. "It sounded like Jared was hoping this warrant would wrap up this case soon. We're busy as hell."

Knox was hoping the same thing. Although it brought up a few other questions, such as what he and Jenna were going to do once the investigation was done. She only had a short-term rental and technically, her life was on the road with political campaigns. He traveled a great deal too. Could they make this work? He sure as hell wanted to.

Stepping out onto the back porch, Knox called Jared back.

"I didn't expect to hear from you this early in the afternoon.

"Let's just say that the party didn't go as planned. We left early."

"That's too bad. I won't ask what happened, though," Jared replied, amusement in his tone. "It sounds like it wasn't at all fun. I do have some information for you about Brett Hedgcock, and also your favorite grumpy detective Mike Bauer."

"Bauer? What do you have about him?"

"I have an explanation as to why he hates his job. Turns out he's third generation cop. His dad, granddad, and all of his uncles were cops."

"Sounds like he didn't have a choice. Poor bastard."

"I dug into his background just to be thorough and he applied to art school. I don't think being a detective was his doing."

"That explains a lot."

"As for Brett Hedgcock...Shit, what a mess. He comes from a

perfectly normal middle-class family. His dad was an accountant and his mother taught high school history. He has an older sister and a younger brother. They had a cat and a dog and his mother was on the PTA."

"The whole suburban dream?"

"Yes, except that Hedgcock was the weird kid in school and at home. His teachers and classmates said that he lived in a fantasy world. He was nice and a good guy but he was a little peculiar. He was described as socially awkward but sweet."

"That sounds familiar. Did he get any treatment?"

Knox had a strong feeling the answer was going to be no.

"He did, but only intermittently. He was able to function most of the time. He was just different. But he went to school, got okay to decent grades, and managed to get through community college to get an accounting degree just like his dad. He's changed jobs several times, about once every eighteen months or so. From what we can tell from his finances, he's a loner who pretty much keeps to himself other than working. He doesn't have a lot of friends, doesn't go the gym, and he doesn't even go see movies. He eats takeout most of the time, watches Netflix, and reads books from the local library. He likes historical biographies the most. He doesn't date at all, although he's on a few dating sites. Doesn't seem to get past the talking stage. He does have one hobby, which is an online history club that meets once a week. He's described as a World War II history buff. Maybe he got the interest from his mom, but that seems to be his only social outlet."

"A loner, huh?" Knox said with a sigh. "That's cliché as hell."

"As far as we can find, he hasn't hurt anyone. There's no history of violence. Everyone describes him as nice and rather mild-mannered. Just a little out of the normal. No alarm bells. The guy doesn't even have a speeding ticket. He's a model citizen."

"You sound like you believe that."

"What can I say? I didn't find anything that makes me suspicious. Doesn't mean anything, though. He could be damn good at hiding it all. What did you think? You talked to him in person."

"I thought he needed therapy," Knox replied. "He clearly doesn't like the real world. He's built up an entire fantasy around Lori that is really creepy. Even if he didn't kill her, it's not healthy. He needs to get some help. I question if he even knows what's real and what's not."

"Search warrants are real. So if they find something, that's hard evidence. Right now, we only have the story of a very confused individual who may or may not be a violent murderer."

"Can I ask why they're waiting until tomorrow to execute the warrant? Why aren't they going in now?"

"They want him to be out of the house. Tomorrow morning he'll be in the office. They'll serve him there and also search his desk as well. I don't think anyone is going to tip him off about the warrant, but just in case they've got an officer watching the house tonight. If he tries to dig up the backyard, they'll go in."

"So in the meantime, we just wait."

Jared laughed. "You sound surprised. Patience is a virtue when it comes to what we do. Take this opportunity to relax a little bit. Tomorrow might get crazy. Take a rest when you can."

It was Knox's turn to laugh. "I can't believe I'm hearing this from you. When I was your deputy, it was never time to rest or relax. You were one hundred percent go all the time."

"I'm a hell of a lot older now," Jared explained with a chuckle. "Maybe I'm just mellowing in my old age. Either way, there's nothing you can do tonight. Take your girl to dinner or a movie. Have some fun."

It wasn't the worst idea in the world. In fact, it just might be exactly what he and Jenna needed right now.

A little fun. But what?

27

Knox was up to something. Jenna didn't know what and to be truthful, it was slightly anxiety-inducing. She'd never been a big fan of surprises and she struggled with spontaneity. In her job, she'd learned to go with it when something out of left field happened but for the most part, she liked having plans. She was definitely not the "fly by the seat of your pants" kind of woman. She was a list maker. If it wasn't written down, did it really even need doing?

So she was on pins and needles when he led her to the vehicle, telling her that they were going out on a date. She was dressed in jeans and a red blouse plus a pair of old tennis shoes. Her hair was scraped up in a ponytail, although she'd managed to put on a face of makeup earlier in the day. He hadn't given her much of a chance to touch up except to freshen her lip gloss.

"Maybe I should have changed. I'm not really dressed up."

"You don't need to be for where we're going. It's casual."

He too was dressed almost identically, in jeans and a button-down cotton shirt. But somehow, he made the outfit look infinitely better. He was a man born to wear faded blue jeans and make them look...very good.

Her fingers pleated the hem of her blouse. She was still a bit nervous.

"So it's not a fancy place?"

"Not in the least. I thought it would be fun to go somewhere we wouldn't have to worry about manners or what we were wearing."

That did sound nice. But...where were they going?

He glanced over and then did a double take. There wasn't any traffic in sight, so he pulled over onto the side of the road.

"Is everything okay? You're acting strangely, babe."

Should she? They'd become so close since last night. It had all been like a fairy tale. She didn't want to ruin it by complaining. He hadn't done anything wrong. But if they were going to make this relationship work - and she hoped that they were - she couldn't keep secrets from him. Not again. She'd learned her lesson the first time. This one wasn't as big but it might be important to Knox.

"I'm not really all that fond of surprises," she confessed, her fingers clenching the armrest of the car. "I'm sorry. I really am. I just...I guess I'm not very fun that way. I'm not very spontaneous, either."

He frowned for a moment and then smiled. "Is that it? You don't like surprises? I get it. I really do. Okay, then I'll tell you where we're going. We're going to a lake nearby to have a picnic. That's it. Shit, I didn't mean to stress you out. I just wanted you to relax and have some fun."

"I like fun. I just like my fun to be...planned."

He nodded, seeming to actually understand. "It's okay, honey. To be honest, I don't really like surprises, either."

He'd been doing it because he thought *she* would like to be surprised. Talk about being at cross purposes.

"I promise to never throw you a surprise birthday party," she said, making an X over her heart with her finger. "But you need to know that I'm not spontaneous, either. I like to make lists, remember?."

"I do remember. I can live with that. Sounds like you're probably organized too. That's usually a good thing from what I've seen."

"What if you want to run off to Vegas at the last minute?"

Laughing, he shook his head. "Then I'll talk to you about it."

"But then it won't be last minute."

"We'll still get to go. That's the important thing."

"You're not mad at me about tonight?"

He cocked his head at her question. "Should I be? Did you want to turn around and go back to the house? That would kind of suck because I'd like to have an evening alone with you, but if you want to I will absolutely take you home."

She didn't want to go back.

"I want to be alone with you too."

"Then on we go." He handed her his phone. "If you want to see exactly where we're going the map's pulled up."

He didn't care. He didn't think she was a pain in the ass.

"I love you," she blurted out, then slapped a hand over her mouth. She could feel the heat rush to her cheeks and she desperately hoped that the floor of the SUV would open up and swallow her.

What was she thinking? People don't say *I love you* in a car when pulled over to the side of the road. There was no romance. No candlelight. No...just no. She was an idiot. Was he already thinking of ways to run?

He simply sat there for the longest moment in her entire life. She could hear her heart pounding in her eyes and her words narrowed down to only the two of them, sitting in the car. The rest of the world dissolved as she waited for whatever his reaction was going to be.

Should I tell him I was joking? Should I just play it off?

His smile widened and those blue eyes...they softened as he reached out to pull her as close as the console between them allowed. His hands were strong and warm and she snuggled into his side, inhaling his heavenly scent. If they bottled it, they could make a fortune.

"I love you too, Jenna Waters. And that was pretty spontaneous, by the way."

"It was, wasn't it? Maybe you're having an effect on me."

"I hope so, but I don't care if you're spontaneous or if you plan everything down to the last minute. I love you either way."

They didn't need candlelight or flowers or champagne. They only needed each other.

They were in love. Officially.

And despite what had brought them together, it was glorious.

KNOX HAD NEVER BEEN in love before.

Sure, he'd thought he was in the past, but clearly it hadn't been the real thing. There had been women - lots of them, to be truthful - and he'd cared about several of them. A few times he'd thought he was *in love*. Now he could see that he'd only been practicing for an actual, authentic love. Everything before Jenna seemed small and unimportant.

She'd been so cute and incredibly adorable when out of nowhere she'd told him she loved him. Her cheeks were all pink and her eyes had gone wide in fear as if she didn't know how he was going to reply. She should have known. She'd had him wrapped around her little finger since the first night they'd met. As he'd said before and he'd say many times in the future... There wasn't anything he wouldn't do for Jenna.

He was only beginning to comprehend how much he loved

her, and how different this was to any relationship he'd had in the past.

She was currently asleep, her golden blonde hair fanned out on the pillow, her body curled around the covers. Knox carefully reached out and plucked at a curl, wrapping it around his finger before letting it softly fall on her silky shoulder.

He was glad that she could sleep, but he was wide awake. His mind was far too active, hopping from one idea to another about what might happen in the morning. There was hope that Hedgcock might be the one, but then if he wasn't, where did they go from here?

Slowly sliding out of bed so he wouldn't wake Jenna, he threw on a pair of sweats and a t-shirt and headed for the kitchen. Maybe a shot of whiskey might help him sleep and settle his thoughts. The house should have been dark but the kitchen light was already on.

"Jesus, do you ever sleep?"

It was Eli, of course, munching on a sandwich and a glass of orange juice. He simply looked up from his snack, not seeming surprised that Knox was awake too.

"I do," Eli replied. "But my body clock is a little messed up. I slept a few hours but now I'm wide awake. Are you hungry?"

"I actually came out here to have a drink. I thought it might help me sleep."

"Couldn't hurt."

Knox reached for the whiskey bottle in the cabinet. "Want one?"

"Whiskey, roast beef, and orange juice doesn't sound like a good combination. I'll pass, but thanks. Why can't you sleep? Worried about tomorrow?"

"A little," Knox admitted. "If they don't find anything, I'm not sure where to go with this investigation."

"We start all over at the beginning," Eli said with a grin. "You know how this works. We've been here a million times. We start again and go over every piece of evidence and information with a fine-toothed comb. We'll find something. You already know that they're getting nervous. They'll show their hand again soon."

"What if they don't?"

"They will. Have some faith."

Knox poured a finger of whiskey and sipped at it, enjoying the burn in his belly. "You sound so calm. Do you meditate or something?"

That made Eli laugh. "Nope, I just don't let the little shit get to me. And as the saying goes...it's all little shit. As long as we keep Jenna and her family safe, we have time to investigate."

Knox emptied the glass. "But where do we go from here? I don't think my brother is guilty, and if Hedgcock isn't..."

"We expand the investigation. We look where we haven't looked before."

"Where is that?"

"You tell me. I just got here."

"I don't know."

And that frustrated the hell out of Knox.

"You will," Eli said, finishing off his sandwich and crumpling the paper napkin between his fingers. "Maybe not tonight, but eventually."

"In the meantime?"

"We place ourselves firmly between Jenna's family and the person that wants to hurt them. That will piss whomever it is off. I kind of like the idea of making a killer mad, don't you?"

"It's one of the better parts of this job."

Eli stood and placed his plate and glass in the sink. "How about we watch a movie? I don't think I'm going to be able to sleep any time soon. We've got about five hours to kill before they serve the warrant."

"Fine, but I get to pick the movie."

"I'll give you a choice. *Die Hard* or *Die Hard II*."

"The original. Is *Die Hard* your favorite movie?"

"No, but I thought we could use some inspiration right about now. What's more inspiring than John McClain taking back an entire skyscraper from terrorists single-handedly?"

"I can't argue the logic. We've got five hours. We could watch both of them."

It wasn't the worst way to pass the time. Did Brett Hedgcock kill Lori Waters? They just might get their answer tomorrow.

28

K nox and Jenna stood a few houses down from Hedgcock's home, watching the police coming and going. Every now and then one of the officers would exit with a brown paper bag but they couldn't see what had been removed from the house. They were on tenterhooks, waiting for the head detective to tell them what they'd found.

It was a warm morning and Knox had started it out by grabbing three coffees on the way along with a box of donuts. They might be sitting in the car for a long time. Executing the warrant could take hours.

He was shocked when he pulled up to find one of his three bosses, Jason Anderson, already there along with his brother West, who used to be a detective in Tremont but was now the mayor. West explained that he was good buddies with the chief of police in Rocky River where Hedgcock lived, and he had been invited to observe the activities. The chief of police was also open to them being a part of the investigation, as this would be the first murder case in their tiny town. They didn't have any experience with that sort of investigation and wanted to make sure that it was done right.

Inwardly, Knox was glad that Brett Hedgcock didn't live within the Douglas town limits because he sure as hell didn't want to deal with Mike Bauer. Twenty miles had made all the difference today.

"Are they checking the backyard?" Eli asked quietly. Jenna was chatting with West. "He could have hidden a body back there right under the flowerbed."

"They are. The house, the garage, the property, and right now they should be checking his desk at work."

"Is she going to be okay if they find a body?" Eli asked, glancing over at Jenna. "I hope you gave her a warning."

Knox had pulled Jenna aside this morning as they'd been getting ready to leave the house. He'd cautioned her about what could happen and what she might see. She'd said she was ready. He believed that she was. She knew that the truth might hurt but in the long run it was better than not ever knowing what had happened.

One of the local detectives strode over carrying three brown paper bags.

"I'm Detective Sheridan with the Rocky River Police," he introduced himself. "We have a few items and we'd like Ms. Waters to take a look at them. We need to know if they belong to her sister."

Jenna had already hurried to Knox's side. "I'm Jenna Waters. What do you have?"

"Some personal items that appear to be female," the detective replied. "We'll bring you whatever we find, but we ask that you not touch anything. It's all going to the state lab."

She nodded. "Of course."

Knox wrapped his arm around her waist, hoping to show support. This had to be incredibly difficult. Jenna turned to him and gave him brave smile.

"I'm ready. Let's do this."

"Okay, this first one has a woman's handbag. Can you tell us if it belonged to your sister?"

The rubber gloved officer opened the bag and lifted out a cream-colored purse. Jenna gasped, her body stiffening next to his, and for a moment she reached out before snatching her hand back. She'd remembered not to touch.

"Yes," her voice choked. "Yes, that's Lori's purse. I gave it to her for her birthday."

The detective nodded and closed the bag. "We had a feeling it was your sister's, Ms. Waters, because we did remove the items inside. Your sister's wallet with her driver's license and credit cards were found, but we needed you to confirm."

He opened the second bag and showed them the various items that Lori Waters had carried in her purse. There was a bright yellow leather wallet, two tubes of lipstick, a notebook, a brush, a small bottle of perfume, and some hair ties.

"Her phone?" Jenna asked. "Those definitely belong to Lori but she always carried her phone in her purse too."

"We're still looking for it," the detective replied. "But we do have a few pieces of clothing to show you."

The third bag was opened to display the sweater that had hung in Hedgcock's foyer and also a paisley print silk scarf.

"Yes, those are Lori's too. Michelle and I were with Lori when she bought that scarf. It was one of her favorites."

Jenna's fingers clutched at Knox's arm, her expression changing from one moment to the next. Happy, sad, angry, and a few more that he couldn't identify. Of course, she would be happy that they'd found some of her sister's belongings but there had to be sadness as well there too. Any hope of Lori being found alive had to be quickly draining away this last week.

"Why don't we go back to the car?" Knox suggested. "You can sit down and I'll get you a bottle of water."

Jenna's gaze never faltered, steady on the house the police were searching. "I'm fine. I need to see this through."

"You can see anything they bring you. I was just thinking that you might want to rest a little."

This time she did turn to him, her eyes bright with unshed tears. "Thank you, but I'm okay. I'll fall apart later. Right now, I'm here for Lori."

He leaned down, brushing her temple with his lips. "And I'll be there for you when you do. You're a strong woman, Jenna Waters."

"I guess we'll see if that's true."

It certainly was true. For the next two hours, the detectives brought out about a dozen items for Jenna's perusal. About half of them she was able to easily identify. The other half Jenna wasn't sure about. They were all going to be processed at the state lab for blood and DNA.

It was after midday when Jason pulled Knox aside. "Looks like they're done. They found quite a bit, enough to take Brett Hedgcock in for questioning. The detective has invited us in. I told him that you should be the one to do it. You know the most about this case, and you've earned it. Looks like you might have found the person responsible."

"It's early yet. I don't want to count my chickens and all that shit."

Chuckling, Jason nodded. "I agree but it's looking good. Are you up for an interrogation? We need to find out where he dumped the body."

It made Knox queasy to even think about asking those sorts of questions in front of Jenna. She shouldn't be listening to the down and dirty details.

"I am, but..."

Jason quickly glanced at Jenna who was talking to Eli. "I get it. You're right. I can have Eli take her back to the safe house."

Knox explained to Jenna that they were going to question

Hedgcock and that Eli was going to take her back to the house. He didn't expect her to object and she didn't. If anything, she seemed exhausted and pale. Eli had assured him that he'd take care of her, but Knox still didn't like not being with her. She needed him. But the investigation needed him too.

Knowing Jenna, she'd be pissed if he didn't put the case first. She was all about getting to the truth.

The Rocky River police station was like so many that Knox had seen through the years. Small, stuffed with desks in every corner, and smelling of burnt coffee. They were led to a back room with two-way glass. Hedgcock was already sitting on one side of the table, looking absolutely terrified. The man was literally shaking in his chair and for a moment Knox felt sorry for him. He was getting a huge hit of reality and clearly unprepared for it.

Knox, Jason, and West had discussed the interrogation on the way to the police station. They had each given their own suggestions which Knox took as being a little more than a mere *suggestion*. Jason was his boss, after all, and West had been a successful cop before becoming the mayor. Knox's priority was to get Hedgcock to tell him where Lori was, which meant that he was going for a confession of sorts. He wasn't thinking he'd get that, though, so he was going to take a different approach. One that might appeal to someone that liked to live in their own world.

Jason handed Knox two bottles of water. "Go get 'em. Let us know if you want us to give you a break. We need to keep the pressure on Hedgcock, so if you get tired just tag one of us and we'll come in."

Knox entered the room, shutting the door behind him, and sat across from Hedgcock. The other man was fidgeting in his chair, looking like he might bolt from the room at any second.

"Are you sure you don't want an attorney present?" Knox asked. Hedgcock had already said that he didn't, but Knox wanted to give him another chance. They had already read his Miranda rights and he said that he understood them. "We can wait if you want to call one."

"I don't have anything to hide," Hedgcock said, his voice thready and weak. "I just want to answer your questions and go home."

Knox slid one of the bottles of water across the table. "You must be thirsty. Have a drink and we'll chat. How does that sound?"

"Okay, I guess."

Hedgcock twisted off the cap and took a large gulp.

"So, Brett...can I call you Brett? You can call me Knox if you want to."

The other man's head bobbed. "Sure, you can call me Brett."

"Okay, Brett. Let's talk about the items that were found in your home that belonged to Lori Waters. Her purse and clothes. How did you come to be in possession of them?"

"Lori gave them to me."

"She gave you her purse? Didn't she need it?"

Brett shook his head. "She said that I needed to keep it safe."

"From what?"

"She didn't say. Just that it was important." Brett rubbed at the back of his neck. "Look, I told you before that Lori will be back soon. When she gets here, she'll explain everything."

"Do you talk to Lori a lot?"

"It's been a few weeks, I think..." Brett frowned and shook his head. "It's normally not that long but she said that she'd be back. I know she'll be back."

Knox decided to try another path.

"Tell me about your relationship with Lori," he invited. "What you two like to do when you're together. That sort of thing."

Brett smiled, his eyes taking on a dreamy look. "We're both homebodies. We don't really like to go out or anything. We stay home. Cook. Watch television. We both like to read. We lead a quiet life, you could say, but we have fun too. We're talking about getting a dog."

"Nothing better than man's best friend. I wouldn't mind having a dog but I'm not home enough to take care of a pet. It wouldn't be fair to the animal."

"We're home all the time. I'd like a big dog, but Lori thinks that maybe we should get a smaller dog. Like a Corgi. I'd like a Golden Retriever."

This was it. Brett had opened the door. Knox was going to walk through it.

"It sucks that you don't agree. That has to be tough. Is there anything else that you and Lori don't agree about? Food, movies, books? Vacation destinations?"

"Not too much," Brett said with a shrug. "Just the normal stuff."

Knox rubbed his chin and stretched out his legs, sprawling casually on the hard wooden chair. "Do you ever argue about that normal stuff?"

Brett went stiff, his eyes narrowed as he shook his head. "No, we don't argue."

"Ever? Even the most devoted couples have arguments. There has to be something that you argue about. Maybe money? Family? My last girlfriend was always pissed off that I worked too much. She was always frustrated with me about that."

Brett's gaze was focused on the table. "I don't work that much."

"What about money? You said that you two were practically engaged. Did you have any differences in spending style? You seem like a saver to me. Did Lori like to shop a little too much?"

"It was her money. I don't have any right to tell her what to do."

"That sounds like something she said to you. Did she say that, Brett? That it was none of your business?"

Shaking his head, Brett shifted uncomfortably in his chair. "No, we never talked about her spending. We didn't argue."

"Not once, huh? That's great. What's your secret?"

Brett shrugged again. "I don't know. We just...don't."

"Not once. That's great."

Knox noted Brett's body language. The other man had almost curled in on himself, his arms crossed over his chest.

Knox sat up in his chair and leaned forward, his gaze on Brett. "I don't think that you're telling me the truth. I think that you're lying."

Brett had stopped shaking but he immediately started again, wrapping his arms more tightly around himself. "I'm–I'm not. Really."

Knox placed his hands palms down on the table between them as if he were reaching out to the other man. "It's okay to argue with your girlfriend, Brett. All couples have fights. They usually blow over and everything is fine."

"We argued about her going away."

Brett's voice could barely be heard, he'd spoken so softly. But he *had* spoken.

"Was this a few weeks ago or longer than that?"

"A few weeks ago. Maybe. I'm not sure when it was exactly. She said she was going away for awhile and I begged her not to. She said she had to. That she had things she needed to do. That's when she gave me her purse. She said that I needed to take care of it for when she came back."

"But she didn't say why she left it?"

"No, just that I needed to take care of it. And all of her things. I told her I would. She could count on me."

"Did you yell? Did she yell, Brett? Were angry words exchanged?"

Brett seemed to get smaller in the chair, his chin to his

chest. "Maybe. I was...mad...and she was too. She said I wasn't listening to her."

"Was she listening to you?"

Brett shook his head. "No, she just kept saying that she had to go. I kept asking her why, but she wouldn't answer me."

"And that you made you mad."

"Yes–No–I–don't know. I guess it did."

"And you yelled."

"Yes."

"And she yelled."

"Yes."

The response was barely audible.

"You argued for awhile. You were both mad. What happened then, Brett?"

Brett buried his face in his arms. "She started to leave."

"What did you do?"

"I don't remember."

"I think that you do remember. What did you do when Lori started to leave?"

"I–I grabbed her arm. I wanted to talk to her. I wanted her to listen to me."

"What happened then? Did you hit her, Brett? She was making you so mad, wasn't she? She wouldn't listen to you. That had to make you angry."

His head popped up, tears streaming down his cheeks, his eyes bloodshot and swollen. "*No*. No way. I would never, ever hit Lori. I grabbed her arm and tried to make her listen but she shook me off. She left after that. Nothing else happened. I love Lori. I wouldn't hurt her. *I wouldn't. She's my whole world.*"

Since Lori had been missing for months, not a few weeks, it was highly likely this entire scenario was completely made up in Brett Hedgcock's mind. There wasn't any real reason for Lori to have even been in the man's home. They'd been co-workers only, not lovers. They had no relationship beyond a casual acquaintance.

But damn...Brett looked devastated, convinced that his recounting of that day was totally real. To him, it had happened and he was haunted by her leaving.

He and Brett talked for a little longer, but the man's story never changed. Lori had been there a few weeks ago. She'd said she was leaving and he'd begged her not to go. He grabbed her arm but she'd shaken him off and left, leaving behind some of her personal effects. It didn't make a lick of sense. If Lori was going on a trip, wouldn't she want her purse and wallet? Her identification and credit cards? Even Brett agreed that it was strange but he was adamant that she'd left those items with him, telling him that he needed to keep them safe.

Eventually, Knox had to give up. He was exhausted and Brett was in far worse shape, sobbing and rocking in his chair while repeating over and over about how much he loved Lori. He left Brett in the room and joined Jason, West, and the detective from Rocky River.

"I don't think we're going to get anything more from him," Knox said. "He believes his story."

Jason nodded in agreement. "He's completely convinced himself, that's for sure. I agree that any more questioning today is only going to stress him out far worse. He needs care and treatment for his delusions."

"That's exactly what he'll get," the detective said. "We're going to take him to the hospital for a seventy-two hour hold for observation. I want him to get whatever help he needs. Maybe a psychiatrist can talk to him. Help him remember what happened. In the meantime, we're sending all of the evidence we collected to the state lab along with his car, which will be stripped down and searched. If there's a particle of blood there, we'll find out. We're also talking to any of his friends, neighbors, or co-workers to see where he was the day Lori Waters disappeared."

The detective and West walked down the hall, leaving Jason with Knox.

"You did good," Jason said, slapping Knox on the back. "Looks like you're close to getting your answers. A good doctor can work with Hedgcock and hopefully find out the truth."

Knox glanced at the closed door to the interrogation room. Through the window he could see that Hedgcock had stopped crying and was now standing at the two-way mirror, looking back at Knox. He had to know he was being watched through the glass. "I just feel so badly for him. He seems to really love her."

"It doesn't mean he didn't kill her," Jason replied, his tone gentle. "I can name about half a dozen murderers off the top of my head who supposedly loved their victim."

"He needs help."

"And he's finally going to get it. He probably should have gotten it a long time ago. He'll be assessed at the hospital. The detective is going to notify his family." Jason's phone buzzed in his hand and he checked his screen. "That's Jared. He says that they were able to successfully triangulate where the texts to your girlfriend were sent from. Brett Hedgcock's home."

"They didn't find Lori's phone."

"Maybe it's hidden in his car. Maybe he destroyed it after he sent those texts. Either way, that's where they came from."

That pretty much sealed it. Brett Hedgcock had killed Lori Waters. Knox turned to look at the man staring back at him through the glass. Brett couldn't see him, of course; he didn't know that Knox was standing only a few inches away. Hedgcock didn't look sad or panicked anymore. He looked...exhausted, as if he'd spent all of his emotion and he didn't have any left.

"What do you want me to do next?"

"We're in a holding pattern until we can build more of a case," Jason replied. "It will take weeks to get the lab results back, and I'm guessing it could take even more time for a doctor to unwind whatever is going on in Hedgcock's mind. I think we put this one on hold until we get more information. Would it be a problem to head back home tomorrow?"

Knox would need to talk to Jenna, but he hoped she'd be up for the trip. It was too soon to take a victory lap. They hadn't found Lori yet, but they'd made progress.

Truth always showed itself in the end.

29

Knox scanned the refrigerator for something to make for dinner. Jenna had gone to visit Anita but she'd be back soon. They needed to eat and then pack so they could get on the road early in the morning. They had a long drive ahead of them.

"Are you sure you don't want to drive back with us?" Knox asked Eli. "You're more than welcome to join us. I wouldn't mind an extra driver on the trip."

Eli grimaced. "I do hate to fly but I don't want to intrude on your couple time. I'd be the third wheel, if you know what I mean."

"I do and you wouldn't be that at all. It's just a drive. We're not planning to elope or anything," Knox chuckled. "Seriously, grab your bag and come with us."

"Jenna might–"

"She brought it up first," Knox said with a shake of his head. "So just pack your bag."

"I don't like to be all scrunched up in those airplane seats," Eli said. "Aw hell, I'll go with you. I'll call the office admin and have her cancel the ticket."

"In a few months you'll have enough airline miles to upgrade your seat," Knox laughed. "I rarely fly coach anymore. And if the flight is over four hours then the firm will upgrade you automatically. Logan, Jared, and Jason don't like folding themselves up in those seats any more than we do."

"They seem like good people to work for."

Knox closed the refrigerator in frustration. They hadn't bought many groceries because they didn't know how long they'd stay. Now they only had remnants of food, nothing that would pull together as a meal. "They're the best. I've worked a lot of places and I can easily say that this is the best job I've ever had. Hands down. It's not even a close race."

"Why don't we just order in?"

"I won't argue that. I need to write myself a note so I remember to clean out the refrigerator in the morning before we go. I don't want to leave a mess behind. Jason said not to worry about cleaning. They'll get a service in here after we're gone, but I thought we might give them a hand and strip the beds. Take out the garbage. That sort of stuff."

Eli held up his phone. "I'll make a note of it right now."

Knox dug into a drawer for the takeout menus. "Maybe we should go ahead and order. Jenna's going to be starved when she gets here. I should probably call her brother Tom and see if he wants to join us. She'll want to see him before we leave in the morning."

"He can't make it," Eli replied. "Jenna already asked him when he stopped by to see Jenna."

Knox frowned. "Tom was here? I didn't realize. I thought he was at his office all day. That's what he told me when I asked if he wanted to be there when they executed the warrant."

Eli shrugged. "Maybe his plans changed. He stopped by while you were still at the station. He and Jenna talked for a few minutes and she told him that she was going to see Anita. She asked him if he wanted to come for dinner but he said that he already had a commitment to his history club. Apparently, they have a meeting tonight. She teased him about being a World War II nerd. They hugged and cried a little - I tried to make myself scarce at that moment - and then he left."

Knox's brain was buzzing, the back of his neck tingling, but he wasn't sure why. Tom had told him he had meetings all day long. So maybe they were cancelled. Meetings get cancelled all the time. Right?

World War II nerd?

Wait.

"He said he was in a history club? Are you sure?"

"That's what I heard." Eli frowned, rubbing his chin. "What are you thinking? Because you've got a strange look on your face."

"I don't know what I'm thinking," Knox confessed. "It's just...Jason told me that Brett Hedgcock was in a history club. That he's also a World War II history buff. Don't you think that's...weird? I mean, what are the chances?"

"Considering I've never in my life known anyone in a history club? Maybe that makes me uncultured, but now you've met two in the space of a week? That's some six degrees of separation shit."

"I don't like it," Knox said slowly, trying to make sense of what he'd learned. "But I'm not sure what it means. If anything. Anyone can like World War II history. It's not a crime."

Knox didn't like knots. He was going to tug on this string because he didn't like coincidences. It might be nothing. Or it might not.

He grabbed his phone and punched in a number. "Jared? Remember you were telling me about Brett Hedgcock being involved in an online history club? I don't suppose you have or can get a list of members?"

"I can get one pretty easily. Are you looking for someone in particular?"

"Yes, Tom Waters."

Because coincidences suck.

He needed to talk to Jenna. Right away.

JENNA PULLED up in front of Anita's home. She'd managed to convince Knox that she didn't need a bodyguard to go see her mother, but it hadn't been easy. He'd wanted to go with her or send Eli but she'd dug in her heels and stood her ground. She needed to speak to her adopted mother privately. Jenna was going to tell Anita about Hedgcock and what the police had found in his home. Knox had argued that she couldn't go by herself but she'd pointed out that the threatening texts from Lori's phone had been sent from Hedgcock's house. He was the one that had been threatening them and now he was locked up for seventy-two hours.

Knox had finally given in but he hadn't been happy about it. He'd had to concede that Brett Hedgcock looked like the person that had probably set the fire. She'd teased him that he simply wanted to be with her wherever she went. He'd laughed and admitted that was true but he understood that this was something that she needed to do herself.

She rang Anita's doorbell and inwardly hoped that her mother would be having one of her good, lucid days. She had spoken with Michelle yesterday and they'd agreed that Anita needed to be told the truth as soon as possible.

Anita answered the door, giving Jenna a huge smile and a hug. "Come in, come in. It's so wonderful to have both of you here to visit me."

Both of us?

To Jenna's shock, Michelle stuck her head around the corner of the kitchen. "I'm here too. I thought I'd surprise you."

"You managed that. I thought you were in Miami."

This was why every time she'd tried to call her sister it had gone to voicemail. Michelle must have been on an airplane.

"I couldn't stay there forever. Give me a minute. I'm making some tea for us all and then I want a big hug from you. I've missed you so much."

"I've missed you too."

When Jenna thought about how Knox struggled with his family, she was even more grateful for what she'd found here with Anita, Michelle, and Tom. And Lori. Although she wasn't around anymore, Jenna could almost feel her presence in the room. Warm and cozy, full of love. That's how she'd remember her sister. Lori was someone who gave of herself selflessly, showing love and kindness to everyone.

Especially to me. Thank you, Lori. I'll miss you every single day and I'll never forget you.

Jenna sat next to Anita on the couch and they hugged again. Apparently, Michelle had listened to her voicemails because she'd already told Anita that Jenna was leaving today and heading back to the Seattle area. Jenna promised that she - and Knox - would visit soon. She just needed to get settled and figure out what she was going to do with her life going forward. She didn't have a job at the moment or a direction, and she didn't want Knox to think her plan was to mooch off of him. She could take care of herself financially, but she couldn't imagine herself sitting around bored all of the time. She needed something to do.

"You bring that handsome young man with you next time," Anita said. "He seemed like a keeper."

"He is," Jenna assured her mother. "And I will bring him, I promise. But today is nice, just the three of us."

Michelle exited the kitchen carrying a large tray with three iced tea glasses and a plate of cookies. "It's hot out today, so this tea should really hit the spot."

She set the tray out on the coffee table and picked up two glasses, handing one to Anita and then Jenna before picking up the third for herself. "I think we should toast to Lori and finding out the truth. What do you say?"

It also appeared that Michelle had already had the talk with Anita. Jenna was slightly annoyed at her sister as this hadn't been the plan at all last night when they'd spoken. It was, however, just like Michelle to do. Since she was the older twin, she always thought she was in charge.

I should be happy. Now I don't have to do it.

They clinked glasses and Jenna sipped at the cool liquid. It was an unusually hot day out there and it felt wonderful sliding down her parched throat.

"So they've arrested that young man?" Anita asked. "He's in jail?"

"No, he's not in jail," Jenna explained. "He's in a psychiatric hospital under observation. They need to see how mentally ill he is. They're hoping they can talk to him and get him to admit what he did."

Anita shook her head, sadness in her eyes. "We may never know where our Lori is."

"We'll find her," Jenna said. She and Knox had had this very same conversation last night and he'd convinced her to have faith. "It just may take some time, that's all. I'm not giving up."

Michelle pursed her lips. "You can't trust anything that man says."

They chatted for a little while, bringing up old memories of Lori and the fun things they'd done and the places they'd gone. They were all a little teary-eyed as they reminisced about the good times as a family. Jenna was particularly affected as she thought about what her life would be like if she'd never met

Lori. It would all be so different and sad. She was lucky she'd had her sister for as long as she did.

Jenna kissed and hugged Anita goodbye and promised to keep in touch better than she had in the past. As she and Michelle were walking to their cars, her phone buzzed and she saw that a message had come in from Knox. She read through it twice to make sure she understood.

"Michelle, did Tom ever mention meeting Brett Hedgcock? They both might be in the same history club."

Michelle shook her head and shrugged. "No, of course not. Why would you think that they knew each other?"

Jenna held up her phone. "Because according to Knox, Brett's only hobby was an online history club. They're both World War II buffs."

"So? I still don't know why you think that they would know one another."

"You don't think that's strange?" Jenna asked. "It's a bizarre coincidence. They both love World War II."

"I think Tom would have mentioned it. It's weird but life is full of weird things. I wouldn't give it any more thought. There must be tens of thousands of people in history clubs, especially online."

There probably were that many or more but she hadn't met anyone - that she knew of - and now she knew two people who loved to study World War II. Knox had said in his message that he didn't like coincidences. He was going to find out the names of the people in the history club, just to be sure.

"If Tom knew Hedgcock," Michelle went on. "Why would he not just say so? If he knew him he would have told us."

"That's true. It's just so...strange."

Michelle sighed. "Everything about this is strange, Jenna. All of this. The whole situation. At this point, I'm not sure anything could surprise me."

"You're right," Jenna replied with a groan. "It's all beginning to get to me. And to Knox too."

They both stopped next to Michelle's vehicle. "What is he going to do? Aren't you guys leaving in the morning?"

"He's going to try and get a list of the members of the online club."

"Can he do that?"

"I don't know. He's going to try."

Tapping her chin, Michelle smiled. "Why don't we both just go and ask Tom? He's at home right now. I know because I got a text from him earlier. We can ask him and get the answer instead of standing here wondering about it."

It would be more efficient just to ask Tom about the history club. For all she knew, there were thousands of people in the club and they might not even be there under their real names. They might have social media personas to hide their real identities for privacy reasons.

"Fine, I'll follow you there."

Rolling her eyes, Michelle popped the trunk open on her car. "I can drive but it's fine if you want to drive yourself. But you need to get a package that came to the house for you. It's in the trunk."

"What is it?"

"I have no idea but it's heavy as hell. Did you order an anvil?"

"Not that I remember, but late-night television, a credit card, and an inability to sleep..."

"I'll get it while I remember and we can put it in your car."

Michelle walked to the back of her vehicle and rummaged in the trunk. "Can you give me a hand? This really is heavy."

Shit, what did I order?

"Of course, I have no idea what it could—"

There was no time to react to what happened next.

Michelle's arm swung wildly in the air, in her hand a heavy

tire iron. Before Jenna could jump away or even call for help it came down on her temple, the pain bursting through her head like a bomb exploding. She felt her legs give way under her as her hands went instinctively to the wound. There was a sticky wetness between her fingers and her stomach tumbled and twisted, making her want to retch from the blinding pain.

She tried to focus but the world was a blur.

"Michelle, I–"

She couldn't get the words out; her tongue wasn't taking direction. It was too difficult. She couldn't keep her eyes open, her lids far too heavy. She let them close, her sister's blurred visage the last thing she saw before falling into unconsciousness.

JENNA WASN'T ANSWERING her telephone or replying to messages and Knox didn't like that one bit. That tingling on the back of his neck was getting stronger and there was no way he could ignore it. So he got into his SUV and drove to her mother's house to find her, watching the opposite direction along the way in case she was stranded with a broken-down car. Out in the middle of nowhere it wasn't that uncommon to be between cell phone towers but it had been too long, in his opinion. He wasn't going to wait any longer.

Eli had insisted on going with him in case they needed someone to stay with the vehicle on the side of the road while waiting for a tow truck. He also knew a bit about cars and said that if she was broken down, it might be something simple and he could get it up and running without too much effort.

When he pulled up in front of Anita's house, he was relieved as hell to see Jenna's car still parked there. His pounding heart could go back to a normal pace.

"I worried for nothing, I guess. She's still here."

Eli frowned. "Then why isn't she picking up your calls?"

"Maybe her phone is dead? Let's go in and find out. You can meet Anita. She's a really nice woman."

Anita answered the door when he rang the bell, looking surprised to see him.

"Knox, I didn't know you were stopping by. Come in."

They entered and he introduced Eli.

"This is my friend, Eli Hammond. Eli, this is Anita Waters, Jenna's mom."

"It's nice to meet you, ma'am."

"It's nice to meet you, too." Anita turned her attention back to Knox. "To what do I owe the pleasure? Come in and have a seat. Relax a little."

Knox's gaze scanned the empty living room. He didn't see or hear Jenna at all.

"Actually, I came to see if Jenna was still here. She's not answering her phone."

Anita frowned and shook her head. "Jenna left quite awhile ago. She's not here."

"Her car is still parked outside."

Anita walked over to the front window and moved the drapes so she could see out. "That's strange. Maybe she left with Michelle."

Michelle? Michelle was in Miami. Knox remembered how Anita could get confused every now and then.

"Michelle is in Miami," he reminded her gently, pulling out his phone and thumbing the screen to call Jenna. The phone rang but there was no answer. "So she couldn't have left with her."

"No, Michelle flew back," Anita said firmly. "Michelle came to see me today and she and Jenna walked out together. We all had iced tea and cookies and talked about Lori."

Knox wasn't sure what to believe. On one hand, Anita seemed quite sure about what she was saying, but on the other,

Michelle wasn't supposed to fly back from Miami until tomorrow.

Eli nudged Knox with his elbow. "There are three glasses in the sink."

Okay, that was an indicator that Anita wasn't confused. But why had Michelle flown back without telling anyone? And why wasn't Jenna answering her phone? He tried calling a second time but once again he ended up being sent to her voicemail. He didn't like this. That tingling in the back of his neck was growing with every passing minute.

"Did Michelle say why she flew back early, Anita?"

"Jenna asked her that. Michelle said that she couldn't stay in Miami forever. I think that she just missed her family. She and Tom have grown so close since they moved in together. It's wonderful for a mother to see that. When they were younger Tom barely acknowledged his sisters, so it's nice to see things change."

Knox had questions about Tom Waters. Anita might be an excellent source for answers.

"I'm surprised to hear that. You all seem so close, especially with Michelle moving in with Tom."

Anita laughed. "No one was more shocked than I was when that happened. When my husband and I got married, Tom Junior didn't like Lori and Michelle at all when they came along about a year later. He was terrible to them as they grew up, calling them names and generally being mean. His father sent him to therapy, of course, and over time things did get better. However, Tom still didn't spend much time with the family, preferring to be on his own. He was starting his career so it actually wasn't that inappropriate. Why would he want to be around young girls? He had his own life and friends. After my husband died, Tom came around more often and seemed to soften some. Then a few years ago, Michelle moved in with Tom. I was happy to see them grow so close. It's wonderful to see all the children together on holidays and truly enjoying each other's company."

At some point Eli had gone outside to check Jenna's vehicle - see if it was locked or if she'd left her purse or phone, since she wasn't answering. He came back inside, wearing a grim expression and holding up Jenna's handbag.

"I found this on the curb by the mailbox. There are blood droplets on it and the grass."

Fuck. That tingle in the back of his neck was now a voice screaming in his ear to find Jenna. Now. Something was wrong. He didn't know what yet, but clearly, she wouldn't walk away from her purse willingly and leave it on the side of the road. And Michelle? How did she fit into this? Was that blood Jenna or her sister's? Or both?

"We need to make sure Hedgcock is still locked up," Knox stated. "We also need to try and get a BOLO out on Michelle's vehicle. Anita, do you know where Tom is?"

"He should be at the office," she replied, her brows pulled together. Her cheeks were red and she was becoming agitated. "Are my girls in danger? Do we need to call the police? I thought they had him behind bars."

"That's what we thought," Knox said grimly. He needed to find Jenna, and he didn't have a clue as to where to start. "Did Michelle say where she was going?"

"Home...I think." Anita's eyes widened, and she reached for her phone on the end table. "About a year ago, Michelle and Lori said that I needed more security for the house. They had one of those doorbell cameras installed. It can see the street where the cars were parked. I can see the video on my phone but I don't think I've tried to since that first day."

Knox said a silent thank you for modern technology. It had saved his ass more than a few times.

"We're going to need to see that footage, Anita."

Eli's phone beeped and he checked the screen. "That's a text from Logan. They tracked Michelle's phone back to her house. That's where she - or it - is now."

"Then that's where we're going, just as soon as we see what happened."

Somehow Tom and Brett were connected. And now Michelle and Jenna weren't where they were supposed to be, plus there was blood.

He had to get to Jenna. Right now.

30

Groggy and disoriented, Jenna pried her eyelids apart and blinked against the lamp shining in her eyes. Her head hurt like a bitch, the pounding at her temple relentless. She lifted a hand and touched the wound gingerly. Wincing, she muttered an expletive under her breath as her fingertips came away red and sticky. Even the pillow she'd been lying on had spots of blood on it.

Dragging herself into a sitting position, her gaze ran around the room as she fought to shake the brain fog away. She was in the guest bedroom back at Tom and Michelle's, lying on a bed all alone. That realization, however, raised more questions than it answered.

How did she get here?

Why was she here?

And the biggest one - why the fuck had her own sister hit her in the head with a fucking tire iron?

What in the hell was going on? None of this made any sense. Had Michelle lost her mind? Had the stress of the situation gotten to her and she'd snapped somehow? She and

Michelle had never so much as yelled at each other, and now her sister had tried to kill her.

There were more questions but she first needed to tell Knox where she was. He had to be worried if he hadn't heard from her by now. Looking around the room, she didn't see her purse or phone.

Maybe I dropped it when Michelle hit me? And that leads to the question again...Why did my own sister hit me? The world doesn't make sense right now.

Head pounding, she slid off the bed and walked quietly to the bedroom door, turning the knob and peeking out. She could hear loud, angry voices and she recognized them immediately - Michelle and Tom. They were arguing, another rare occurrence. Jenna couldn't remember the last time that had happened. The two siblings barely used a harsh tone with each other. The Waters' family didn't argue or raise their voices.

Everything was topsy-turvy and Jenna didn't quite understand what was going on in her world. But one thing was clear; her intuition was telling her that she needed to tread carefully here. Her heart was pounding against her ribcage so loudly she was sure her brother and sister could clearly hear it over their heated disagreement. Her muddled brain was finally beginning to function again and it was telling her to be suspicious. Tom might have known Brett through a history club and now Michelle had become violent. Her heart kept saying one thing, but her head was saying something far different.

Quietly, Jenna crept to the end of the hallway, not wanting Tom or Michelle to hear her moving upstairs. She knelt down and leaned against the wall, listening in to their argument.

"I can't fucking believe you could be so stupid," Tom yelled, his anger clear in his tone. "You stupid, stupid cunt. You've ruined everything. Now I'm going to have to fix it all."

"It's only a matter of time of time before that boyfriend

figures it all out," Michelle screamed back. "He's already figured out that you're connected to Brett. He'll figure it all out and then we'll both go to jail."

Jail?

Jenna's heart dropped to her stomach, the bile rising in her throat. Clearly, Tom and Michelle were somehow mixed up in some bad situation. And Lori? How did she fit into this?

"We're not going to jail," Tom replied, sounding exasperated. "If you hadn't fucked up and knocked her out, I could have talked our way out of this. I could have explained it and blamed it all on Brett. But shit, now we've got that bitch passed out upstairs and when she comes to, she's going to run off to her cop boyfriend. This is all on you. You did this."

I'm guessing I'm the bitch. So much for familial love.

"I was only listening to you. All of this was your idea. I was just doing what you told me to."

"I never told you to hit Jenna and knock her out. You should have come to me and we would have figured it out. Just like we figured it out with Lori. I handled that, didn't I?"

Jenna's ears perked up at the mention of her sister. Just what had they *figured out*?

"You didn't handle it so well if that ex-cop can connect you with Brett."

"He can connect Brett with hundreds of people in that club. It doesn't mean anything. It's all just circumstantial. There's no evidence linking us to Lori's disappearance. I made sure of that."

Her blood running cold, Jenna had to clap her hand over her mouth not to be sick right then and there.

They'd said it out loud. *Out loud.* They'd admitted it.

Tom and Michelle were responsible for Lori's disappearance. Not Cal. Not Brett. Not some unnamed stranger. Lori's own flesh and blood.

But *why*? Why would they do that to their own sister?

"Now I need to clean up after you because you're a fucking idiot," Tom went on. "We can't let Jenna run to her boyfriend or the police. We're going to have to make sure she can't do that."

"If something happens to her, he'll never let it go."

"Then we damn well need to make sure that it looks like an accident."

They were going to kill her and try and make it look like an accident. And Knox thought he had a shitty family. It turns out her family was far worse.

Survival was priority number one. Knox had no idea where she was so she couldn't depend on him to ride in like the cavalry and save her. She had to save herself. She didn't have the luxury of sitting around and pondering why Tom and Michelle had become killers. She could think about that later. She needed to be concentrating on how to get out of the mess she was in currently.

She was stuck on the second floor of the house and it was too high to jump from a window. She'd likely break an ankle and then really be at their mercy. Could she sneak down the stairs and run for the door? Depending on where her siblings were located - and she couldn't see them from her position in the hallway - she might make it. Or might not. There were two of them and Tom kept himself in good shape. She wasn't sure she could outrun him if it came down to a sprint for the road. Several possible scenarios played out in rapid succession in her brain but she tossed each one aside. Every one of them sucked and would surely get her killed.

She couldn't talk her way out, run her way out, and she sure as hell couldn't fight her way out either. It would be two against one.

I'm fucked. What now?

Too late. She could hear the sound of footsteps on the stairs. Instinct took over and she lunged down the hall blindly, not even sure where she was headed but knowing she needed to get away and fast.

Her head still hurt, her lungs were painful as she gulped in oxygen, and her legs were wobbly but she made it to the end of the hall. Her only hope was to lock herself inside the master bedroom and then again in the ensuite bathroom. There would be two doors between her and danger. She didn't know how long they'd last but hopefully by then she'd have figured something else out. She wasn't thrilled that she'd basically be cornered, but she didn't have any other ideas. Every option was shit.

Her hand connected with the doorknob just as another larger, and stronger, hand landed on her arm, yanking her back roughly. Tom had caught up with her and he was pulling her kicking and screaming back down the hall. Would anyone hear her? They were so far from the road that the chances were remote.

But she wasn't going to let him kill her and make it look like an accident. She was going to fight tooth and nail until the bitter end. If both she and Tom were covered in bruises and scratches, she had to depend on Knox to know that she hadn't gone quietly. That is was no accident. She'd been murdered in cold blood.

I might be dead but Tom? You're going to prison. Knox will make sure of that.

Raking her nails down Tom's arm, she kicked out at him, exhausting herself but managing to connect with his legs several times. He growled and cursed, slapping at her face as he dragged her down the hall and stairs, and into the living room where Michelle was waiting.

"Stop it," Tom ground out, pulling Jenna to her feet. "Just fucking stop it. You're already dead. None of this matters."

"Knox will never believe it was an accident," Jenna spat back, sucking air into her starved lungs. She was completely exhausted, covered in sweat and dirt. "You'll go to prison. Both of you."

"I don't think I will. Let's just say that the police are on my side," Tom said with a mocking smile. "Knox will go back to where he came from and life will go on."

Tom picked up a gun that had been sitting on an end table. He immediately pointed at Jenna's temple. "Now settle down or this might accidentally go off."

Trying to be as still as possible, Jenna looked up into her brother's face. She barely recognized the man she saw there. Angry and hateful. So different than the person she'd grown up around. Had he been hiding his true self all this time? And what of Michelle?

"Why did you kill Lori?"

Jenna's voice was quiet, not wanting to spook Tom, but she couldn't stop herself asking the question. All of this didn't make any sense.

"She stuck her nose where it didn't belong and now so have you. That was a mistake."

"And Brett, what about him?"

"He's served his purpose. Your boyfriend caught him and that's exactly what was supposed to happen. He just wasn't supposed to link him to me."

"You ruined a man's life."

"He didn't have much of one to begin with. Now stop stalling." His fingers tightened painfully on her arm and the muzzle of the gun felt cold against her skin. "This is going to look like a murder-suicide."

"No one will believe that I killed myself. Or murdered anyone else, for that matter. Knox won't believe that."

Her voice shook but not because she was unsure of what she said. She was terrified, her heart racing, thundering in her ears. Sweat poured down her back, her shirt sticking to the damp skin.

I don't want to die.

"I'll make them believe it."

"Michelle, don't let him do this," Jenna said, her tone full of desperation. Just how far into this was her sister? Did she truly understand what Tom had done? "We're sisters. We're family."

"We're not family," Michelle said indignantly, her lips curled into a sneer. "We were never family. Lori picked you up like a stray dog and then I had to share her and everything else with you. You took my twin sister away from me. You took my parents away from me. You got all of their attention and I got none."

"That's not true," Jenna protested. "They loved you. You're their daughter."

"And you're not," Michelle shot back. "But they treated you like you were. No one asked me if I wanted to share my sister or my parents. No one cared what I thought. They only cared about you and Lori. Now Mom is going to care about me. I'll be all she has left. I'm going to make her beg for my attention."

Jenna truly had no idea that Michelle hadn't welcomed her into the family. She'd never acted as if Jenna joining in was an issue. Had she? Now she was questioning everything. Every look, every smile, every curse. It had all been a lie, and she'd fallen for it hook, line, and sinker.

"Shut up, both of you," Tom roared, pressing the gun more firmly against her temple, the metal icy cold even in the heat. "Just shut the fuck up. God, I hate to hear your fucking whine, Michelle. That's all you ever do. At least now you'll be quiet."

He pulled Jenna closer and then swung his arm out, pointing the firearm at Michelle instead of Jenna. "First the murder. Then the suicide."

She didn't have a clue what he was talking about until the gun went off and Michelle stood there, her eyes wide with shock and a growing crimson blood stain on her abdomen.

Jenna screamed as her sister pressed her hands to her belly and then crumpled to the ground.

He shot Michelle. He just...shot her.

"Are you insane?" Jenna cried, tears blurring her vision. "Have you lost your mind? You shot our sister."

"Why do you care? She hated you, Jenna. And she hated Lori for bringing you into our family and replacing her. She's hated you all these years."

"I don't believe you." Jenna struggled but his grip was like iron. "What about you? Do you hate us too?"

I don't want to die. I want to see Knox again. I want to feel his arms around me.

"I do. All of you, especially that bitch Anita. She took my father from me and then she took everything else. I'm going to get it all back. She'll be living on the streets and wishing she'd never been born when I'm done with her."

"You are crazy," Jenna choked out. "You don't make any sense. Anita loves you as if you were her own son. Just drop the gun, Tom. We'll call an ambulance for Michelle. I'll tell everyone it was an accident. You don't have to do this. Just let me go. I won't tell anyone what happened."

She was pleading for her life now, knowing that Tom could easily shoot to kill. She wouldn't have a chance of surviving either at point blank range.

"It's too late for that."

Sirens. She could hear sirens in the distance. They were faint but audible. Were they coming here? Or heading to some unknown destination, passing by the real and true emergency.

"They're coming," Jenna said, more tears falling down her cheeks, the words choked. "They're coming and they'll know that you did this. They won't believe any of your lies. Not anymore."

"They're not coming."

But they were. Getting louder with every passing second.

She could feel Tom beginning to tremble next to her, drops of his sweat falling on her neck and shoulder.

"They're coming for you. It's too late."

Tom's breaths were coming faster, his shoulders heaving with each exhale.

"It's not too late. It can't be too late."

"The police are coming. They'll shoot you, Tom. They'll kill you and not think a second about it. Do you want to be dead? Or do you want to live? I don't think you want to die."

"I'm not going to die."

His head swiveled so that he was staring at the back of the house.

"You can't run," she said, the adrenaline rushing through her veins. She wanted to run too but he was holding her far too tightly. "They'll catch you. It's too late."

"Shut up. Just shut the hell up."

This time he sounded far more frightened and desperate. She could practically hear the wheels turning in his brain, trying to figure out his next move. The world had slowed down to a crawl, and the seconds felt like hours as she waited for what he was going to do. She could hear her own heartbeat like a marching band in her ears, yet she could also hear and see every single breath that her brother took. Every twitch of his fingers, his furtive glances. She just needed him to lower his defenses for a single moment.

"Give yourself up, Tom. Maybe they'll go easy on you if you surrender. We can tell them that the gun went off and it was an accident."

His head jerked back and forth between the front door and the back, his entire body shaking. The gun muzzle slid lower onto her jaw and she was able to pull her head away slightly.

The sirens were louder than before, definitely coming closer. Tom's face contorted, his throat making a garbled sound that wasn't any recognizable words. With a loud yell, he shoved Jenna down onto the floor before bolting for the back door.

Stunned, she didn't move for a moment, still not believing that she was alive. But she was alive, and Tom was on the run. She was going to go in the absolute opposite direction. Levering up from the floor, she stumbled out of the front door and into the long driveway before pain and exhaustion drove her to the ground. Her limbs weren't taking orders from her brain anymore. Her body was shutting down.

The sirens were incredibly loud now and vehicles began to fly onto the property, careening to a stop near her. She sobbed in relief when she saw Knox's SUV and then he was jumping out of it, running straight for her. He lifted her into his arms, his hands cradling her head, examining the wound.

Nothing in this world had ever looked or felt better than this man holding her at the moment. She'd thought she'd never see him again but here he was. She was alive and she could feel him. His touch, his nearness. She could trust him and lean on him while she was weak. Later she'd be stronger.

"Are you alright? Are you okay? Fuck, we need to get you to the hospital. You need to see a doctor."

She didn't disagree, but there was one more pressing thing to be done first. She pointed toward the backyard, trying to speak but what came out didn't even resemble a coherent sentence.

Eli knelt down next to her. "Is that where we need to go, Jenna? Do we need to go that way?"

"Tom," she croaked, her throat like sandpaper. "He shot Michelle. He was going to shoot..."

She didn't have the energy to continue but the guys seemed to get the message. Eli took off after Tom, but Knox didn't budge. His hands were soothing, rubbing her back and crooning sweet words softly as if she was a child.

"You...have...to...get...him."

"Eli and the others will get him. He won't get away. We won't lose him. I have to take care of you, babe."

Someone wrapped a blanket around her and Knox lifted her to her feet. She saw a gurney being rolled into the front door and she prayed that Michelle was alive. No matter what she'd done, she didn't deserve to be shot down like a dog in the street.

Clinging to Knox like a life preserver, she laid her head on his chest, his heart pounding underneath her ear. Strong, but fast. He'd been scared too. Had he thought he wouldn't make it in time?

"How did you know?"

"I knew you weren't where you were supposed to be, along with Michelle. I knew for sure that Tom and Brett were in the same history club. Jason called me with that information on the way here. And I don't like coincidences. I also knew that your purse was found on the side of the road and there was blood there. Your mother pulled her doorbell camera footage and we saw that Michelle hit you on the head with a tire iron. From that, we called the police."

"Tom and Michelle killed Lori, but I don't know why."

Knox glanced over his shoulder, his expression grim. "We'll find out why. In the meantime, we have to get you to the hospital."

She didn't argue, letting him sweep her up into his arms and carry her to the ambulance. He gently placed her on the gurney and then stepped away so the paramedics could do their job. But she didn't want him that far away. She needed him close.

"Hold my hand. Please."

Smiling, he did as she asked, his flesh warm and comforting.

"I love you, Knox."

She didn't have any clue as to whether this was the right

moment to say it. They had several witnesses but they were acting as if they heard stuff like this all the time.

She only knew that she felt it. So...overwhelmingly. In every bone, muscle, and pore. This man was everything. Far more than she'd ever hoped for, to be honest.

"I love you too, babe. Don't worry. I'm not going anywhere. I'm staying right here with you."

There was no better place to be than by Knox's side.

31

T *wo months later...*

"How about spaghetti? Or we could order in."

Just home from work, Knox held up a few takeout menus, waving them in the air. Jenna pulled a face and shook her head.

"We've ordered in too much lately. Let's fix dinner. I'll help."

Not that Knox needed help making an easy dish like spaghetti but they'd found that they liked cooking together. They liked working together too. Jason had offered Jenna a temporary job helping to work up profiles with his investigators. It was good work and she enjoyed it, but her long-term plan was to head back to school for her doctorate.

"Sounds good to me. I'm starving."

They both shuffled around the kitchen getting the boiling water and the ground beef started. Knox popped open a bottle of beer and then poured a glass of wine for Jenna. She accepted it gratefully, taking a sip.

"Am I going to need this? You haven't said a word yet."

He took a long draw from the bottle before answering.

"Michelle made a deal with the prosecutor. She tells all against Tom for a reduced sentence."

"What sort of a reduced sentence? A few years?" Jenna was pissed off. "Is that all they think Lori's life was worth?"

"More like a few decades. Fifteen to twenty-five. That's a hell of a lot better than life without parole, which was what she was looking at. She has to tell the whole story and also reveal where Tom hid Lori's body."

Jenna squeezed her eyes together, a few tears slipping out. Tom had been captured that day but he'd stubbornly kept quiet, only saying that he was innocent and Michelle was guilty. That was easy while Michelle was fighting for her life in the hospital. No one had thought she would make it but she had. Now she had turned the tables on her half-brother had taken a deal.

"She gave a statement, Jenna."

Taking another fortifying sip of her wine, she then placed the glass on the counter.

"I assumed she would have to before they'd negotiate."

"I can tell you about it or not. It's up to you, babe."

She wanted to know. She'd had so many questions but hardly any answers. How many nights had she lain awake trying to wrap her mind around the fact that her two siblings were cold-blooded killers? How many times had she wanted to visit Tom in prison and ask him why he'd done it? Not that he would have told her.

"I do want to hear about it. I *have* to know the truth."

Knox sighed and pulled her close, letting her head rest on his chest. He was solid and warm and comforting. "I don't want you to hurt anymore. I want to make this better for you."

He'd been saying that almost daily for the last few months. She'd started into therapy and he would often attend as well. She had much to grapple with when it came to her family - or what was left of it - and he did too. It was healthy for both of them, especially if they wanted to have a future together.

They both wanted that. Very much.

They hadn't known each other long but they both knew that what they had was special and important. They wanted to build something together that would last.

"You make everything better," she replied with a smile. "And you weren't the one to hurt me."

"I hope I never hurt you."

"We'll hurt each other at times. I'm not sure we can completely avoid that. I think the important thing is that we don't do it on purpose." She stepped back and looked up into his soft blue eyes. She could see the love there, revel in it. It was still so unbelievable that something good had come out of such complete shit. "So what did she have to say?"

Knox leaned a hip against the counter, rubbing the back of his neck. "Apparently, Tom had been angry ever since his father married Anita. It only got worse when they had Michelle and Lori."

Jenna nodded. "Lori said once that Tom had some anger issues in the beginning."

"He did and he went to therapy for them. It looks like all he learned was how to hide all of the anger that he had. Otherwise his father would have drummed him out of the family. It simmered in him for years until Lori brought you home. That's when he realized that Michelle resented you. From what she says he stoked that hate for years, constantly saying that someday they were going to do something about it."

It was hard to believe that Jenna had been the catalyst for all of that hate and anger. She'd honestly never suspected, although now looking back she could see a few tell-tale signs in Michelle, but nothing overt. They'd been excellent actors. It had helped that the Waters family frowned on displays of anger. Jenna could now see that there had been a great deal of repressed emotion in that household.

"What were they going to do?"

"Michelle didn't say. Just that Tom was furious when his dad left almost everything to Anita and not to him. He was even more angry when he found out that Anita intended to split the inheritance four ways - Tom, Michelle, Lori...and you. He said that he wouldn't stand for it."

Poor Anita hadn't taken the news about Tom and Michelle well. She'd collapsed and had to be taken to the hospital, staying overnight for observation. Her memory issues now seemed even worse and she rarely smiled. She didn't, however, blame Jenna. Instead she was clinging to her last remaining child like a lifeline. Jenna and Knox had already talked to Anita about possibly moving to the Seattle area so they could stay close and visit often.

"But he didn't do anything."

"Actually, he did. He started stealing from the family company, siphoning money into dummy corporations with phony invoices. He was bankrupting the family but taking it all for himself. Then he got found out. Lori was at his house and accidentally knocked over a stack of papers. When she went to tidy them up, she looked through them and realized that Tom had been sending money into offshore accounts. She told Michelle about it, thinking that her sister would be on her side. Trusting was her mistake. Michelle and Tom had to get rid of Lori or be found out."

Physically shaking, Jenna had to sit down on a kitchen chair. "Oh my God, I still can't believe that they killed Lori. How does Brett come into this?"

"Tom sort of knew Brett from the history club. He got Brett a job at the same company Lori worked for. It wasn't difficult. He'd helped Lori get a job there too."

"He couldn't have known that Brett would become obsessed with Lori, though."

"He didn't. That was pure luck. Lori started to complain about Brett and that's when they figured out that they could use him. So he and Michelle played with Brett's reality. She pretended to be Lori, leading him on, but making it look like he was stalking her at the office. They planned to pin Lori's disappearance on him. You threw a spanner in the works on that by insisting it was my brother Cal."

She rubbed at her pounding temple. The same one Michelle had hit. Luckily, Jenna's sister was in terrible shape and she'd only given Jenna a concussion, not a lethal brain injury. She also liked to fool herself by thinking that maybe Michelle's heart wasn't really in it when she'd hit her. That maybe she'd only been doing it half-heartedly.

I am a fool.

"I owe your brother an apology."

"Trust me when I say that he owes many apologies to many people. He can wait."

Knox had put his family on something of a *timeout*. They were still his family but he had decided to keep them at arm's length. Even Randy. He wasn't happy about what his little brother had pulled at the birthday party. As for Ben Owens? Knox was officially done. His dad had already had drinking issues in the last few months. Nothing had changed.

"It doesn't make any sense. Michelle and Tom wanted me to hire a private investigator."

"Yes, because they wanted to gently prod the investigation toward Brett Hedgcock. Michelle even continued to pretend she was Lori, visiting him and leaving Lori's things at his house. The poor bastard never had a chance."

Brett was currently receiving outpatient treatment and supposedly making good progress.

"That's so cruel, playing with his mind like that. He wasn't crazy at all. He really was seeing Lori and talking to her."

"I don't think Tom really gave a shit. Just like Detective Mike Bauer. Your brother got lucky there, as well, with a detective that hated his job and didn't want to do it. Tom thought he'd won the lottery and that the investigation would stay closed. If it didn't, and you kept pushing it, he would put Brett up as his star suspect."

"But just because they got rid of Lori didn't mean they were in the clear. There was still me."

"My boss Logan says that criminals are rarely brain trusts and I think he's right. Your brother was pretty smart, actually. He played the long game and he came close to winning it. His mistake was staying in the history club with Brett."

"And hiring you," Jenna said. "Any other investigator would have just gone with Brett and been done with it."

"I'd like to think that most others would have done what I did. Of course, the big break came when Michelle made her mistake and hit you in full view of your mother's security camera. She should have known better."

"I think she was scared."

"She should be."

"So was she the one that sent me the threatening texts from Lori's phone? And what about the garage fire?"

"She did send the texts. She was visiting Brett again as Lori and sent them. As for the fire, Tom set that, hoping that it would scare me off. He also sent Michelle to Lori's townhouse to make it look like a break-in. Apparently, there were more copies of that key than you thought. Tom liked the status quo of the cops thinking that Lori ran off on a vacation but he realized when I came onto the scene that he wasn't going to be able to hold onto that. Also, Michelle never went to Miami. She stayed in the area but out of sight, gaslighting Brett."

It was a lot to take in and digest.

"They were eventually going to kill me? And then the inheritance would be split between them?"

"And make it look like an accident. Tom had suggested cutting your brake lines or putting poison in your food. They were going to wait, though. Probably next year. Michelle had suggested making it look like a suicide, and that you were bereft from Lori's passing."

Finally, the last question to be answered.

"Where...is Lori?"

Clearing his throat, Knox's own eyes were glittering with tears. "Tom buried her on the property where the family cabin is located. The police will start looking for her right away."

Jenna's dad had had a fishing cabin up in the mountains near a lake. He'd go there with his buddies to get away for a few days and drown some worms. Tom had liked going there with his dad as well.

"They were...diabolical. All the effort, lying, subterfuge. I never wanted the money. I would have given it to them if they'd just said to me that they didn't think it was fair. I just wanted the family. I didn't care about the inheritance."

"It was about more than just money, babe. Michelle resented you for years. As far as she was concerned you'd taken her sister, mother, and father. She wanted you out of her life. Tom just resented everyone. Period. I don't think he ever planned to share with Michelle when it came right down to it. I think he eventually planned to get rid of her too at some point."

Jenna still had nightmares watching Tom shoot Michelle...the bloodstain, her sister's shocked face. Michelle hadn't expected Tom to turn on her.

"Does Tom know that Michelle made a deal?"

"He does by now. I don't know whether that will change his defense. They'll point fingers at each other but I don't think that's going to work. They have a star witness in you. He held a gun to your head and told you that you were as good as dead. That's pretty powerful."

"I dread testifying."

"I know. If it comes to that, I'll be there for you every second. Hell, everyone is going to be there for you. They won't leave you alone."

His friends and their wives had truly been a blessing since she'd come back here and lived with Knox. His co-workers were amazing and she'd made friends with the females as well, now counting them as her friends too.

"I guess you and I are going to have to build a new family."

Kneeling down in front of her, he cupped her face in his hands. "I've been thinking about that a lot. I know it's fast and that we should wait, especially after everything that you've been through, but dammit, I just love you so much, and want to spend every day with you from now on. You're my future and my whole damn world."

It was the greatest and most wonderful run-on sentence she'd ever heard. The words had come tumbling out so quickly she almost hadn't understood. But she did comprehend. His expression said more than all the words he'd just spoken.

"I love you too, Knox Owens, and the answer is yes, I will spend the rest of my life with you."

His smile widened and his blue eyes had turned a deep color. "You're saying yes? Because I asked you to marry me, woman. Just in a sort of roundabout way."

She pressed her lips to his, her heart fluttering in her chest. He was the light in the dark. She'd follow him anywhere and everywhere.

"I said yes. You can't back out now."

"I don't want to back out. I want to build a family with you."

"You mean kids?"

"At least two. Maybe three. And maybe a dog too."

She reached over and turned off the burners on the stove. "Then dinner can wait. We better get started on those kids."

To her delight, he swung her up in his arms and carried her toward the bedroom. It wouldn't be easy; they both had scars, some deeper and uglier than others. They'd fight, they'd make up, they'd love and grow, building a life and a family together. As a team.

She couldn't wait for the future.

I HOPE *you enjoyed Deceptive Truth! There will be more in the Serials and Stalkers series coming soon.*

Thank you for reading.

ABOUT THE AUTHOR

Olivia Jaymes is a wife, mother, lover of sexy romance and cozy mysteries, and caffeine addict. She lives with her husband, son, and two spoiled dogs in central Florida and spends her days typing on her computer with a canine on her lap.

She is currently working on a new cozy mystery series – *A Ravenmist Whodunnit* - in addition to her other ongoing romance series world – The Cowboy Justice Association.

Visit Olivia Jaymes at
www.OliviaJaymes.com